Crazy for the Competition

A HOPE SPRINGS NOVEL

CINDI MADSEN

Entangled Publishing, LLC
2614 South Timberline Road
Suite 109
Fort Collins, CO 80525
Visit our website at www.entangledpublishing.com.

Bliss is an imprint of Entangled Publishing, LLC. For more information on our titles, visit http://www.entangledpublishing.com/category/bliss

Edited by Stacy Abrams
Cover design by Jessica Cantor
Photography by iStock and Shutterstock

Manufactured in the United States of America

First Edition June 2015

Bliss
an Entangled imprint

For everyone who's felt like they didn't quite fit in.

Chapter One

Impressing boyfriends' parents wasn't something Quinn Sakata was known for—well, she definitely left an impression, just not the good kind. Her first awkward meet-the-parents moment had been when she was sixteen, after she'd accidentally stranded herself and her boyfriend at the time in the middle of Hope Springs Reservoir and they'd had to call his parents to rescue them. In her defense, there'd been maneuvering around in the tiny boat for kissing purposes, and while she'd known she'd knocked something over, the splash had seemed so inconsequential with his lips against hers. Turns out oars are more important than you'd think.

Then there was the summer after junior year, when Jackson Cooper's mama had come home unexpectedly and found Quinn and him making out on the couch, clothes askew, damning empty beer cans on the table. His mother had asked for her name, but only so she could call her parents, which had resulted in one of many groundings.

Which was why being in a church with her current boy-friend's family meant sweaty palms and second-guessing every movement she made and word she said.

I knew getting involved with the brother of the groom was a bad idea.

It didn't help that her sister, mother, and aunt were all eyeing her, giving her looks that screamed *you'd better be on your best behavior* as the wedding rehearsal kicked off.

It's like they think I'm some kind of ticking time bomb. Their worried looks only made her nerves bounce that much higher, so she told herself if she did slip to make sure she transitioned to speaking Japanese, so at least the Rutherfords wouldn't understand what she'd said.

Quinn took a deep breath and then slowly let it out. *I got this. I make risky acquisitions with my father constantly looking over my shoulder. Impressing my boyfriend's parents is a cakewalk in comparison.*

Mmm. I can't wait for the cake tomorrow.

The incessant hammering echoing through the church made it hard to hear the preacher's words as he detailed exactly what would happen tomorrow when her little sister, Maya, and her fiancé, Steven Rutherford, got married. Not that Quinn was paying that close attention. How much prep did walking down an aisle at the speed of nail polish drying take, anyway? Being in the middle of a business deal that had nothing to do with her regular job wasn't helping her concentration, either.

As the mother of the bride, Haha beamed, absorbing a moment she'd obviously waited for all her life—of course her mother made sure to mention to Quinn that as the eldest, she always thought *she'd* marry first. No thanks on that. Chichi stood next to Haha, also beaming, and backing her up whenever she needed help with the wedding prep—Quinn had always admired the team her parents made.

Quinn peeked inside her purse at her phone, silently begging it to ring. The town committee had promised a decision by five, and it was a quarter till. She'd get a dirty look from Haha for answering, but there was no way she'd miss it. Chichi would assume it was a business call, like 90 percent of her calls were, and let it go. This *was* business, but it was also personal, and what she hoped to one day turn into professional. If the deal did go through, Chichi would no doubt be disappointed in her decision to move another way, but she couldn't dwell on that right now.

"Quinn-chan, come stand off to this side with Maya-chan," Haha said, directing her to the left of the altar, where the hammering noise only grew louder—apparently there were a few last-minute touch-ups going on to make sure everything was ready for tomorrow's ceremony.

Maya bumped her hip into Quinn's. "Just another hour and it'll be over. And then tomorrow"—her face lit up and her voice pitched higher—"I'll be married!"

Before Quinn could give her sister a hug like she'd planned, Haha grabbed her shoulders and twisted her to stand sideways. "Turn this way. No slouching. And would a smile kill you?"

"Maybe," Quinn said. "Is that a chance you really want to take?"

Oops. Those are the inside thoughts today, remember?

Luckily Haha didn't bother with a response—she was used to the sarcasm. With the Rutherfords lined up on the other side, they probably hadn't heard, either, so no harm done.

Haha continued rearranging everyone in place, making the groomsmen switch order when she didn't like the height differences. "Perfectionist" was an understatement, not to mention how determined she was to show the Rutherfords that a small-town celebration could be just as extravagant as one in the city. There were caterers driving in from two towns over, and the decorators had driven up from Salt Lake to deck out the town square. The entire reason Maya had wanted to be married in Hope Springs instead of Cheyenne, where all of their family had relocated for the time being, was the small-town charm. Despite their many moves through the years, the sisters both considered it their real home—it was where they had their best memories.

But the Sakatas were big on impressions, especially when clients were invited and they were trying to one-up the Joneses. Or Rutherfords, as it were.

Quinn had asked Maya if she wanted all the fuss, and while she could tell her sister didn't, Maya asked her to let it go. So for her sake, she'd be compliant. She reached over and squeezed her sister's hand. "It'll be like in *The Little Mermaid*, when the whole kingdom's there to see."

Maya laughed. "My dress *is* sparkly."

"We just need to get you a gold tiara real quick. Do you think Chichi would hold a trident?"

"And sprout a tail?"

The image made them erupt into the kind of silent laughter where you hold in the sound but your entire body convulses with it.

When they'd played *The Little Mermaid* growing up, Maya was always Ariel and Quinn was Ursula. It was more fun. Until that whole getting-rammed-through-with-a-sharp-pole-and-dying-an-electric-death thing. The characters they'd gravitated toward pretty much summed up their polar opposite personalities.

All growing up, Quinn heard things like, "Why can't you be more like your sister?" and "Look at Maya. She's the younger one, and she's the better example." From her parents, teachers. Other family members. Pretty much everyone except their maternal grandmother, Sobo Machi, who was one of the few people who'd actually understood Quinn.

While that might lead some to resent their sibling, Quinn had never felt that way about Maya. She wanted to protect her sister's shiny, hopeful outlook of the world and make sure all her optimistic dreams came true. Maya's one rebellion through the years was to sneak into Quinn's room after Haha and Chichi were asleep. They'd whisper and giggle and tell stories long into the night, and Quinn often had to carry Maya back to her room after she fell asleep so they wouldn't get caught. So despite their different personalities, they'd always been close, and Quinn would do most anything to make her sister happy.

"It's going to be perfect," she whispered to Maya, giving her hand another squeeze.

When she glanced up, Mrs. Rutherford quickly looked away, as if she'd been studying her. It hadn't been easy to hold back snarky comments when the woman remarked on the quaintness of the town in that condescending, grating way people did when they tried to make insults sound like compliments.

Hope Springs was Quinn's town, even if she didn't currently live here. Although if this deal she was waiting on went through, she'd change that soon. *Please, please, please let it go through.*

Grayson flashed her a smile from the Rutherford side. They'd started dating because his brother had been dating her sister, and they were always together anyway, so it made sense. Haha and Chichi approved, which always made it easier, if a little less fun, and he fit in with her new plan to date boys who wouldn't stomp all over her heart for sport. She was trying to be more mature, as her father constantly pointed out she needed to be.

Maturity blows. And it's boring.

The truth was she missed the excitement of dating someone…not so calm and predictable. Not to mention she always felt like she fell a little short of who Grayson wanted her to be.

What's wrong with me? He's a successful man who treats me well. He…talks about his stocks a lot.

But that was easy enough to tune out. When she'd dared to suggest to Maya that he might not be the guy for her, her sister had freaked out and made her promise not to break up with him before the wedding. Which was good, she supposed. It gave her a couple more days to see how he interacted with his family and hers and decide if it was time to end it or take things to the next level. Plus, having him in Hope Springs would give her the chance to introduce him to Sadie, and her best friend would help her figure out her next step.

A calm washed over her at the thought. She'd been so antsy on this trip. It was hard to concentrate when her dream hung in the balance, so close she could taste it.

The hammering continued, the noise pounding behind Quinn's temples. She was tempted to march over and yell,

What are you doing back there? Building an ark? Can you maybe just shut up for fifteen minutes so we can get through this and go home?

Instead she tried to concentrate as the preacher went over the final details.

Yeah, yeah, let's wrap it up. We walk down the aisle, and then they exchange vows. People cry. Then they go eat and dance in the town square. It's not exactly rehearsal-worthy.

Quinn peeked at the screen of her phone again and then made sure the sound was on. *It's all going to work out. It's got to.* First, she'd use the money she'd scrimped and saved to secure the run-down Mountain Ridge Bed and Breakfast she'd fallen in love with as a child, then she'd turn it into a beautiful property where she could finally be free of her father as a boss and a job that she was good at but didn't love. Free from all feelings of obligation, and no dealing with implications that she'd only gotten where she was because of who her father was. She couldn't wait to have something that was 100 percent hers.

Just call already. I've jumped through all your hoops, and now I'm ready to turn my dream into a reality.

Haha cleared her throat, and Quinn glanced up. Oops, everyone else had moved. Quinn's heels tapped a quick rhythm against the hardwood floor as she hastened toward the end of the aisle to do another trial run, just in case someone had forgotten how to walk in the last ten minutes.

Quinn ended up next to Mrs. Rutherford, and the woman's eyes went to Quinn's necklace. More accurately, the diamond hanging from it. Grayson had gifted it to her a few months ago—it'd nearly sent her running because he was obviously more serious about her than she was about him.

But then she'd remembered being serious about relationships was something she was looking for. In theory.

Guilt swirled through her gut, but she told herself that
she did care about him. She'd even let him know she wasn't
ready to get too serious yet, so it wasn't like she was leading
him on.

"My son has good taste," Mrs. Rutherford said.

Quinn smiled. "Yes, he does. He's a very bright boy."
Were those words actually coming out of her mouth? She
didn't say things like "bright boy." But she didn't think she
should mention that the first thing she'd noticed when Maya
introduced them was how nicely he filled out a suit—especially from the back. So she nodded like the good little girl
her family expected her to be.

And Mrs. Rutherford actually smiled what appeared to
be a perfectly nice, genuine smile.

Here I am, impressing my boyfriend's mother. Go me.

If her phone could just ring right now and she could excuse herself before she said or did anything wrong, that'd be
great. Or maybe the phone call would screw it up, but not
knowing if she'd gotten the property or not was making her
crazier with every minute closer it got to five.

The hammering stopped, the quiet suddenly loud in its
absence. Then the embodiment of every fantasy she'd ever
had—every bad boy she'd ever dated or lusted after rolled
into one—stepped out from behind the podium, hammer in
hand, a light sheen of sweat on his forehead.

His arms were ripped and tattooed, his ears pierced, and
his jeans and T-shirt snug. Her knees trembled, her mouth
went dry, and her heart beat faster than it had since she'd
had that regrettable treadmill-tripping incident at the gym

a few months ago—she'd given up exercise *for* her health after that. The guy lifted the bottom of his shirt and wiped at his face, exposing glorious abs covered in more tattoos.

"Holy shitballs," Quinn said, and although she'd meant for it to be a whisper, it more burst out of her and echoed around the room, filling every corner of the chapel, drifting across the preacher, and bouncing right back to the entire wedding party.

Maya fought back a smile but hid it with her fake flower bouquet prop, Haha shot her a death glare, and Chichi's mouth formed a line so tight it looked like he'd lost it altogether. As for the groom's side?

It was dropped jaws, hands thrown over hearts, and a general mix of shock and awe that she'd enjoy under other circumstances but didn't strike her as particularly amusing now, especially combined with the pale pallor of the new town preacher.

At least Grayson was more caught in a permanent flinch than a disapproving scowl.

Well, hell. Did she mention she wasn't particularly good at first impressions?

• • •

Heath fought back a laugh as he glanced at the woman who'd just sworn in the chapel. The bride-to-be—who he assumed was her sister—looked amused, but everyone else wore horrified expressions. A few of them inched away as if lighting might strike her and get them in the process.

At first glance he'd noticed she was pretty, but as he took in her long dark hair and exotic Asian features, the adorable blush on her cheeks, and the deep red lips, he thought pretty didn't quite cut it. In fact, he was thinking he'd like to know more about the hottie with a sailor's mouth.

She was probably only in town for the wedding, though—he definitely would've noticed her earlier if she lived here. There was no place to hide in Hope Springs. Oh, sure, you could try to hide out at home, but the busybodies in town wouldn't allow it for long.

Speaking of townspeople… Heath glanced at the time. Nearly five. He'd picked up odd jobs here and there since he'd gotten back into town, but within a few minutes, he should be finding out if he was going to win the property he was eager to get busy fixing up. Then he could focus on building the dream he and his brother had talked about since they were old enough to think about the future.

The town committee moves about as slow as a snake on a cold day. Not that they were cold-blooded. Well, not all of them, although it was a possibility with a few of the older ladies. The thought of other people holding his future in his hands made a lump form in his gut.

If only he hadn't left such a bad impression back in high school. But he couldn't do anything about that now. Just keep proving he'd changed and hope for the best.

The hottie glanced back toward the wedding party. She carefully schooled her features, but the blush remained. "Sorry about that. I just…remembered that I need to make a call. For work. Please excuse me." She rushed out of the chapel, moving surprisingly fast considering the super-tall heels on her feet.

Heath dropped his hammer in his toolbox and gave the floorboards and formerly wobbly bench another test. "Did you need anything else?" he asked, addressing Preacher Hadfield.

"No. Thanks for taking care of it on such short notice. I meant to get it fixed weeks ago."

Heath took up his toolbox, ignoring the disapproving looks he got from the wedding party—he didn't even have to swear in church to earn them. It was another thing that had him worried when it came down to getting the town committee to accept his proposal. Add being from the wrong side of the tracks and having the wrong dad, and sometimes he thought he was stupid for even dreaming Mountain Ridge could be his.

It'd be easier if Cam were here—he was the charmer, the courageous soldier, and the more impressive of the two of them by far. But he was out there fighting for their country, so Heath could fight for this.

His friends Royce and Sadie were currently the town's golden couple, and with any luck, the good words Royce had put in about him—as well as the fact that he was in a band with Sadie—would go a long way. The property he was after was right next to their place, after all, and if they weren't afraid to be his neighbors, surely the committee would see that as a good sign.

When he'd first heard the property was going up for sale, he'd had no idea how many hoops he'd have to jump through to try to buy it. Who knew there were still places where the town committee got to decide who bought land and what the owner could do with it? That was Hope Springs, Wyoming, for you, though. It both irritated him and endeared the place to him at the same time, although he wasn't sure how that made any sense.

Man, he couldn't remember the last time he'd been this anxious. It was so much nicer to keep his nose in his business and not care about much else.

When he pushed out of the church, his pulse quickened at the sight of Miss Holy Shitballs herself leaning against the brick exterior. She had one foot propped against the wall, which had her skirt hiked up to midthigh territory on that side.

He grinned at her. "Hey."

"Are they sending the preacher after me with some holy water?" she asked, craning her neck to glance behind him.

"I think they're gathering wooden stakes, actually. But I guess if you're standing out here in the sun, they're not going to be very successful."

She placed a protective hand over her heart. "Vampire or not, I don't think a wooden stake to the chest would feel very good."

"True. If it gets ugly, I'll step in. Vouch for you. Considering the way they looked at me, though, I don't know if that'll help or hurt your case."

One side of her mouth kicked up, but as her gaze rose to his face, her almost smile faded and her eyebrows drew together. "Hey, you're Heath Brantley, aren't you? I didn't recognize you at first."

He tried to place if he'd met her before, but he was sure he wouldn't have forgotten a girl like her. But then pieces from town gossip, talk of the upcoming wedding, and Sadie's stories clicked into place. "You must be Quinn Sakata."

"*Must be?* So you don't remember me from high school?"

He shifted his toolbox to his other hand. "Nooo. Should I?"

"*Pfft.* Probably not with all your girls."

Dang, did I hit on her before? He knew she was Sadie's age, and he'd always made sure to stay away from the younger girls in high school—he was already the town rebel and hadn't needed to give the quilting ladies another reason to send the police after him. Judging by how many times cops had showed up at his house to "just ask a few questions," they'd thought he committed every crime in town. Not that there was much to report. It was usually about tracks in fields that broke trespassing laws, disturbing animals with loud noises, or the infamous cow tipping, with a few minor theft complaints and "someone smelled marijuana" thrown in.

Quinn straightened and poked a finger at his chest. "You once called me squirt. I came up to you, said hi, and you said, 'What do you need, squirt?'" Her eyes flashed and she advanced a step closer. Even with her giant heels on, she was pretty damn short, but he didn't think now was a good time to mention that.

"Uh, are you sure that was me?"

"Of course I am! I had a huge cr—" She clamped her lips together and shook her head, her cheeks coloring again.

He lightly cupped her elbow to see if he could fluster her a little more and get her to finish that sentence—he liked where it was going. "Go on."

She shook her head and then lifted her chin. "If Sadie hadn't spent the past few months saying nice things about you, I'd have some choice words for where you can stick your flirtation."

"But I won't call you squirt anymore, I promise." He shot her a grin. "How do you feel about half pint?"

"Ah!" She smacked his arm, and he laughed. It only took her a second to join in.

"Quinn?" The bride-to-be stuck her head out of the door. "Hey, we've got to wrap up the rehearsal so we can run the last of the errands and head to dinner. Hurry up and get all your swearing out now, then get your"—she glanced back into the church and lowered her voice—"butt back in here."

"How mad are Chichi and Haha?" Quinn asked.

"They haven't said a single word. Just lots of polite nodding."

"Uh-oh."

Heath assumed they were talking about their parents. He'd noticed the two older women on their side had occasionally given instructions in another language. Chinese or Japanese, or maybe Korean. Or maybe something else. He wouldn't know the difference.

"Yeah," her sister said, eyes wide. "And the Rutherfords are asking the preacher about the history of the church and where the stone came from, even though they clearly couldn't care less. Now tell the guy who caused the swearing good-bye and come on." She flashed Heath a quick smile and ducked back into the church.

Heath put a hand on his chest. "*I* caused the swearing?"

"Oh, no," Quinn said, sticking one finger in the air. "I've got a swearing problem. Just ask my parents. Actually, don't ask them, because it's kind of a sensitive subject. Ask Sadie, she'll tell you. It most *definitely* didn't have anything to do with you." The way she avoided his gaze made him think that wasn't totally true. A smug sense of satisfaction wound through him. He was about to ask if she was going to be in town for a while when his phone buzzed. Quinn's did, too, and she reached into her purse, her movements slightly frantic.

Heath took his cell out of his pocket, wondering if simultaneous texts meant another town drill was in effect—the last one was to prepare them for a stampede, even though he doubted there'd been any since the West was won, and before that, it was to alert everyone to an emergency meeting called because their usual float supplies vendor had gone out of business and they were worried about how it'd affect the Frontier Days parade.

But then he read the message.

The town is split on the bids for Mountain Ridge. We will have a meeting tonight at seven thirty to discuss the matter further. Your attendance is required.

"Tonight," Quinn muttered. "How am I going to pull that off with all the wedding stuff?"

Foreboding pricked Heath's skin. "You're not…"

She looked at him, confusion clear on her features, and then she noticed the phone in his hand. She leaned in and read, and since she'd find out eventually anyway, he let her.

"You're the other bid?" she asked.

"I'm going to be the winning bid."

The muscles around her jaw tightened, and something hard and—to be honest—scary overtook her expression. "Over my dead body. If you're my competition, I'm going to crush you."

A moment ago, he'd been thinking he should ask the girl out, and suddenly he wanted nothing more than to get away from her. "Don't count on it, squirt."

• • •

Hot bursts of anger traveled through Quinn's veins as she stomped back into the church, and it seemed like more swearing was inevitable. There was no way Heath Brantley could do a better job of running Mountain Ridge Bed and Breakfast than she could. In her practically nonexistent spare time, she'd studied different design themes, envisioning everything the eight-bedroom building could be. She wanted to keep the charm and hominess, but renovate more on the simple and sleek than frilly, overly floral side. She knew about the dozens of certificates she'd need, everything for renovations, starting an LLC, and the other documents required to open a business. She knew Wyoming commercial law like the back of her hand, and she was disciplined and driven. She'd wanted Mountain Ridge for longer than she'd wanted anything, and there was no way any guy — regardless of how hot he was — was taking it from her.

Is he seriously going to take phone calls and greet guests? Sit in the main room and organize family activities? Go ask people if they need more towels? How does he think he can run a bed and breakfast?

"You okay?" Grayson asked, putting his hand on her arm. And she got angry all over again, because the soft touch didn't ignite near the desire that the brief brush of Heath's callused fingers had brought. Of course Grayson had soft hands. He typed on a computer, made phone calls, and spent hours in meetings. There was nothing wrong with that. "Don't worry about my parents. They'll forget your slip in no time."

Slip. Right. Who the hell cared about that at a time like this? Her bid was in danger. She'd spent the last three years working at her father's commercial real estate company, starting with leasing offices and eventually moving up to acquiring and selling properties. She closed deals. Oversaw remodels. Clients liked her—loved her, actually. But she always had Chichi over her shoulder, telling her the things she did wrong and frowning at her if—heaven forbid—she showed excitement about closing a deal. The rest of the guys got to slap each other's backs, go out for beer and a game of golf, and she was supposed to nod quietly and go about her business.

Every time she'd had a bad day at the office lately, she told herself that it was only temporary. The end was in sight. Soon she'd have her own bed and breakfast where she could laugh as loud as she wanted, make small talk, meet new people, help arrange relaxing vacations, and live within walking distance of her best friend.

"Quinn, darling?"

Quinn glanced into Grayson's clear blue eyes and faked a smile. "I'm fine. Just hungry. Let's get this done and then we'll grab dinner."

And after that, she'd call in reinforcements and figure out a game plan to meet with the town committee and do whatever it took to close this Mountain Ridge property deal.

Chapter Two

Quinn didn't need to ask Grayson what he thought of Seth's Steak and Saloon, or what most locals referred to as the Triple S. He'd given the old western-style exterior scrunched-up eyebrows, and his footsteps slowed as they pushed inside—no swinging door, for the record. Wyoming got way too freezing in the winter for that madness.

His obvious trepidation only grew as he swept his gaze across the wooden interior, from the tables dotting the room to the large dance area complete with a country music–filled jukebox. A twangy country song filled the air—someone had obviously lost a tractor or a cow. Probably his girlfriend, too, so double whammy.

Quinn grinned, the feeling of being home washing over her. When she'd first come through Hope Springs as a little girl, she'd immediately fallen in love. Haha had been on Chichi to take a family trip and they'd brought Sobo Machi along with them. They'd stayed at the Mountain Ridge Bed and Breakfast for ten amazing days.

A few years later, when she'd been about ten and Maya was six, they'd tried to stay there again, but it was closed. Since the beautiful town was a central location to Chichi's properties, which spanned across southern Wyoming as well as northern Colorado and Utah, her parents eventually decided to build a summer home/place for Chichi to stay while going back and forth. After another year of Quinn begging them to move to Hope Springs full-time, they'd finally given in and let her spend her high school years there. It meant Chichi had to travel a bit more, but at that time, he'd been traveling nonstop to acquire more real estate anyway.

Now she was the one traveling all the time, when all she wanted was to find her way back home to Hope Springs again.

"Come on," Quinn said, nudging Grayson. "It's fun and different."

Grayson wrapped his arm around her waist. "I like calm and the same."

Which is pretty much the opposite of me, in case you didn't notice. Quinn spotted Cory, Royce, and Sadie at a table in the corner. Sadie looked up and shot out of her seat. They met in the middle and crashed into a hug.

"Why if it isn't the Asian cowgirl in the flesh," Sadie said with a laugh, low enough for only Quinn to hear. Quinn had always joked she was going to be the first famous Asian cowgirl, but then she and Sadie had found out it was a slang term for a sex position and it became a running joke. One they were careful to use just between them, because guys always took it a level or five too far.

"I missed you so much," Quinn said. During the six long

years Sadie had spent in Nashville, they'd only gotten to communicate via phone and email, but after coming back to Hope Springs a couple of months ago for what was supposed to be a temporary stay, she was back permanently. "Being able to hang out like we used to over the summer only made me realize how sucky it is when I don't get to."

"Same." Sadie stepped back and glanced at Grayson. Before Quinn could introduce him, Royce and Cory showed up. They exchanged hugs, and then Royce's arm wrapped around Sadie.

Their eyes locked, and they kissed. She couldn't believe either of them had ever doubted they were meant to be together when it was so clear to everyone else. Which reminded her… "The ring! I need to see the ring!"

Sadie held out her hand. Quinn had gotten a picture of the western-style wedding band with the diamond, but in person it was so much better. Not that it looked any different, but this way she got to exchange excited smiles with her best friend.

"I've learned a ton helping Maya throw this wedding together record fast, so we've got to talk wedding deets," Quinn said.

Grayson cleared his throat and Quinn shot him an apologetic smile. "Sorry." She introduced him to Sadie, Royce, and Royce's best friend, Cory. All four of them had spent their high school years together. Cory had even taught her how to ride a horse. Considering the guy was a complete commitmentphobe, it was surprising she hadn't fallen for him. Probably because despite the tan skin, jet-black hair, and piercing blue eyes, he still had a good-guy look to him. In high school, she'd preferred the tattooed bad boys who'd crush her heart and never look back.

Guys like Heath—hell, Heath had been on her crush radar since her freshman year. Now she knew better. No getting distracted by the sexy tattoos... *Next time I see him, I'm going to have to see what they are.*

Wait. No. I'm going to crush him, not crush on *him. Come on, brain. Get it together.*

"Are we going to sit down?" Grayson asked.

"Of course," Quinn said, realizing for the second time that night she'd forgotten about her boyfriend. "Sadie and I will go get drinks!" It came out way too excited, but hey, alcohol was exciting, so she stood by it.

Sadie turned to Royce. "Coors?"

"Make that two," Cory said, apparently so used to them talking two inches from each other's faces he didn't mind interrupting.

"Hurry back." Royce slid his hands into Sadie's rhinestoned back pockets and kissed her like she'd be gone for weeks.

"You got it, cowboy. And just so you know, I'm dragging you on the dance floor later, so be ready."

He sighed as if it were a huge inconvenience, but the passion in his eyes gave him away. They were so cute that if she didn't love them so much, she might hate them. They'd earned their happiness the hard way, though, reuniting after six years apart. Now Sadie worked at Second Chance Ranch with Royce, helping rehabilitate at-risk youth, all while recording an album and traveling with her band, Dixie Rush. A band that happened to include Heath, but Quinn was trying not to think about that and focus on how well Royce and Sadie seemed to be handling the transition, despite the long stretches apart they occasionally had to endure.

They were only a few steps toward the bar when Sadie raised an eyebrow. "So what's the deal with the boyfriend? There's definitely an absence of sparkage."

Quinn's shoulders slumped. "I'm trying to date safe guys, remember?"

"There's safe, and then there's dead in the water. You know I love you, and if you tell me it's working—"

"I keep trying to make it, but I'm just not sure…" She sighed and ran a hand through her hair. "He's smart, polite, and successful, and in the beginning I was sure he was exactly what I needed to prove to myself that I could be attracted to nice guys. And you saw him—he's easy on the eyes. But sometimes it feels more like I want to want him than that I want him, you know? I worked so hard to impress his family today, too. I'm not sure swearing super loud in the church during the wedding rehearsal was the kind of impression I was going for, but that's how I roll."

A laugh burst out of Sadie. "Did your parents have mutual heart attacks?"

"Heart palpitations were definitely involved. Probably more on my part, though. You failed to mention that Heath Brantley's the kind of hot that makes swearwords fly out of your mouth."

Sadie shrugged. "You've seen him before. I didn't know it was news."

"Do girls constantly throw themselves at him after your shows?"

"Yes," Sadie said matter-of-factly. Which was another reason Quinn shouldn't give a second thought to the guy. They'd had such great banter going on before finding out they were on opposing sides, too.

They reached the bar, and Quinn plopped herself on an empty bar stool, hooked her heels on one of the rungs, and folded her forearms across the well-worn wood. "And did you know that he's the other bid for Mountain Ridge Bed and Breakfast?"

Sadie flinched. So yes. "I'm sorry, Q. You know I want you here more than anything, but I also need Heath to stick around now that Dixie Rush is taking off. So I've been waiting for the town committee to make their choice, trying to stay out of it and hoping you both somehow get it."

"Don't you go Switzerlanding on me."

"If Switzerland were a verb, I'm afraid I'd have to." Sadie held up her hands. "Seriously, I can't get in the middle of you guys. Please don't ask me to."

Quinn scowled at nothing in particular. Their high school classmate Seth, who'd inherited the Triple S, came over, familiar green cap covering his red hair. "What trouble are you girls planning to get into tonight?"

"Same old same," Quinn said. "General destruction and debauchery."

"So tequila?"

"And Coors for the guys," Sadie said.

"And a…martini for…yeah, just a martini." Quinn doubted many people ordered martinis here. Not that it wasn't a perfectly okay drink. Bond made do with one, so it's not like it made Grayson less of a man. Now the trips to the salon to get his hair just so…

Better abandon that train of thought right now.

The jukebox transitioned, another loud song blaring through the room. Seth glared at the box, rolled his eyes, and headed to get drinks. While she loved the jukebox with its never-ending supply of country tunes, Seth felt quite the opposite, which cracked her up. Last time she and Sadie had been in the Triple S he'd told them he wanted to get rid of the dance floor and go all bar and restaurant, but apparently the town committee wrote him a letter demanding the dancing go on. Now that they had *her* future in their hands, she didn't find it nearly as funny.

"It's just all I ever wanted," Quinn said, turning to Sadie, who'd taken the next stool over. "You know how long I've talked about Mountain Ridge."

"I know." She bit her lip. "Did you hear from the committee, then?"

"Heath and I have been summoned to a meeting later tonight, right when I'm supposed to be helping out with the last-minute wedding stuff and entertaining the Rutherfords, so I'm going to have to come up with a good excuse to sneak away." Quinn ran her thumbnail over the edge of the bar. "How does Heath expect to run the place when you guys have to travel to shows all the time?"

Sadie shook her head. "I don't know. He talked to Royce about the property before we got back together. Whenever it came up the past few months, I told them I wanted to stay out of it, because I knew if he talked to me, I'd be obligated to talk to you, and I really was trying to stay clear. Honestly, I figured you'd easily win over the committee. I wanted deniability on both sides."

"I *am* going to win."

"Good luck. And I mean that in the sincerest, I-shouldn't-be-saying-this-out-loud-but-you-know-I'd-pick-you way. Now, back to the guy over there…" Sadie glanced at Grayson and so did Quinn.

"Maya made me promise not to break up with him before the wedding. It's a good thing, though, because it's given me a chance to see how easy things are between our families. Grayson was actually nice about the swearing, too, even though I could tell he was embarrassed by it."

"That makes more sense—the first part, I mean," Sadie said. "Getting along with your family is good, and being nice about the swearing is all fine and well, but I'm not sure that means he's right for you. The real you."

The real her. People tended to scare when she fully freed the real her. "Despite the cultural differences, my parents have accepted Steven. Of course the Rutherfords' wealth, high business standing, and the fact that they lease our biggest building obviously helps. Plus Maya's the golden child and therefore would only fall for a good guy. But they also like Grayson, which has never happened with any of my boyfriends before. We've managed to make it past my usual relationship benchmarks, and it really is a more mature relationship than I've had with other guys. Maybe I should stick it out." She told herself that they could work on the chemistry. Most relationships needed a good shake-up now and then to keep them fresh. "He's good to me and gives me a sense of security, even if I am a little bored sometimes."

"I think you deserve better than boring," Sadie said.

Easy to say. The problem was the guys Quinn wanted— the guys that were the opposite of boring and secure—all had the same expectations. Sadie didn't quite understand, because while she had never slept around, sex was part of the equation when it came to her relationships.

While Quinn had wrestled with her decision and

occasionally still did here and there when it pushed her and a guy she liked to the breaking point, she hadn't given in. Because while there were many principles and beliefs her parents and she disagreed on, waiting until marriage for sex was one that had stuck. She didn't judge people who didn't do the same, but she couldn't help but judge guys who walked out when they realized she truly wasn't going to sleep with them, especially not as an ultimatum.

So far, Grayson had respected her boundaries, even though he occasionally tested them or asked if she'd changed her mind. So maybe it wasn't the sparks Sadie and Royce had, but sparks meant getting burned, and after enough of that, she liked to think she'd learned her lesson.

• • •

The bolt finally came free, and Heath maneuvered to the side so that the oil would spill into the pan and not onto him. The last oil change of the day, and then he'd need to race home, shower, and get ready for the town committee meeting. While he'd sworn he'd never work for Dad at Rod's Auto Repair again, when he'd come back to town, he'd had to swallow his pride and find a way to make money and get away with free rent. Free rent came with so many strings attached, he wasn't sure he could actually call it that, though.

It's just a means to an end. A way to make sure I never have to work for anyone else ever again. Another month and I'll be done with both this job and my current living arrangements.

Just as soon as he got Mountain Ridge. The old building would need to be demolished and replaced with the lodge, and then he planned on erecting a garage where he could work on his custom motorcycles during the slow season. He wasn't even sure if there'd be a busy season—he just knew that one night in high school, when he and his brother had decided they weren't going to end up like Dad, they'd started talking about how to make money at something they'd enjoy. After joking about things like professional motorcycle testers, sports car drivers, and the snort-worthy suggestion of being gigolos, the hunting lodge idea had come out.

He and Cam had practically grown up on the mountain range behind Mountain Ridge, hiking, camping, fishing, and hunting. Any time they got a chance, they'd pack their gear and disappear for as long as possible, and they knew those trails, hills, and lakes like the backs of their hands. Whenever they'd see that abandoned B and B, they'd comment that whoever ended up with the building would be lucky to have such an amazing place practically in their backyard. That night when they'd discussed their futures, they'd decided *they* could be the lucky ones.

For years it was more of a pipe dream, but shortly before Cam enlisted, he'd taken Heath out to the Mountain Ridge property and said, "When it goes up for sale, we're building that lodge. Look at all that space. Think of how easily we can head into the mountains on a whim. People will come from all over to get away from their lives, and ours will involve taking them to hang out where we most want to be anyway. Can you see it?"

And Heath *had* seen it. He saw freedom from Dad's mood swings, beers on the porch of a large log cabin with his brother, and guys coming and going for the various hunting seasons. Now he also saw his motorcycle garage off to the side. Custom bikes had started as a hobby, but word of mouth spread, and now he had a decent amount of high-paying jobs lined up. He'd saved every single spare penny, and the shows he'd played with Sadie and the album they'd recorded had helped push his bank account to the respectable range. Add Cam's contribution, and now the hunting lodge was so close he could close his eyes and see it.

By the time his brother got back from his last deployment ever, it'd be ready to open—Heath would make sure of that.

Three more months. Then we'll be together again, and all the family drama won't seem so bad.

"Heath?" The small voice drifted across the room, and then two untied shoes came into view.

"Under here, buddy. Give me just a minute."

"Dad didn't pick me up from baseball," Oliver said. "I can walk home if I need to."

"I'm almost done here. Why don't you go grab a pop out of the machine? By the time you're done drinking it, I should be finished up." Heath wiped his hand on his jeans, leaving smudges of black—he should've pulled on the coveralls, but another stain wouldn't hurt his already beat-up pants. He dug into his wallet and produced two dollar bills.

Oliver bent sideways and stuck his face in the gap beneath the car. He still had on his baseball mitt—he rarely took it off these days. "This means I get to ride on the motorcycle, right?"

"Right." He extended the money to his seven-year-old brother. "How was practice?"

"Made it to second base once. A grounder came up and hit me in the chin." He rubbed a red mark on there, the dollar bills crumpling with the effort. Then he looked at the green papers, straightened them, and ran toward the pop machine.

"Tie those shoes before you trip," Heath called, even though he knew it was too late. The focus was on pop now—no going back.

Like the rest of the women Dad chose, Oliver's mom was pretty and completely unreliable. She was half Dad's age, and only a year older than Heath. Their relationship—if it could even be called that—had only lasted a few months. Just long enough for Oliver to happen, really. The poor kid had no parents—not functional, responsible ones, anyway—so Heath tried to pick up the slack now that he was here. He knew all too well how hard it was to grow up like that, but unlike Ollie, at least he'd had Cam living under the same roof.

Heath finished up the oil change, parked the car, and told Mrs. Perkins she was good to go. He headed back to the garage to check on Oliver, who was downing a bottle of Mountain Dew, his swinging legs rocking the chair he perched on. Probably should've specified a pop without caffeine, but it's not like the kid had a mellow mode, caffeine or not. "Ready to—"

"Excuse me." A man in a suit appeared at the garage entrance. Heath knew he'd seen him before, and it took a moment to connect the dots. In the church today. The father of the bride. And of the woman he'd had a hard time not thinking about ever since he'd talked to her outside of the church. He kept reminding himself he was up against her for Mountain Ridge, so asking her out was absolutely out of the question.

Maybe a consolation dinner would help her not be too angry when I win, though.

"I need someone to look at my car," Mr. Sakata said.

"Sorry, but the shop's closed for the night." Heath needed to get Ollie home and make sure he had some dinner to go with the fizzy bubbles pumping through his system. Then he needed to jump through the shower and haul ass to the committee meeting.

"I'll make it worth your while. I won't have time tomorrow with my daughter's wedding."

Inwardly Heath sighed. He mussed Ollie's overgrown blond hair. "Give me a few more minutes," he said and then he turned back to Mr. Sakata. "What seems to be the problem?"

The gleaming Mercedes caught the dying light of the day, reflecting orange and pink on the silver hood. Mr. Sakata ran his gaze over him, a whole lot of judgment filling the brown. "This isn't just any car, you know. Everything's controlled by the internal computer. Are you even qualified to work on it?"

Qualified? The guy insisted on him looking at it, and now he was going to insult him? Dad was the one with all the official certification. Heath had worked on cars since he could pick up a wrench, but technically, he didn't have a certificate qualifying him for the job. Not that he was going to tell Mr. Sakata that while he looked down his nose at him. "Why don't you tell me the problem, and we'll go from there."

"The check engine light came on."

Heath looked inside, and sure enough, the light glowed orange.

"You're going to put some type of protection on the seat before you sit in it, aren't you?" Mr. Sakata asked. "You're covered in grease."

Heath straightened, fighting the urge to drag his dirty hands across the gray leather. "Why don't you pull it in, and I'll get the scan tool. And don't worry about your seats. I'll make sure they stay in their pristine condition."

If Quinn was as concerned with fancy cars, he probably couldn't afford a big enough consolation prize. Then again, if she was loaded, she could offer more for the property. His heart sank at the thought. It'd take everything he and Cam had saved to get the property, and they'd still need to take out a loan for the construction. All she'd have to do is bat her eyes at Daddy and he'd probably hand over a couple extra grand.

Mr. Sakata got out of his car, and Heath took the keys and ushered him into the office where he could wait. The man looked around at the chairs and apparently decided they'd get his suit dirty, because he remained standing.

Let him stand, then.

Heath hooked up the scan tool to the car, found it was an emission error, and checked the gas cap—it'd come loose. He contemplated letting Mr. Hoity-Toity stew, but Ollie had finished his pop and was starting to pick up stray tools. Which usually meant about five minutes before he destroyed something, either other tools or body parts.

Heath took the keys back inside the office and explained the error. "So just double-check your gas cap next time, and you'll be fine."

Mr. Sakata reached for his wallet. "What do I owe you?"

"No charge. Have a good day. And enjoy the wedding tomorrow." The man probably didn't know that Heath would be at the reception afterward. They'd asked Sadie to sing, and that meant he'd be on the guitar.

As Mr. Sakata walked away, Heath gripped the edge of the counter. The Sakatas owned a ton of real estate—they obviously knew how to work the system. If they outbid him enough to sway the committee...

I could get a bigger loan and pay it off after the album releases. I'll just hope the record hits it big.

Desperation crept in, and it only got worse as he thought about Cam's last email. He'd been so excited about the lodge, and he'd detailed the tours he'd already mapped out to the best spots, from easier and a day trip to extreme and camping up to a week. He'd also mentioned that if he didn't have that to come home to, he probably would've had to reenlist again.

More than anything, Heath wanted his brother to have a place and a job he loved to come home to. A place where they could make good memories to overtake the bad. From their past and from the war.

So he wouldn't just roll over and watch their dream go to someone else—to people who already had dozens of properties at their disposal. *I'll do whatever it takes. Even if it means taking on one of the most powerful real estate families in the state.*

Chapter Three

Quinn marched into town hall, head held high. The majority of the time getting what you wanted boiled down to confidence. And okay, money factored in there, too, but no one would entrust you with money if you didn't have confidence.

The usual suspects had gathered, the who's who that'd run Hope Springs forever. Patsy Higgins sat at the head of the table. The woman somehow knew everything that took place within the town limits mere minutes after it happened. Quinn and Sadie used to joke that her grandmotherly exterior was a front to hide the fact that she was a former CIA spy who'd take you out if you didn't participate in town functions.

Good thing I stopped myself at the one tequila shot more than an hour ago, with a giant steak and fries to help absorb it. With Cory teasing her that she'd turned into a soft city girl, it hadn't been easy to resist his dare to do more shots, but she needed her head straight for this.

See. I totally know how to be mature when I have to be.

The door swung open with a *creak*, and heavy, booted steps echoed through the room. Somehow she knew it was Heath, even before she turned around to confirm it.

Whereas she'd put on her lucky power suit, he wore the same clothes as earlier today, only now they were smudged with black—the guy hadn't even shaved or showered. It looked damn good on him, too, and even as Quinn told herself not to check him out, her pulse steadily inclined as she took in the intricate tattoos, muscles, and scruff. A black baseball hat sat on his head, covering the light brown hair that'd probably been blond as a kid, and unlike the majority of men who lived here, his black boots were more motorcycle than cowboy.

He stopped right next to her and flashed her a smile that turned her insides to mush. "Hey, squirt."

The mush hardened and she curled her hands into fists. Oh, he wanted to play that way, huh? "You know, you probably should've dressed up to make a good impression. Lucky for me, you're out of your league."

"Pardon me if I didn't line my pockets with my daddy's money first. Some of us have to work for a living."

That stung, a dozen needles right to her chest. The whole point of this was to *not* be tied to Chichi's money or the marionette strings that came with it. In fact, if he knew she was here, he'd tell her to stop playing around and focus on her job. Another reason to stay and get what she wanted. She couldn't be a puppet anymore. The money she'd bid was all hers, savings from three years of working for Sakata Real Estate. She wished it were more, but the first year she hadn't been thinking long-term. Honestly, she'd been thinking house-decorating stuff! Clothes! *Shoes!*

But she'd turned it around when she realized that a fancy townhouse and wardrobe wasn't making her the kind of deep-down happy she craved and she needed a long-term plan to get what she truly wanted.

"Looks like we're ready to get started," Patsy Higgins said. "Thank you both for coming on such short notice. We figured you'd want to hear this right away, and Quinn, we know you're in town for your sister's wedding, which gave us a small window to work with. The committee has gone the rounds over the Mountain Ridge property. We see advantages in having a bed and breakfast where tourists can bring their entire families to come and enjoy our little town…"

Quinn straightened, pride and determination buoying her. She knew she could accomplish that better than Heath.

"…but we also see the benefit and tourist draw of a hunting lodge."

"A hunting lodge?" It burst out of Quinn, the way her thoughts tended to. She spun to Heath. "You want to turn my beautiful bed and breakfast into a freaking *hunting lodge*? Over my dead body."

A gavel banged—what was this, court? The committee's faces ranged from annoyed to angry to bored.

"Miss Sakata," Patsy Higgins said, pointing the gavel she was wielding at Quinn. "If you'll kindly keep from interrupting…"

Heath chuckled under his breath, and Quinn crossed her arms as tightly as she could to keep from smacking him. "Of course. Sorry. I just didn't realize there was a chance Mountain Ridge Bed and Breakfast would be anything but what it was *historically* built for."

Okay, adding the "historically" was a bit of a jerk move, but it was also accurate.

"Do you know how much tourism hunting brings to Hope Springs?" Mack Gardner, one of the men on the committee, asked. "People come from all over to hunt game here."

"The lodge would be for more than hunting, too," Heath said. "Snowmobiling, motorcycle rides, tours of the rivers, lakes, and mountain ranges. It'd be a more *authentic* Wyoming experience."

"Yes, yes," Patsy Higgins said. "We've read the proposals from both of you. If you'll listen, we'll let you know what we've decided."

Pressure built within Quinn, hotter and hotter, seeking an escape. If she were a teakettle, she'd be whistling.

"Neither one of you has lived here for several years, which worries us."

Quinn opened her mouth to argue and then clamped it closed, her teeth clicking shut. She glanced at Heath and found him looking back at her. Apprehension showed in his features as well—he wanted this badly, too, she could tell.

Taking it from someone only mildly interested would be so much easier.

"With Frontier Days coming up, you both have the perfect opportunity to show us how much you're willing to dedicate to this town. The Morris family has been dealing with medical issues, which means we're shorthanded this year. There are floats to finish and the parade to put on, as well as the barbecue and other town festivities. We plan on making our decision at the end of the festival, when we've seen how well you work with the committee and what you're willing to do for the town."

"But..." Quinn's stomach bottomed out. "I could help with anything during the festival, but my office is in Cheyenne. I'm not sure I could be here during the week to build floats."

Patsy Higgins's face grew grim, as did the faces of the rest of the committee members. She nodded tightly. "I see."

"I'm here," Heath said. "I'll clear my afternoons and evenings and help with whatever you need."

Patsy Higgins brightened, and once again, everyone else followed her lead, as if their expressions worked as one. "That's so good to hear, Heath. Pleasantly unexpected, truly."

Quinn was pretty sure a muscle in his jaw tightened, but he held the plastered-on smile. Her bed and breakfast, with its gourmet meals, never-ending stream of happy couples and families, and fun activity-filled days, along with the childhood memories it held, started to drift away, like a cloud she'd caught hold of only to find nothing substantial to grip.

"I might need a few days," Quinn said, "but I'll find a way to help. I'll take leave from my work, and you can count on me, too."

The grin on Patsy Higgins's face widened—clearly she'd just gotten everything she wanted. "Excellent. Quinn, we'll give you a few days, but with the celebration only a month away, we must get on this. Meet at the bus garage Friday evening and we'll dole out assignments. Until then, this meeting is adjourned."

As she and Heath walked toward the exit, Quinn muttered under her breath, mimicking his earlier statement. "I'll clear my afternoons and evenings and help with whatever you need." Of course he was free. Just her luck.

"Did you say something?"

"I have a full-time job in Cheyenne. I can't just ignore everything and be here. It's so unfair."

"Not my problem."

"How about how much you travel with Sadie? How do you even think you're going to run this, this"—she forced the words out, the image of rough wooden walls and floors, along with orange vests, camping gear, and muddy boots strewn about, making her wrinkle her nose—"hunting lodge, while being on the road?"

Heath pushed out one of the large double doors of town hall and held it open for her. "Hunting season is the band's slow period, and I plan on having help. Don't worry about me. *I've* got it under control."

She stepped past him, onto the large concrete step in front of the tan brick building, and then spun to face him as the door closed with a loud *clang*. "I don't care how much you *think* you've got it under control. There's no way I'm letting you turn my classy bed and breakfast into a lodge with animal heads and antlers tacked on the wall so that a bunch of guys can scratch their balls and drink beer by a fire while congratulating one another over an archaic so-called sport."

"Big surprise. You're a snob. Didn't see that one coming," he deadpanned.

"A snob?" All her life people had accused her of that. Said things about how her family was rich so of course she didn't understand. That it must be nice to buy anything she wanted. That she was spoiled. Stuck-up.

Sticks and stones. They didn't realize how suffocating it

was to live under a roof where she was never allowed to go out and where her attitude—which she thought of more as her personality—was a problem. Where she'd been grounded more than not. And in spite of counting the days to get away from it all, after college, she'd given in to pressure and joined the family business, foolishly thinking that being a grown-up would mean things would be different. Now the suffocating happened at work and she was counting down the days again, scared of dishonoring her family but even more scared she'd never break free. Trying to explain that to the jerk in front of her would be a waste of breath, though, so she didn't bother.

Right as she was about to make a dramatic break for her car, Heath leaned in, a challenge glinting in his eyes. "And as for the *letting* me build my hunting lodge, go ahead and try to stop me. If you need me, I'll be volunteering for float duty."

• • •

Heath couldn't believe he was living in his childhood house again. When he'd left at eighteen, he hadn't even cast a last glance at the place, glad to be rid of it. Coming back certainly hadn't ignited any fuzzy feelings. His pride nearly stopped him from moving back in with Dad, but he needed every last cent for Mountain Ridge.

As he parked his truck in front of the run-down three-bedroom bungalow, he took a fortifying breath. When it came to Dad, Heath never knew if he'd get drunk and disorderly or the jokester or just plain mean. It depended how many drinks in he was, and if he'd pulled out the hard stuff.

Pocketing his keys, because Dad never bothered locking the door, Heath walked up the cracked sidewalk overgrown with weeds and then stepped inside the cluttered house. At first he'd tried to straighten up, but Dad seemed to take offense to that, so now he simply left the bottles and cans alone. Not to mention he didn't understand the "organizing system," also known as the way Dad stacked hunting and gun magazines going back years in piles around the room. Target practice, fishing, and hunting trips were some of the few good memories he had with Dad. Especially during the earlier years, when Dad had had something to live for and at least tried to control how much he drank.

But then Dad had injured himself on the job—an accident with a tractor that'd nearly torn his arm off. After that, his drinking spiraled out of control, Mom left, and subsequently, he got fired from the job that'd left him injured. Instead of trying again, he'd decided to collect disability and call it good. It was almost enough to feed and clothe his kids. Almost.

As soon as Cam was old enough to drive, he and Heath would escape to the mountains as often as possible, taking every opportunity they could to be away from the house. It also gave them the chance to catch enough fish and game to keep the freezer well stocked.

Eventually Dad had sort of recovered and bought the garage with a loan from the bank he probably still owed a ton on, considering that before Heath came back to town, the hours it'd been open were hardly regular or enough to sustain a business.

Dad glanced up at him and patted the threadbare tan couch he'd never bothered replacing, even though it'd been a hand-me-down when he and Mom had gotten married. Who knew how many years of alcohol had been spilled on it. "Sit. Watch the game."

Heath looked from the TV to the mitt on the coffee table. "Did Ollie's mom come pick him up?" If she had, Heath would have to run the mitt over—the kid would need it tomorrow.

"No, she wanted to go out tonight. Said it was my turn to watch him. He's in the back room playing video games. It's all kids do these days, apparently."

"I'm going to check on him." Dad shrugged and turned up the volume on the TV.

Heath opened the door to Cam's old room. In the middle of stacked battered furniture and boxes containing clothes Cam hadn't worn in years sat a bed. Ollie's blond head stuck out against the navy bedspread. Trigger lay next to him but perked up his ears when Heath stepped inside.

Within seconds, his blue heeler puppy jumped off the bed and bounced around at his feet. Heath bent down and petted his gray-and-tan coat. One spot of black circled his left eye, and his opposite ear matched it. When Heath had come across a family selling the blue heeler puppies a couple of weekends ago, he'd known he wanted this one. Someday, he was going to be a great hunting dog.

He scooped up Trigger and scratched behind his ears as he plunked down next to Ollie, who had his gaze glued to the small TV on the dresser. "Get that guy in the background or you're dead."

A grin spread across Ollie's face when he fired with his controller and the other guy went down. "Yes," he said, pumping his fist as the screen announced his team had won.

"I'm just like Cam now, huh?"

"Pretty close," Heath said. While Ollie had barely met Cam during his last leave, he already admired him. The kid was obsessed with all things army and marines.

Ollie flung aside the controller and glanced around. "When Cam gets out of the army, where am I gonna sleep when I stay the night? He'll need his room back."

"By the time Cam gets out, he'll have somewhere else to sleep." Heath almost told Oliver that he could have a bedroom in the lodge, too, but the kid had enough people who made promises they couldn't keep. He knew he couldn't take care of a kid full-time, but he'd make sure Ollie had a place to come play when both of his parents were pointing fingers and shoving the kid back and forth like a toy they'd tired of playing with.

His thoughts turned to the two bikes he was working on, the three gigs he and Dixie Rush had booked, the hours he needed to put in at the station, and on top of all that, he now got to squeeze in float building. He didn't have the first clue about how to build a float, but he'd do the dance.

For just a moment, Heath dropped his internal defenses and let Quinn's image pop into his mind. When he'd seen her standing there in the town hall, his heart had thumped hard in his chest. It'd been a long time since he'd seen a girl and lost the ability to speak.

But then she'd spoken, and it was clear she thought as little of him as her father had. He'd nearly been late because of the guy, hadn't charged him, and he'd still looked at Heath like a spot that needed scrubbed out.

After his flirtatious interaction with Quinn at the church, he'd been disappointed to see she felt the same. Still, something about the flash of anger and the way she'd practically stomped her foot over the committee's decision made a dart of desire shoot through his system.

The girl was damn cute, he'd give her that.

But that was all he was going to give her.

Chapter Four

Quinn tried not to stare at Heath as Dixie Rush set up on-stage for the reception. A long-sleeved white button-down covered his tattoos, although a hint of them showed through. There was no covering up the earrings, and he hadn't bothered shaving, something she knew her parents would notice and shake their heads over—once Sadie sang, though, they'd forget their complaints.

The postwedding glow must be responsible for making her more wistful than bitter as she took him in, her joy over her little sister's happiness combating the irritation from last night. The ceremony had been short and sweet, simple yet beautiful, and filled with the townspeople who'd shaped a big part of their lives—everything Maya had wanted to achieve by having it in Hope Springs.

Even better, Quinn had managed to avoid blurting out any swearwords to ruin the mood. The preacher had kept giving her worried looks, each one adding more pressure and paranoia she'd somehow screw it up. But vows were exchanged, tears shed, and now Maya was Mrs. Maya Sakata Rutherford.

People were still over by the chapel congratulating the couple, but Haha had rushed Quinn and the rest of their family over to make sure everything was perfect for the reception.

I'm simply doing my job, Quinn thought as she continued to stare at the stage. *Making sure Heath looks perfect—er, the band looks perfect.*

When he picked up his guitar, her knees wobbled. As if he needed anything to make him hotter. She'd always chosen her crushes well, and the residual nervousness of seeing him in the school halls hit her. Of that day she'd finally approached him, thinking she'd throw out a flirty line, only to stand and blink at him.

This is stupid. I'm not in high school anymore, and last night he became nothing more than the competition. Infuriating competition who wants to replace my B and B with a hunting lodge, at that.

And I have a boyfriend, she reminded herself as an afterthought.

But looking was free—as long as he didn't catch her.

"Can you fix that string of lights over there?" Haha pointed. "See how it's sagging? It looks awful!"

"Yes, Haha," Quinn said. The string of lights brought her closer to the band. Not that she noticed the mere fifteen feet or that Heath glanced her way. Or that he looked away so quickly.

Clearly he knows I'm not someone to mess with. She pulled a chair toward the sagging strand of lights, hiked up the skirt of her red dress, and balanced, heels and all, on the seat. As she wiggled the lights and the accompanying multicolored paper cranes into place, she prayed she wouldn't topple off the chair and break her neck. With Heath most likely watching, that'd be especially embarrassing.

Enough caring what he thinks. Focus on how he called me squirt. Told me I was a snob. Heat rose up and uncurled in her chest. *Yes, focus on the anger. On how I'm going to crush him before he can take away my dream.*

The bride and groom arrived as she was replacing the chair at the table she'd stolen it from, both grinning and glowing. Wedding guests trailed after them, the nearly empty reception area slowly filling with people.

Arms wound around her waist, and then she was pulled back against a firm body. A check over her shoulder confirmed it was Grayson. He spun her around and kissed her, and she closed her eyes and tried to let it take away the tension she'd felt since last night's nondecision from the town committee.

Grayson's lips moved next to her ear. "So, I was thinking we sneak away to my hotel room as soon as possible."

Quinn's shoulders stiffened. "Oh, yeah?"

He wrapped his arms tighter around her and kissed her neck. "Come on, Quinn. It's been six months."

"And…?" She knew what he was getting at, but time wasn't the issue. "You know my stance, Grayson. I made it clear that it's important to me."

"Maya and Steven didn't wait till the wedding, you know."

Every muscle in her body tensed. How did he know? And if he was telling the truth, why wouldn't Maya have told her? They'd always talked about how hard it was to find a guy willing to wait and how she'd been so happy that Steven was. "Well, I'm sure they at least waited until they were engaged…"

"You're saying either I ask you to marry me or it's not happening?" The cold edge of his words dug at her.

She pushed him back. "I'm not asking for that. I don't even want to get married right now. I'm just reminding you that I told you where I stood, and that hasn't changed."

Frustration wafted off him. Well, he wasn't the only one dealing with that feeling, which meant she had to work twice as hard to remain calm. Over the years, this same fight had escalated to yelling and nasty words between her and her boyfriend at the time. With their families now joined together—and all only a few yards away—discretion was key.

"Come on," he said, running his fingers down her necklace. "I've shown you I'm serious about you."

The diamond charm suddenly weighed a hundred pounds. She reached back, undid the clasp, and thrust it toward him. "Sorry, I'm not for sale."

Grayson set his jaw, not making a move to take the necklace. With his neat brown hair, dimpled chin, and pale blue eyes, he always seemed classically handsome, but right now she wanted to punch him right in his perfect nose. The emotions she'd tried to contain broke through, too. Disappointment and animosity and pain. She'd thought she'd finally found a guy who understood, but he was just like all the others.

"Now, don't go doing anything rash," he said, an unspoken threat in his words.

"Rash? You're the one pushing. Aren't you always

saying good investments are worth waiting for?"

"Yeah, but you've got to know when to walk away, too. Some things aren't worth the time you put in."

"What the hell's that supposed to mean?" Despite her attempts to keep it down, the question burst out of her, earning them a couple of looks.

Grayson wrapped his hand around her arm and walked her a few feet away, where a pillar wrapped in red ribbon and white lights blocked them from view. "Seriously, can you not keep it together, even in front of my family?"

She jerked free. "You're the one who came over and demanded sex. My swearing, my stance on waiting—it's a package deal. You either take me as I am, or we might as well end this now."

The fact that he didn't immediately tell her he wanted her as she was said everything. Tears pushed at her eyes. She shoved the necklace at Grayson again, slamming it to his chest and letting go, and then headed to the parking lot to collect herself so she could force on a happy face and get through the reception with her freshly exed boyfriend and his entire family.

• • •

Heath glanced at the stage where Will was still fiddling with his drums and then scanned the area, hoping to find Sadie, but she was nowhere to be seen. Probably got pulled away to chat.

Should I go hunt her down, or... Quinn quickened her pace, rushing in the direction of the parking lot, and Mr. All-American Douchebag headed back toward the crowd, clearly not going after her. *It's not like I can do anything to help.*

But the reception was starting, and he'd bet a missing bridesmaid would mess up the plan. Judging from the pain that'd crossed Quinn's features at whatever that yuppie had said to her, it'd be a while.

Just leave it alone. You don't have the first clue on how to deal with a crying woman, anyway, and that one would probably just call you a jerk or accuse you of taking advantage of her pain. He took a step toward the safety of the drama-free stage and then stopped in his tracks. *Damn it.*

He spun around. Maybe they could make a few vampire jokes and then she'd be okay. Even as his feet moved for the parking lot, he could hardly believe he was going after her. But what was he supposed to do? Just let her cry because they wanted the same property?

A more qualified search party would probably be the wiser choice, but he knew what it was like to need to be away from everything.

He found her leaning on a silver Mercedes similar to the one her father drove. The reminder of who she was almost made him turn back, but then she glanced his way.

The dying afternoon light caught the teardrop on her cheek. She quickly wiped it away and straightened, making a good effort at an *I'm-all-good* front. "I…" Her voice cracked, and then she closed her eyes and shook her head.

"I saw." He pointed his thumb back toward the festivities—the entire town square had been transformed with colorful paper lanterns and cranes, glowing lights, tables and chairs for a huge crowd, and a temporary stage. "I was making sure we were all plugged in and…I didn't hear the fight, just could tell that there'd been one and that it hadn't end-ed well." He took another hesitant step toward her. "You okay?"

"Not really." She cast a worried glance at the square. "There are slim-to-none odds that no one else noticed that fight, and if everyone at the reception starts talking about it, it'll be one more time I managed to mess up a nice family event with my 'bad attitude,' aka, the fact that I have a mind of my own."

"Don't worry, I hear wedding cake is magic. The sugar coma that follows tricks people into only remembering the good—it's how weddings continue to happen, despite the drama that inevitably goes down at them."

A smile tried to catch hold but only made it halfway across Quinn's lips before it lost steam.

"Plus, I really don't think anyone else saw," he added. "Like I said, I was back behind the stage, and all the decora-tions give pretty good cover from everything else."

"The hours I spent helping arrange them must've given me a little good karma to work with. If only it would've been enough to delay that fight a bit longer." Her lower lip quivered, and unshed tears made her eyes go glossy. "I should've known he was just like the rest."

"Clearly not right for you?"

She whipped her head toward him, and he held up his hands.

"I'm just saying, I could've told you that. He looks like a tool and you…" He ran his gaze down the fiery red dress that matched her personality, getting a little lost in the way it clung to her body and the sexy legs that led to those crazy-tall heels—without the help she could barely clear five feet.

"I what?"

"Look like that," he said, gesturing to her.

"Like a snob?"

Heath sighed and glanced back the way he'd come. He should've known after their last interaction that it'd go like this, regardless of his good intentions. "Maybe I should go."

Quinn slumped back against the car. "Sorry. It was nice of you to check on me, and the cake sugar coma theory was really funny…I'm just experiencing a mini crisis and I'm having a harder time than usual powering through. Don't worry, I'll be done in a quick sec." She sucked in a breath and let it out.

"You want me to go get Sadie?"

She shook her head and took another deep breath. Then she transformed before his eyes, blinking away the tears and pulling out a smile that made a strange sensation go through his gut, despite knowing it was fake. "Ready."

They headed back toward the buzz of the crowd. The girl must be a pro at shoving down emotions, because no trace of her sorrow remained. It'd probably freak him out if he wasn't too busy being intrigued by it.

"Thank you," she said, placing her hand on his arm. The glow from the decorations lit up her dark brown eyes and the featherlight touch on his arm made his stomach tighten. Entertaining thoughts of her was a bad idea all around, even if he ignored the property bid.

In spite of that, he still found himself looking forward to their forced interaction preparing for Frontier Days more than he should.

She dropped her hand, and he couldn't help saying, "A very pretty snob with a killer smile. For the record."

The corners of her mouth trembled as she tried to fight the smile, but then it broke free, and now he could see the difference between the fake one and the real one. From now on, only the real one would do. "From a Neanderthal, I'll take that as a compliment."

"Touché," he said with a laugh. Then he glanced at the stage, where Sadie and Will were scanning the crowd, most likely looking for him. "Catch you later." He backpedaled a few steps before turning around. Right before he reached the stage, he glanced to the spot where he'd left her.

He caught her watching him and winked.

She rolled her eyes, but he got another one of her killer smiles. Little girl was trouble with a capital *T*.

Come to think of it, it'd been way too long since he'd been in trouble.

• • •

"What were you doing talking to him?"

Chichi's stern voice cut through the happy vibes, a hot knife through butter. Quinn smothered her smile and turned around. "Who, Heath? I was just talking to him about the band, Chichi. He plays with Sadie, see?"

Chichi glanced at the stage and frowned. Sadie grinned and waved, and his stern expression softened. While he might not always approve of Sadie's choices—he'd literally said that before—she'd always had a way of charming people, and even the ever-serious Mr. Sakata wasn't unfazed.

He nodded at her and then turned back to Quinn. "Make sure you remember your priorities. It doesn't look good for you to be seen alone with someone like that, especially with your boyfriend and his family here."

Yeah, about that... She could only imagine the discussion their breakup would cause. Chichi always thought she was too wild to hold on to a man, and she'd always been too mortified to reply that she'd lost most of them because she wouldn't have sex with them. She and Chichi simply didn't have that kind of relationship. Neither did she and Haha, for that matter. If it weren't for Sadie, she'd likely implode. She always loved that despite the different decisions they'd made about having sex, Sadie never held back about that part of her life or talked to her like she was naive. Her best friend got that she'd made a decision, whereas a lot of people treated her like she was clueless about the particulars and needed shielding.

So while she definitely needed to have a lengthy discussion with her best friend about everything that'd happened with Grayson, she needed to wait until Maya was on her way to her honeymoon. For now it was time to pretend everything was butterflies and unicorns.

"Yes, Chichi. Looks like the place is getting busy. I'd better go see where I'm needed." Quinn purposely kept her gaze straight, no looking at the stage. Her parents would have a heart attack if she brought home someone like Heath.

It'd be slightly entertaining until the disappointment set in. She was so sick of being the family failure, which was why for the rest of the reception, she also avoided Grayson. Not too hard to do, because he was clearly doing the same to her. When people asked her questions, she smiled and nodded, never letting the slam from earlier show—good thing she'd perfected faking it till she made it.

There were forced posed pictures with Grayson in them,

of course, but keeping on opposite ends was easy enough. Once the car with JUST MARRIED drawn on the back window pulled away, the Rutherfords disappeared, her ex included.

At least Maya had gotten to drive away believing everything was picture-perfect—she deserved that kind of a fairy-tale ending.

The fact that the discarded decorations and overflowing trash cans made Quinn want to wax poetic about how she totally knew how they felt meant it was probably time to go home. If only she wouldn't get accused of ditching out of her responsibilities.

Just a little longer and I can leave and have a real cry, she thought as she grabbed the guest book and cleared the table it'd been on. It wasn't so much that she'd been super attached to Grayson—although his rejection had stung more than she would've guessed—but more like the idea of him. A nice guy her family liked who didn't give her a sex ultimatum. Until he did.

If even the straitlaced "safe" guys ran at the mention of celibate dating, what chance did she have with a guy she was crazy about? She already knew, because she'd attempted to date plenty of them. It never worked, smoking-hot chemistry or supposed security. Eventually Chichi would have to recruit one of his friends' sons to take pity on her and drag her down the aisle. Yeah, that sounded hot.

Sadie leaned on the table, placing herself in Quinn's line of sight and crossing one ankle over the other. "What happened with the boyfriend?"

"Oh, you know. Same thing that happens every time. Did Heath tell you?"

Sadie's eyebrows drew together. She glanced Heath's

way—he was putting his guitar case into a black truck with raised tires and a roll bar. A motorcycle was strapped in back and a gun rack hung across the rear window. The dude was country through and through.

She'd always liked country boys. There was just something about their rugged manliness that made her heart pump double time and her common sense fly right out the window.

"Earth to Quinn?" Sadie snapped her fingers in front of Quinn's face. "I just noticed that you guys kept your distance, and obviously he's not here now, so I figured something had happened. How does Heath know?"

"He saw the fight—didn't hear it, thank goodness, because then I'd have to die of mortification and call it good."

Anger flickered through Sadie's eyes. "He really dumped you because of sex?"

"Yeah. It's been six months. Apparently that's supposed to be long enough to change my mind. Oh, and he brought up Mr. Sparkles, like gifting me with an expensive necklace obligated me."

"Well, I hope you told him he could stick his present where the sun don't shine."

"I should've. I just told him I wasn't for sale and gave it back." Quinn sat on the edge of the table, beyond caring if she ended up with icing on her butt. "It's never going to change, is it? I'll go through this same cycle three hundred times and learn the same thing again and again. Guys only care about one thing."

Sadie sighed and tipped her head. "You know that's not true."

"I know there are good guys out there, and I'm happy

you found one. That doesn't mean even some of the good ones are willing to wait." The urge to wave the white flag on relationships slammed into her, draining her of her energy. "I'm too outspoken and wild in my family's eyes, and to the rest of the world, I'm too conservative and old-fashioned. I don't fit anywhere, and I can't win."

Half of the people in town thought she slept around, and the guys she'd actually dated thought she was a prude. Hard to be slutty and frigid at the same time, but she somehow pulled it off. Her frustration must've shown, because Sadie stepped forward and hugged her tightly.

While it didn't magically fix everything, she'd desperately needed it.

"Think you can sneak away to the ranch?" Sadie asked. "We can get drunk and eat chocolate like we did when I was sure Royce and I'd never get back together. In a few hours, it'll almost be like your breakup never happened."

"Maybe I'll sneak out of my bedroom window, too, so I can relive the glory days."

"If you get yourself grounded, don't go blaming me."

Quinn laughed.

Her parents came over, the craziness of the past few days showing on their faces, but pride was there as well—they'd married off one daughter to a successful, wealthy business-man. They probably believed eventually they'd succeed in doing the same with Quinn, to the same family, even.

"Thank you for the music, Sadie," Chichi said, and Haha echoed the sentiment.

Sadie flashed them a warm smile. "Anytime. It was my pleasure, really."

Chichi wrapped his arm around Haha and she leaned in,

letting him hold her up. They'd met through family friends. Apparently Haha was so shy and demure that it'd taken three dates before Chichi had even gotten a full sentence out of her. Her mother, Sobo Machi, had been the wildest family member before Quinn had come along, which was why it'd hurt so much when they'd lost her. Since she'd lived with them for the ten years after her husband passed away, most of Quinn's childhood memories included her, and while Sobo Machi always tried to remain straight-faced when Quinn got grounded—yet again—she'd slipped and laughed a few times.

Instead of constant reprimanding over Quinn's so-called rebellious nature, she'd always referred to it as "strong spirit." She'd gotten Quinn's humor when no one else did, and when it came to talking about her problems and frustrations, Sobo understood. *Man, I miss her.*

"I wish my mother was here to see this," Haha said, apparently noticing the same absence.

"Me, too," Quinn said. "It was a lovely wedding and ceremony—you did a great job of making it all come together." She rolled her tight neck, her thoughts on kicking back on Sadie's comfy couch as she unwound from the long day. "I'm going to head to Second Chance Ranch with Sadie and stay the night there."

Frown lines puckered Haha's face. No doubt she was thinking about how Sadie practically lived at the ranch, despite the fact that she and Royce weren't married yet.

"Quinn can stay in the spare bedroom," Sadie offered with her signature wide grin.

That didn't seem to ease the concern, but since Quinn was now a grown woman, there wasn't much her mother could say. Didn't stop disapproval from oozing from her.

"I'll be home early tomorrow morning so we can head back to Cheyenne." With a giant hangover, most likely, but she'd wear her dark glasses and doze in the backseat. Then she'd have to deal with the office and sorting through anything Grayson might've left at her place, and finish axing that relationship.

The more she thought about it, the more she wanted to put Cheyenne in her past and make Hope Springs her future. Now she'd have to feel bad about beating out Heath for the property, but it was easier to be her weird, clashed self here. If she didn't get away from everything, she'd go completely crazy.

She inwardly cringed just thinking about asking Chichi for time off. No need to tell him it was to get the property in Hope Springs until it was a done deal.

No, she'd cross that sucky, shard-strewn bridge when she got to it.

Chapter Five

All week long, Quinn had been looking forward to this moment. It was just after three on Friday afternoon when she pulled her car up to the Mountain Ridge Bed and Breakfast.

As luck would have it, Chichi had wanted her to do a final check on a property in Casper first thing this morning, which led nicely to heading from there to Hope Springs for the weekend.

She'd figure out how to get enough time off next week when it came around. Put it right up there with breaking the news that there wouldn't be a second wedding involving the Rutherford family. Maya already knew. While Quinn had planned on waiting until she got back from her honeymoon to tell her, apparently Grayson had already told Steven, which meant Maya had texted to ask her side of the story. Grayson had made it sound like she didn't care as much about him as he did about her. Possibly true, but totally spinning it to make *her* sound like the bad guy. And he'd had the gall to leave an apology on her voicemail the next day when she didn't pick up, as if he hadn't thrown her under the bus with her sister and new brother-in-law.

I swear, next time I see him, I'm going to give him a piece of my mind. I might've already given him back the necklace, but I've got plenty of things for him to stick where the sun don't shine.

Anger rose, taking over the calm she'd felt when she first pulled up. She exhaled and took a drink of the large Coke she'd grabbed when she'd filled her car with gas. No letting that guy ruin the moment she'd looked forward to for days. No letting him into this special place at all.

After a quick glance around to double-check she was alone, she ditched her pants suit and heels for shorts and her canvas ballet flats, sticking with the lacy tank top she'd worn under her jacket. Then she stepped outside and took a breath of the crisp, earthen air.

Ah, I'm home.

The large Victorian building in front of her had seen better days. Each year it'd gotten more run-down, and Quinn took in the barely-hanging-in-there shutters, the sagging porch, and the roof stripped of most of its shingles.

The porch steps creaked under her weight, conveying their offense at being neglected for so long. Quinn placed her hand on one of the weather-roughened beams. "We'll get you all fixed up, don't you worry."

She talked to buildings regularly, although usually not so lovingly. But this one—this one was going to be her baby. Quinn looked around again, a tinge of worry pinching her gut. Technically, she might be trespassing. But was it really trespassing to inspect a property you'd put a bid on?

Total gray area, if you asked her, and gray areas were her home base. The screen door screeched as if it meant to make her eardrums bleed, and then it went ahead and clattered off its hinges, nearly hitting her on the way down. She stared at the warped metal, now diagonal and propped against the old swing where she and Sobo Machi had spent several hours together. They liked to watch the sun dip low in the sky and marvel at the way it turned everything orange and pink right before dusk. They'd never seen sunsets like that in the city. Too many buildings in the way.

Quinn pushed open the heavy door that'd held up rather well compared to everything else and stepped inside. Dust and cobwebs covered every inch, and a bird's nest sat on top of the mantel of the fireplace. Sunlight streamed through the hole in the roof where the birds must've come in, spotlighting the warped wooden floor planks.

Last time she and Sadie had sneaked into the place back in high school, that hole hadn't been there. Everywhere she looked she noted more repairs that needed to be done. She'd thought she was prepared, but the weight of the project and how much money it'd cost pressed against her. *It's okay. That's what loans are for.*

I make a good loan candidate, right? Ignoring the anxiety trying to bind her lungs, she passed the large rooms where people had gathered to enjoy the fire or board games, walked through the dining room where she'd sat around the table with her family, two other families, and the old owners, and peeked inside the kitchen.

"This room's not so bad." Her voice sounded so loud in the quiet that it didn't even seem like hers. But the kitchen had obviously been remodeled shortly before they'd shut down. The walls, ceiling, and counters were dusty, but not broken. Large gaps remained where the appliances had been—they'd probably sold those. But a good scrubbing and coat of paint or two, and this room would be good to go. Since the heart of most homes was the kitchen, she took that as a good omen.

I can't wait to make those vanilla-almond Belgian waffles with fruit and whipped cream and serve them to guests so I can watch their faces light up, the way mine must've when I first had one. She'd thought she'd died and gone to food heaven.

She and Sobo Machi had sneaked seconds and called it brunch, even though they'd already had breakfast and had gone ahead and ate lunch at the diner a few hours later as well.

After checking upstairs, her hope and excitement grew. The animals and weather hadn't hit it as hard as on the bottom floor, and the bedrooms, while dirty and sporting peeling floral wallpaper, were also in pretty good shape. The bones were all there.

Quinn ducked into the last room—the one she, Maya, and Sobo Machi had stayed in. She leaned against the wall and closed her eyes, thinking back to when Sobo had pulled her aside—Quinn had made a loud joke during dinner, which had earned her dirty looks from her parents, so she'd been sure she was about to get into trouble.

Sobo had patted the bed and Quinn had sat next to her, hanging her head.

"Quinn-chan, you are a very smart, funny girl," Sobo said. "You will move mountains. It's important to be respectful and learn when to speak, but it's also important to keep that spark. To apply it for good. *Wakarimashita ka?*"

Quinn had nodded to show that she did understand, although she wasn't sure she did. Not then.

But now she did. Sobo had seen how driven she was through the jokes and inability to keep from saying whatever popped into her head. She hadn't wanted to put out the spark but teach her how and when to use it. Quinn could've used her guidance longer, but she'd never forgotten that talk.

"I'm trying to apply it for good, Sobo," she said to the dusty room, envisioning it the way she wanted it to be when she got through with it. The wallpaper would be replaced with a vintage-looking wall treatment; a big four-poster bed would sit in the center of the room, a cozy bedspread draped across it, and she'd place antique touches here and there, to give it that country-meets-luxury sort of feel. "I think I can make a difference here in Hope Springs. I can be the person who introduces it to people, the way that I got introduced to it when I needed it most."

Sure, there was the gossip and everyone in your business, but those people were also the ones who spread the word when someone needed help. As a community, they took care of one another, and all the wide-open space after living in the city made Quinn want to go outside and spin circles until she fell in the grass, the way she used to as a girl.

She headed downstairs and paused at the doorway, glancing at the front area where people used to check in. She wanted to be the one there to greet travelers who were staying for a while or just passing through. She wanted to give families outside activities to grow closer. Wanted to be a reprieve from busy life. She wanted to sit around that big table in the dining room and meet new people over amazing food.

Longing wound itself around her heart and spread

through every inch of her. *This is where I belong.* Maybe she'd never find a man who would respect her decision about sex and marriage, but if she had this place, she was pretty sure it wouldn't matter. She could laugh and be herself, and she knew she could help people have one of their best vacations ever.

If that was all she had in her life—that and Sadie living next door—that'd be enough.

Quinn headed back outside, blinking at the bright sunlight. She dug her keys out of her shorts, thinking maybe she'd head over to Second Chance Ranch and try to catch Sadie. Even tagging along as she fed horses or talked to the teens would be a nice way to end her hectic week.

A loud rattle cut through her thoughts and she glanced down just in time to see her foot hovering over a massive rattlesnake, pale yellow and brown, blended perfectly into the tall grass. A scream burst out of her mouth, and she jumped back, flinging her arms. The keys went flying, and the snake rattled louder, raising its head from its coiled body, arching and ready to strike.

Quinn's heart hammered against her rib cage, pumping fear and adrenaline in massive waves that took her breath away. The snake sat between her and the door of her car and she wasn't even sure where her keys had landed—with her luck, probably right by the snake. The dark forked tongue darted in and out of its mouth as it continued to rattle.

Her brain chose that moment to recall facts about how fast rattlesnakes struck, along with images of bruised and swollen skin from the poison-filled bites. If that thing got her, someone would find her days later, swollen like a black balloon and not even resembling herself. Not to mention the fried red skin from the sun and any other critters who came along and decided to take up residence in her carcass.

The snake reared up again and Quinn backpedaled, spouting swearwords and shuddering. She quickly checked around her feet to make sure the cold-blooded creature hadn't summoned its family members to surround her and take her out. The coast was clear, so she took a few more slow steps backward. Another couple landed her on the porch.

Her rapid pulse throbbed through her head, and she wasn't sure her heart rate would ever return to normal again. She dug into her pocket, pulled out the phone that she thanked the stars she still had possession of in spite of the fact that these pockets left it hanging halfway out, and called up Sadie.

"Oh, thank goodness," she said when Sadie answered. "I need you and Royce to come rescue me. I'm at Mountain Ridge and there's a giant pissed-off rattlesnake next to my car."

The few seconds of silence nearly gave her a stroke. "Royce and I are at a horse sale," Sadie said. "We're *hours* away."

Quinn gulped. "What about Cory?"

"He's with us. And Royce's mom is off with Sheila— they're doing a spa day, since we're between groups of kids at the alternative youth camp right now."

"Shit. I'm not even really supposed to be here. If I call anyone in town, word will spread and then I'll never get the property. Either they'll be upset I checked it out without asking for permission, or they'll think I can't handle it."

"Just a second…"

Sadie explained the situation to Royce and Cory, who

laughed—she was seriously going to kill them next time she saw them. Sadie scolded them for her. Then she heard Royce say, "Tell her to get a large stick and scare if off. Make sure she keeps the head back so she doesn't get bitten, though."

"You've met Quinn, right?" Sadie asked, which was exactly what Quinn would've said to him. She wasn't going near the thing. Not with a ten-foot pole. And not so that she could enrage it further and give it a reason to hunt her down and poison her with as many bites as possible.

Quinn didn't quite catch the next thing Royce said. Then Sadie's voice came through loud and clear again. "Call Heath."

"Are you insane? I'm not calling him of all people! He'll use it against me."

"He won't."

"The last time I talked to him I was crying in the parking lot over my breakup," Quinn said. "If he sees me as weak, he'll use it."

"Or maybe you'll use it, because you'll show him that while you're terrified of snakes, you're a shark when it comes to real estate."

"I'm not calling him. I'll…I'll figure out something."

"Quinn, come on. I'm going to be so pissed at you if you die right now."

"I'll just wait out the snake. It's good—gives me time to explore the place a little more. You enjoy the sale."

"…me know if…okay?" Wyoming was half dead zones, with internet capability on the road nonexistent, so even getting through to Sadie in the first place was rather miraculous. Sounded like their five minutes of clear service was up. At least now someone knew where to find the body if the worst happened.

"Don't worry," Quinn said, not even sure Sadie could hear her anymore. "If the snake's still here after I'm done looking around, I'll call someone." It was a bluff. She couldn't risk it. Worst-case scenario, she'd wait here until Sadie, Royce, and Cory got back. Maybe she'd test out the dusty beds—that'd be fun.

Sadie's response was too garbled to make out.

After Quinn hung up, she tucked her phone in her bra, thinking it'd do a more secure job of holding it than her tiny pockets, and surveyed the area once again. Exploring wouldn't seem so intimidating if she wasn't now paranoid there were dozens of snakes waiting for her. Careful of where she stepped, she headed around the back of the B and B. She checked out the rusted, dirt-encased patio furniture—that'd definitely need to be replaced. She sat in the cracked tire swing, bouncing to make sure it'd hold her, and then kicked off and pumped her legs.

Swings always seemed so magical as a kid, but while soaring through the air still made her stomach rise up, the tire hurt her butt and the off-balance twisting made her dizzy. The rope kept creaking, too, and she eyed the branch, sure it was about to crack. *Okay, now that I feel old and heavy…*

She jumped down and checked her phone. She'd managed to kill almost thirty minutes. Her stomach growled, and she put a hand over it. In her excitement to get here, she hadn't bothered with lunch.

Two large rocks caught her eye. Quinn wiggled them from their half-embedded spots in the dirt and gripped one in each hand. *Maybe this will work. At least they've got a farther-distance-away-from-the-snake-reach than a stick.*

She hoped she wouldn't need them, but fortune didn't

seem to be on her side today, so backup was a good idea. She rounded the house and crept closer to her car, still keeping a generous amount of space between her and where she'd last seen Mister Fangs. No rattling seemed like a good sign, but as she hesitantly moved closer, she saw the fat snake coiled in the same place, happily soaking up the sun, the bastard.

Quinn launched one of the rough, coconut-size rocks at the disgusting reptile. It landed about a foot in front of it, not even getting a reaction. *Guess I should've paid more attention in PE.*

Come on, you can do it. Then you can get in your car and reward yourself with a large burger and fries, followed by a banana split at the Dairy Freeze.

This time, she put more oomph into her throw. The rock pelted the side of her car with a loud smack, denting the door. It then bounced close enough to the snake to send it rattling and doing the wavy head dance while poking out its tongue—she swore it was mocking her.

"Argh! Just move already!"

The sound of an engine droned in the distance, growing louder by the second. She squinted at the road, and in between the trees and cloud of dust, she spotted a familiar black truck. *Oh, Sadie, what have you done?*

While she wanted to be mad, a traitorous surge of relief calmed the panic that'd taken up residence in her chest. Her car and her nerves could only handle so many more rock tosses.

The truck turned, the motorcycle strapped in back like it'd been last weekend, and then Heath's features sharpened into relief. Same scruffy chin, same black hat, same criminally good-looking face. He parked and got out of the truck.

She'd started to think she'd exaggerated how hot he was, but nope. The guy was hotter than any guy should be allowed to be. She lifted her chin, doing her best to act nonchalant. "I told Sadie I was fine."

"Well, she told me that if her best friend died of a rattle-snake bite, she'd hold me personally responsible. With how much time I have to spend with her, I'd rather she not be plotting vengeance during it. I'll turn around to tune my guitar one day, only to get choked by the cord of a microphone. No, thanks." Heath reached into the back of his truck and lifted out a shovel. "Now, where is it?"

Quinn pointed. The closer Heath got to the snake, the more space she put between herself and the two of them. "I think this is a bad idea. Don't you have a gun? I think long-range killing would work best."

"So now you're okay with guns?"

She opened her mouth and then snapped it shut. No matter what she said right now, he'd use it to defend his hunting lodge—this was exactly why she hadn't called him. Maybe she should've taken her chances with someone from the town committee. "If you get bitten, I'm not taking responsibility. I'll try to get you to the ER, but considering the snake will probably come after me next, your odds aren't going to be great."

He chuckled and looked at her, amusement clear on his features as he continued to advance on the snake.

"Pay attention to where you're stepping! It's going to bite you and then you're not going to be laughing." Quinn slapped a hand over her eyes, not wanting to watch. But then not watching seemed freakier, so she took another step back and bit at her thumbnail.

The snake rattled as Heath approached, shovel in hand. It struck and Heath batted its head away with the shovel and then brought the blade down on its neck, leaving the air blissfully rattle-free.

And that instinctual caveman-cavewoman–type attraction that must've occurred when the man brought back a saber-toothed tiger for dinner twisted Quinn's gut. She hated to admit it, but holy hell, that was hotter than it should've been. Her ovaries stood at attention, shouting, *You man, me woman. Put baby in here now.*

Heath picked up the back half of the snake. "I like to use everything I hunt. So I'm thinking rattle bracelet for you, and we can share some rattlesnake stew. Sound like a plan?"

She wasn't sure if he was kidding or not. "I'm...good."

He laughed and tossed the snake's tail at her. She shrieked and jumped out of the way. "Jerk!"

"I believe the words you're looking for are 'thank you.'" He bent down and picked something off the ground that rattled in a metallic, non-snake way. "Did you toss your keys at it?"

"Not on purpose. It startled me and they sorta flew, so..." She stepped over the first rock and took the keys. "I tried rocks." She wasn't sure why she admitted that.

Heath squatted and ran his hand over the ding in her door. "I can see that." He twisted his face toward hers. "Bring it to Rod's Auto Repair and we can fix it up. I'll only charge you double," he said as he shot her a grin.

When he straightened, their bodies were suddenly only a few inches apart. Too close, but she couldn't seem to make herself move away.

"So, what?" he asked. "You came here to count your

chickens before they hatched?"

She crossed her arms. "Just checking the place out."

"You realize that if you get the property, there are going to be animals and the occasional unwanted creature involved. How are you going to take care of that? How about the remodeling and the electricity and the plumbing?"

Offense pinched her gut and stepping back didn't seem so hard anymore. "I know, and I'll deal with problems as they arise. There are people for those kinds of things, and if the place was mine right now, I would've been able to call them. What? You're planning on doing it all yourself?"

"Yeah. I mean, I'll hire help for the construction of the lodge, but I'll also be using my own two hands to build it."

"That doesn't mean you want it more than I do."

"I didn't say it did. Just pointing out that I might be better qualified. Do you even know anything about the rest of the land?" He swung his arms wide. "It's more than this crumbling building."

She clenched her jaw, the anger that came out around him rising up again. How could she be so attracted to someone who also made her so furious? "Of course I do," she said, even though she hadn't really thought about the rest of the land. She just liked that there was so much of it between everything else.

Heath tilted his head, his skepticism clear.

"Okay, so I don't know where all the property lines are or much about the rest of the land, but I'll learn. I'll do whatever it takes."

Heath glanced at his truck, and some kind of internal debate took place. Resolve replaced the back-and-forth and then he said, "Come on, then."

"Come on? I've got my car. I'm going to—"

"If you're serious about this place, you should see it, and you should see it with someone who knows it. I'll get my bike out of the truck." He set the shovel in the bed of the truck and then climbed up and unfastened the motorcycle.

"How do I know you won't drag me out there and leave my body?" Quinn asked. "Weed out the competition?"

"Because I could've let the snake do that for me. I'd just tell Sadie I was too late."

"So you thought about it?"

A grin spread across his face, as if that were actually a funny question. He set up a ramp, backed his motorcycle down it, and then scooted forward on the seat and gestured for her to get on.

Quinn looked at her car and considered telling him to forget it. But now she was curious, and she'd always been a sucker for motorcycle rides. Plus, the guy *had* killed a snake for her, and despite the jokes, she knew she'd be safer checking out the property with him than on her own.

She stepped over the headless reptile, wrinkling her nose, and then swung herself onto the bike. Her front slid against Heath's firm back, the curved seat not allowing for any space between them. She loosely wrapped her arms around his waist.

He revved the engine and glanced over his shoulder. "Better hold on tight. I want to keep you around so I can see the look on your face when I win over the committee."

Before she could answer that, the motorcycle shot forward, dirt spitting behind them, and she had no choice but to cling to him and hope that this whole venture wouldn't end up biting her in the butt.

Chapter Six

Heath rode higher and higher up the trail, until the dirt slipped under the motorcycle's tires and the rocks got big enough to bounce them a few inches off the seat. Quinn clung onto him, which tempted him to push farther up the steep hill, but in the end, he decided safer would be better than wrecked. On his own he'd done it, but another person switched up the dynamic, and they weren't wearing helmets.

He maneuvered the bike to a relatively flat area and shut off the engine. "We've got to walk for a bit. You okay with that?"

"Bring it," she said. She was too competitive for her own good. She climbed down from the bike and his gaze snagged on the tiny shorts that displayed lots of smooth skin. She pulled her dark hair into a high ponytail and secured it with the band she had around her wrist. She had a bright red stripe of hair underneath that wasn't visible when her hair was down but practically glowed now. "You coming?"

He made sure the kickstand would hold the bike, pocketed the keys, and then started up the trail. He stopped when he spotted several deer up ahead. Keeping his movements slow and his voice quiet, he pointed them out to Quinn. "See them?"

Her eyes lit up as she looked at the group—there were five feeding in the clearing, including a tiny one that must've been born this spring. "It's kind of crazy that so much wildlife is only a few minutes from home."

"That's why I love it here," he said.

"So you can hunt them down?"

He frowned at her. "You really think I just go shooting anything that moves? I enjoy seeing the wildlife same as you. Have you ever gone fishing?"

"Well, yeah, but—"

"And I suppose you've had a burger."

She rolled her eyes.

"I hunt for food and for sport, and if it wasn't allowed, there'd be overpopulation problems. It just shows that you don't know anything about the land."

"How many times am I going to have to hear that today?"

"Until you open your eyes."

She looked like she wanted to punch him—maybe this was a bad idea. Clearly they'd never agree. The wind shifted and the deer caught their scent and darted away.

"You want to go back?" he asked.

"No. I want to see the rest of the place. Regardless of having a stubborn, condescending tour guide." She shot him a tight smile and then charged up the hill, her ponytail swinging—apparently it didn't matter to her that she didn't know where they were going. It gave him a good view of her backside, so he simply followed, calling out a "go left" or "veer right."

When they reached the creek, he found a place where the water was about shin-deep with lots of rocks to cross — mostly for Quinn, because his boots would keep his feet dry as long as it didn't go over the top of them.

She bounced from rock to rock, having to jump when her strides weren't long enough to follow the path he'd taken.

"Watch that last one," he said. "It's — "

She leaped onto it and her foot slid out from under her. She fell backward, barely getting her hands down to semi-catch herself as she hit the water with a small splash.

"Slippery," he finished. He took a step back into the stream, sure she was about to freak about getting her clothes wet. All he could really do now was make an attempt at damage control. "You okay?"

"I'm fine. Help me up?" She extended her hand, and he took hold of it. He was surprised she'd asked for help. Usually she was so —

She yanked on his arm and swept her leg under his. He landed hard on his butt and she erupted in laughter. "That's for throwing the snake at me."

For a moment he didn't move, simply sat and gaped at her smug expression as cold water seeped into his jeans. Her impressive takedown move and laughter were so completely at odds with the prissy reaction he'd expected that it took his brain a few seconds to catch up. "Nice ninja skills."

She jumped up and grinned. "It's in the blood, you know. That, and my father forced my sister and me to train in aikido."

He pushed to his feet and shook water off his hands. "So

that makes you…"

"I'm Japanese. With or without the aikido. And no, I won't make you Japanese food, and I especially won't make you Chinese food—just putting it out there now, because guys tend to ask, like, first date. Not that this is a date. Obviously."

"Obviously," he said, not bothering to mention it was the closest thing to a date he'd been on for a while. "And I wouldn't dream of asking you to cook for me. You'd probably poison the food or sweep kick me as I was eating and then stab me with your chopsticks."

She laughed again, more happy than evil sounding this time, and it echoed through his chest.

"And you don't ask me if I make good moonshine." He heaved a sigh. "I get so sick of girls asking me that. I'm good for more than providing booze, you know."

She laughed again, and he leaned in as if he were about to divulge a huge secret. "Actually, I've got a really good batch in my bathtub right now, so maybe you should ask."

"Then I guess I'm coming over tonight."

Suddenly he realized how close they were and the way he had to work harder for every one of his breaths. Quinn coming over tonight sounded good—guess he'd have to figure out how to make moonshine after all.

Even with their constant clashing, he felt an inexplicable draw to her that made him want to know more. "So, I hope I don't come across as stupid asking this, but I'm guessing you speak Japanese as well?"

"Hai."

"I'm going to assume that means yes."

A smile curved her lips. "Yes. And it's not a stupid

question, by the way." She walked past him, toward the bank of the stream, and he followed. He offered to go back if she didn't want to continue the hike in wet clothes, and she declined, stating that between the heat and the hiking, the cool water had been refreshing.

As they continued up the hill, side by side, he picked up the get-to-know-you conversation again. "Were you born here or in Japan?"

"Here. Well, not Hope Springs, here, but in Cheyenne. My mom's parents came over when she was a girl, and my dad's parents relocated to the States when he was a teenager. He had to work really hard to learn English—he always talks about how difficult it was, and how long it took for other people to understand him clearly—so he made sure my sister and I learned early. We spoke a combination of both languages at home, and I'll admit to being very Americanized, but my parents always wanted us to maintain our heritage, too."

She paused, her chest heaving with labored breaths. This last climb had him feeling the exertion, too. "Most people just assume instead of ask," she continued. "I think they're too uncomfortable."

"Well, I'm probably just too backward to know polite conversation."

She placed a hand on his arm, her soft touch bringing back that stomach-tightening sensation he'd felt at the reception last weekend. "Not at all. I tend to be the person who blurts things out without thinking. Despite our differences of opinions on pretty much everything, you're not half bad."

"I can't tell if you're extending an olive branch or

smacking me with it."

She laughed again—he was quickly becoming addicted to the sound. "Right now I'd say extending. But I'll hang onto the end so that in a few minutes when we disagree on something, I can use it for smacking.

"So what about you?" she asked, ducking under low pine tree branches that made a canopy over their path. "Were you born here in Hope Springs?"

"Yep. Lived here until I graduated high school, then I wanted to get away for a while. I traveled all over and did a dozen different jobs, everything from construction to mechanic work. Played the guitar whenever I could and built motorcycles in my spare time. I never thought I'd miss Hope Springs, but then I started to, and when I found out about Mountain Ridge, I knew it was time to come home. Meeting Sadie and forming the band made it feel a bit like fate—if I believed in that kind of thing."

"But you don't?"

"No. I believe in making your own destiny, not waiting for the universe to line up for you. If I'd waited for that, I'd be my dad." It'd come out before he'd thought it through, and now he wanted to pluck it out of the air and take it back. Instead of waiting for her to ask about his dad, he charged on. "Anyway, just wait till you see this view."

The hill turned even steeper, and the gravel under their feet slid. Every foot placement became important, every branch a lifeline to hold onto. Quinn was doing fine, but once he crested the hill, he extended a hand anyway. She took it, and he pulled her the rest of the way up, their bodies bumping together for a brief moment before she turned to look at the grassy valley spread out before them. On the far end, jagged blue-gray mountains with white tips touched fluffy white clouds, the pine trees scattered across the lower two-thirds reduced to specks of green that blurred into each other.

"Wow," she said, her voice filled with reverence and awe. "You can see Second Chance Ranch from here. And Hope Springs Reservoir—I got stuck in a boat there once. Word to the wise, keep a tight hold of your oars, because those things are important."

He smiled at her, fascinated by how different she was from who he'd expected. "I'll keep that in mind next time I'm out there."

She plunked down on a patch of grass, leaned back on her palms, and tipped her face to the sun. Serenity showed on her features, along with genuine happiness that made her skin practically glow.

What were you thinking bringing her up here so she could get even more attached to the land? Now you'll feel extra horrible when you get it instead.

Too late to undo it now, so he sat next to her.

"So, where exactly are the property lines?" she asked, looking at him. "You know, so my eyes can be more open."

There was a hint of sarcasm in there, but he could tell she wanted to know. He pointed east. "Right along the ridge there, across the base of the mountain to the river, all the way to up here. Second Chance Ranch borders to the west, but to the north it's national forest land—that's where I'd take the hunters. They'd have to draw licenses through the Wyoming Game and Fish Department, and they limit how many go out in an area—I'd double-check that they had them before I took anyone out, too. I already talked to Royce about renting his horses, so we'd be able to ride far and cover both big game units—"

"Big game units?" Quinn asked, wrinkling her forehead.

"That's where you can hunt. Like I said, the Wyoming Game and Fish Department limits licenses, and they also tell you where you can hunt—you draw for which type of game in a certain area. Since Mountain Ridge is central and easily accessible to both areas, it makes it the perfect location for a lodge, and with the different game and seasons, we could be busy most of the fall."

"We?"

Again he wondered how wise it was to give up all this information. But the town committee knew, so it wasn't anything she couldn't find out by asking a couple of questions. "My brother Cam and me. We're going to run it together— that's how I'm going to run the lodge and stay in the band. He's been in the army for ten years—he enlisted as soon as he was eighteen—but he's only got two more months left of his tour and then he'll be getting out. We've talked about doing this together for years."

Quinn's shoulders slumped and her chin dropped.

"If we get it," he quietly added.

"When I was a little girl, I stayed at the B and B with my grandmother and the rest of my family. Some of my best memories are there, and they mean even more now that she's passed on. I want other people to be able to find this magical place where their parents *actually* take a vacation and spend time with their kids. Where they can have space to run and play and discover the beauty and welcoming people of Hope Springs. Ever since the place shut down, I swore I'd find a way to make it mine. After my grandmother passed away, I only became more determined. It's a piece of her, and I don't want to let it go."

Here they were, back to their impossible situation. "So I'm competing with a dead grandma."

"And I'm competing with someone who's given ten years of his life for his country," Quinn said. She turned to him and sighed. "I figure this can go two ways. Either we try to undermine and backstab each other…" Her eyebrows arched. "Which I don't want to do, because it feels icky and politician-like, and, well, you're a decent guy who killed a snake for me…"

He couldn't help leaning in, propping his hand in the grass so that his face and hers were lined up—man, she was pretty, the sun highlighting her unique features and shining off her dark hair. "What's behind door number two? I think I'm already voting for it."

One corner of her mouth twisted up. "*Or* we can understand that we both have good reasons for wanting the property. We can play the town committee's game and give our all to get it—on the up and up—and at the end, we shake the other person's hand and wish them good luck."

"Maybe we should throw in a congratulatory kiss, too," he said. "For good measure."

A shaky breath escaped her, and he was glad he hadn't held that thought inside like he probably should've. "Well, if it's in the name of good sportsmanship…"

His gaze moved to her lips. Maybe they should seal the agreement with a kiss, too.

"So it's a deal?" she asked. "We agree to make the best of the situation and not turn this into a smear campaign?"

"It's a deal. Although now I'm wondering what skeletons

you have in your closet."

"Good thing we already have a deal, then," she said, grabbing his hand and shaking it. Instead of letting go, he held on for a moment longer and dragged his thumb across her knuckles.

Then both of their phones went crazy.

"Wow, I'm surprised we get service up here," Quinn said, pulling her phone out of her bra, which made him jealous of a phone for the first time in his life. "And I'm glad I didn't have my phone in my pocket when I fell into the water or it would've been toast."

"It's hit-or-miss. Cross over the ridge and nothing gets through, but this spot's high enough to get pretty good reception." Heath lifted his phone, thinking he was glad he'd shelled out money for the LifeProof case. Years of working on vehicles and traipsing through the mountains had caused several broken phones.

He'd expected the text to be from the town committee and include more hoops to jump through. Instead it was a group text to him and Quinn from Sadie.

Hello?! Are you guys alive? It's not cool to tell me you're cornered by a deadly snake and then not let me know if you're ok. Of course I haven't had service until now, but that means I should DEFINITELY have a text letting me know.

Quinn's answer popped onto his screen.

Sorry, Mom. I know how you worry :P Since Heath did save me from the snake, I'm only a little mad at you for sending him when I told you not to. We're actually hiking now, safe and sound, and we just agreed to a truce as well, so your side mission also succeeded. Try not to let it go to your head.

"Side mission?" Heath asked.

"For you and me to get to know each other enough that we don't kill each other," Quinn said, like he was a little slow for not already figuring that out. "Sadie can't handle people being upset or not liking each other, and this has *Parent Trap* written all over it."

"Parent trap?" The more she talked, the less sense she made.

"You know, getting the two people trapped together, so they see there's…" Quinn blinked at him. "So they see they should be friends."

"Oh-kay."

Quinn stood and brushed the dirt from the seat of her shorts. "I'm almost dry from our impromptu swim—"

"Next time we should choose a deeper spot."

"I'm down."

And we should wear a lot less clothing, too. He shook his head. Bad idea. Good thing he hadn't said that one out loud.

"Anyway, I'm starving and I need to check in with Patsy Higgins so I can get to work being her lackey for a few weeks," Quinn said.

"They want us in the garage at seven to work on floats— she's reminded me every time I've seen her this week, and she came by the shop today for good measure, just in case I managed to forget since yesterday."

"Then I really better get some food in me, because I'm guessing it's going to be a several-hour gig."

They made their way back down the hill, and when they reached the stream, he offered her a hand. She stared at it for a moment before slapping her palm in his. Even after they reached the bank on the other side, he didn't see any reason to let go, so he didn't. She didn't say anything about it, so they walked hand in hand back to his motorcycle.

She climbed on behind him and wrapped her arms tightly around him. His pulse thrummed through his veins as he felt her warm body press against his back. He could get used to this.

Only he couldn't—not really. Regardless of their goodwill talk, he knew that bitter feelings would arise as they exhausted themselves working on the festival preparations, especially whenever they thought of the other person getting the property. At the end, there'd be resentment that'd leave little chance of the possibility of remaining on friendly terms.

Even if the circumstances were different, it wasn't like he was looking for a relationship anyway. Between the lodge and the band, he didn't have time, and he wasn't going to half ass one the way Dad always had—he'd seen how damaging it could be to everyone involved.

Still, he couldn't help taking advantage of the current situation. He wrapped his hand around her bare knee and glanced over his shoulder. "Ready?"

"This time, don't be such a grandma. I wanna go fast."

A thrill shot through his gut. Oh, he'd show her fast.

Chapter Seven

Okay, Quinn. No falling for the sexy country boy's charms. Flirting and joking around were fine, but for her, guys like that were more addictive than nicotine. She'd think she could handle just one puff, and then suddenly she'd be shaking without the whole pack.

The whole six-pack... She curled her hand into a fist and dug her fingernails into her palm. *No. Bad thoughts. Get it together up there.*

Quinn stepped into the enormous school garage where people worked on floats for the Frontier Days parade. The place smelled like dust and stale air, and the fluorescent lights emitted a droning buzz.

Her gaze skipped from face to face and locked on the sexy country boy in question. Then she was thinking of his strong muscles against her body as they flew down the hill and across Mountain Ridge. She'd told him to go fast, but she'd never expected him to go quite *that* fast.

She'd loved every second of it, too. The wind whipping her hair behind her and the buzz of the motorcycle. The way the guy driving moved with the bike, like he'd become an extension of it.

Be cool, be cool. She walked up to him. "He-i." So much for cool. She'd gone to say hey and then decided on hi and ended up with a word that wasn't quite either.

He turned eyes that couldn't decide if they were blue or green on her, and the corners crinkled as a smile spread across his face. "Hey, speed demon."

"I'll take it over squirt."

"Good to know, squirt."

She shoved him, and he laughed. For all her goals about not inhaling and getting hooked, she caught a whiff of a soapy-fresh scent mixed with musky cologne and couldn't help sucking it into her lungs. *Puff.*

Then Patsy Higgins stepped in front of them, a clipboard tucked under her arm—at least she hadn't brought the gavel. "You guys are already behind, so there's no time for horseplay."

Quinn had never gotten that expression. There'd been no neighing or running on all fours. How did messing around equal horseplay?

"...plans drawn up and the materials you need," Patsy Higgins continued, and Quinn forced herself to listen. This was important. She and Heath might have formed a treaty of sorts, but Patsy Higgins would take her out with a cold stare if she screwed up. Then she'd never get her B and B. "The Morrises drew up plans and ordered supplies before they had to step down. You two simply need to execute it."

Quinn looked from the woman with the head of gray

curls to Heath—quite the contrast, by the way. "Heath and I are working on a float together?"

"Is that a problem?" Patsy Higgins asked, peering down at her through the round, thick glasses that magnified the exasperation in her eyes.

"No. It's just that I…"

Heath's eyebrows drew together and if she wasn't mistaken, a hint of mistrust pinched his features.

"I'm a beginner-level float builder. Now, I'm a fast learner, and I'm sure Heath is, too, but it's a really big project and I just want to ensure it gets done right." She turned to him, working up a glimmer of hope. "Or maybe you've built floats before?"

Heath gave a small shake of his head. "Thanks, Patsy." He took the sketch and supply list from the top of her clipboard. "Quinn and I are happy to help—we won't let you down."

"I'll be around here and there, but I'm a very busy woman, so you do what you can, and if you need help, I'll try to find you someone." The way Patsy said it made it clear that if they needed help, she'd be deducting points and offering no gold stars.

Heath put his hand on Quinn's back, and the touch combined with the bomb that they were going to have to pull this off even though neither of them knew what they were doing made the butterflies going through her stomach turn into clumsy drunks that stumbled into one another.

"I thought you were going to slam me after your goodwill talk there for a second," Heath said.

"I wouldn't do that. And I'm sure you'll be more fun to work with than anyone else, but look at this!" She tore the plans that showed how the float was supposed to turn out from Heath's hand and then looked to the sad flat trailer bed in front of them. Cardboard had been attached, but that was it. She glanced back at the colorful drawing with the title "Spread Your Wings and Fly" across the top. "Where are the giant butterflies going to come from?"

Heath opened one of the boxes atop the cardboard, and a sea of colorful materials she had no idea what to do with greeted them. "We'll figure it out. How hard could it be to build a butterfly?"

"That's not going to stand on its own," Heath said.

"Yes, it is," Quinn said, wadding the thick squishy purple paper into a wing-shaped blob.

"You're going to mess up the paper, and we don't have an endless supply of materials."

Quinn fought the urge to throw the makeshift wing at his head to show him exactly how heavy it was. Clearly, they'd never agree, regardless of their truce. They seriously thought the opposite about *every single thing*.

Wielding the giant stapler—we're talking industrial size and weighing enough that she'd definitely have sore arms tomorrow—she walked back to the float and stapled the purple paper to the base of the baby butterfly.

The wing and base slowly flopped over, and she could feel Heath behind her, an *I-told-you-so* superiority radiating from him. They'd been at it for two and a half hours, and she was ready to chuck the stapler and scream. But she'd done enough denting objects for one day, so she set everything on top of the float and slowly spun around.

Heath must've noticed the simmering tension and decided not to say anything. But his smug eyebrow twitch was enough.

"You think you can do better?" she challenged.

"I think that according to the laws of physics, we need something to get it up and keep it that way."

A laugh burst from her lips. "That's physics, huh? Brings something else to mind."

It took him a moment, but then he laughed, too. A deep sexy laugh that took the edge off of her frustration. "I can see where your thoughts are at."

Oops. Those kinds of comments only got her in trouble down the line, when she had to explain that while she understood the mechanics, it wasn't an invitation. She started past Heath, eyes on the blob that—if she was being honest—didn't come close to resembling a butterfly wing.

He wrapped his hand around her arm, stopping her midstride and bringing her right in front of him. "I think we need a break. And we need to come up with a better plan, otherwise we're just wasting our time."

Her pulse ratcheted up a couple of notches. The rings on his fingers provided a cool contrast to his warm callused fingers, and her skin hummed under his touch. She wanted to lean against him, wrap her arms around him like she had on the motorcycle, and take the weight off her feet for a while. The fact that it would put her body against his would be a bonus. She'd never liked feeling out of her league on a project—not that she imagined most people did. But not being able to do something as simple as float building dug at the insecure part of her.

"There's nothing sturdier in the box of supplies," she

said. "Plan or not."

"We'll think outside of the box, then. Come on." He slid his hand down to hers and led her out of the garage. The cool night air smelled much better than the stale dust-filled cloud they'd been sharing with a dozen other people who were nearly done with their extravagant floats. One had a five-foot Oscar the Grouch leaping out of a trash can.

It only made their sad, still mostly cardboard-covered float look more devastating.

Goose bumps broke out across her skin, and she rubbed her arms in an attempt to ward off the chill. With the sun down, the temperature always plummeted. She should be used to it, but the difference wasn't as extreme in Cheyenne.

Heath opened the door to his truck, and, instead of questioning where they were going, she just climbed in. The cab smelled like him, with a hint of grease mixed in. She filled her lungs and held her breath for a moment before letting it go. *Any more puffs and I'm likely to get addicted.*

When Heath got in, he reached behind the seat and pulled out a leather jacket. He handed it over to her and then fired up the engine. She slipped her arms into the sleeves and tugged it closed. It was gloriously huge, and she wanted to wear it for the rest of her life. *Okay, maybe I've tiptoed into addiction territory already.*

But I can quit any time, she mentally added, like any good addict in denial.

Heath drove toward the older part of town. She'd only been to this side a couple times. The other side had all the shops and the hills and streams. They drove past the low-income housing, and then Heath pulled up in front of a small house that was barely in better repair than the B and B.

Heath glanced across the cab. "It's probably for the best if we stay out of the house. But the shed will have what we need."

She reached for the door handle. "Okay."

Quinn followed him into the wooden building off to the side of the house. Heath flipped on the lights, illuminating dozens of parts and half-built motorcycles. A large work-bench sat on one side, and one of those metal toolboxes with several shelves stood out as the shiniest item in the place.

He lifted an old tire off another small bench, the muscles in his arms popping out as he maneuvered it into the corner. Then he wiped a hand across it. "Sorry, it's a mess. You can use my jacket to sit on if you want."

"That's okay." Using the jacket would mean taking if off, and it was warm. Plus she didn't want to mess it up—her shorts would wash much easier than the leather would. She sat down on the tire and crossed her legs.

The jacket, checking on her when she'd fallen into the water, holding the door open at the courthouse, even as they'd been arguing...for a bad boy, Heath certainly had a lot of gentlemanly manners.

He grabbed a yellow legal pad and sat on a small roller chair. She caught sight of a motorcycle sketch before he flipped the page.

Without thinking, she reached over and lifted the paper so she could get a better look at the image. "Is this...whatever blueprints are for motorcycles? Or do you just like to draw?"

"I do custom bikes on the side," he said. "Haven't been able to build as many since I moved back, but I'm about to start on this one for a guy in Laramie. The projects are usually big and time-consuming, but they pay well, and I like that every time's different—I tend to get bored easily."

Quinn twisted the pad closer and studied the streamlined frame and large handlebars. "Did you build the bike we rode on earlier?"

He nodded. "From the ground up."

"Wow. That's impressive. And a little scary, considering I rode it without giving it a good once-over."

"Hey! I thought you were going to be nice from now on."

She laughed. "I agreed to no such thing. *Truce* and *nice* don't mean the same thing."

"Yeah, I can see that."

Now she was the one who said, "Hey!" as she shoved his knee.

They shared a laugh and she got a little lost in the sound of his. Most of the guys she'd dated—even the wilder ones— were more on the serious side. Heath had a great sense of humor. Add his passion for his custom bikes, and his attractiveness was only growing more with every minute she spent with him. "It's cool you know how to do so many things— that you can build something so amazing from scratch. I'm good with making people accept lower bids than they wanted to for commercial buildings. And I'm a pretty good chef. Not sure either of those will help much with our project, unfortunately."

"If our butterflies don't start behaving, you can fry them up," Heath offered, once again showing off his quick wit.

"I'll add them to the snake stew." With her thoughts returning to how hot she'd found him earlier, she decided it was time to redirect back to float decorations. She flipped the page over so he'd have a blank paper to work with. "Ooh! I'm good with color palettes, so once we figure out how to build a butterfly, I'll be able to make it look pretty."

"Perfect. So, this is what I'm thinking." On the page, a wire skeleton of a butterfly started taking shape, but Quinn found herself focusing more on Heath's hands and the way they moved across the paper.

• • •

Heath glanced up from his sketch—if anyone had told him he'd be filling a page with butterfly drawings one day, he would've laughed in his or her face. With the leather jacket on, Quinn almost looked like she belonged here. His thoughts had been so focused on figuring out the float mess that he hadn't had a chance to second-guess his decision to bring Quinn here until he'd noticed her looking at Dad's house, eyes wide.

It reminded him that they'd grown up very differently, and the last thing he wanted was for her to see the mess inside or to meet Dad. He'd probably hit on her—in spite of his hard living, he still looked good for a man in his forties, and it'd given him a false sense of how old he was. Or maybe not, considering Ollie's mom.

Nope, he wouldn't be submitting Quinn to his old man's advances or the mess. Having her in his workspace made him feel exposed enough.

He cleared his throat. "Thoughts? I'm sure you'll probably want to build it the exact opposite way."

That got a smile out of her. "I'll reserve my right to argue for when our butterfly can't get it up."

He covered his laugh with a fist and shook his head. "That's so wrong—I'm never going to look at butterflies the same way again."

"Mission achieved, then." Quinn leaned over the paper, and with her hair up in that ponytail, her neck was fully exposed. He fought the urge to move closer and kiss the skin there. See if it tasted as good as it looked. "So we build the wire thing and then drape the paper over it? How's it going to stick?"

"Glue?"

Quinn dug out her phone—of course she had it in her bra again, which made it impossible not to focus on her cleavage. "I'm going to see if there're any tips on Google." She frowned at her phone. "I can call or text, but it looks like internet's not gonna happen. I'll have to research it tonight when I get home with my wifi."

She stood and walked around, brushing her fingers across stray parts and tools. His jacket looked damn sexy on her. Of course, she could make a potato sack look sexy.

He tried to think back to high school—how'd he miss a girl like that hitting on him? He'd been so focused on counting the days until he could leave. She was at least three years younger, too, and again, he'd made sure to avoid crossing that line. Cam would've already moved out as well, which meant he'd been dealing with Dad's antics by himself for the first time. Lots of hours working at the shop alone with nights that ended with calls from Seth Sr. He'd ask Heath to come get Dad from the Triple S, because he'd gotten drunk yet again, which almost always led to starting fights. Finally they'd simply banned him from going back, so then he'd sit at home to drink, which left Heath with the privilege of taking the brunt of his moods.

Heath stood and ran a hand across the whiskers on his jaw.

"Sorry, got a little distracted looking around," Quinn said. "As for your idea for the butterflies, you'd obviously know more about building something than me. Like I said, I'll take color coordination, and I'll even figure out how to get the fancy paper draped across it. Maybe that way we can work together without killing each other."

"Maybe," he said and she raised an eyebrow. Maybe they should work out their tension another way. Sex did wonders for making you forget your differences.

"Let's get started, then."

His head was still on sex, so it took him a moment to realize she meant building the frame. He grabbed wire and tools and then sat down on the floor, because it was the only space large enough.

Quinn sat across from him, and they worked on shaping the wire. She passed him tools and held things in place when he needed an extra hand. Here and there she made a few half-mumbled noises that he took to mean she wasn't sure he was on the right path. She kept her word and let him make the decisions, though.

After a few minutes straining to see the tiny wire, he reached back and pulled his glasses out of the workbench—he really only needed them for intricate parts.

"Bloody hell, you've got to be kidding me," Quinn said.

He looked at her, her features now extra crisp thanks to the glasses. She had these cute freckles across the bridge of her nose, and her bottom lip was between her teeth. "What?" he asked.

She shook her head and swallowed. "Nothing."

Really? The glasses turned her on? Hell, he'd wear them all the time, then. "What's with the bloody? You turning British on me?"

"I'm an equal-opportunity swearer."

"Well, Miss Potty Mouth, hand me the needle-nose pliers next to your feet, please."

She picked them up and extended them to him. He let his fingers brush across hers, testing how far he could milk this. "Can you hold these two pieces together while I twist?"

Quinn knelt next to him. She gripped the two wires, and he took the pliers and twisted. Every time he turned the pliers, his forearm brushed her chest, even when he tried to do the honorable thing and go from another angle. The beating pulse at her neck called to him again, begging to be kissed. She smelled amazing, too, a light vanilla scent that invaded his senses.

"I'll be damned," she said once he lowered the pliers. "It actually looks like a butterfly. Look at you using your manly skills to spread your wings and fly."

His lips trembled as he tried to keep a straight face—she kept him on his toes, that was for sure. "One, never say that to me again, and two, I told you I'd find a way—never doubt me, woman."

"It was a compliment. No need to get your wings in a bunch." She innocently batted her eyes, the amusement in them clear.

Oh, she wanted to play? He could play. All day he'd held back, not taking opportunities he would under usual circumstances, because she wasn't just any girl. She was in a different class and her family already disliked him, she was Sadie's best friend, and most problematic of all, she wanted to take Mountain Ridge from him. But between the flirting and the constant challenges she threw out, he was done overthinking and worrying about making things complicated.

Letting his instincts take over, he reached up and brushed the strands that'd fallen free of her ponytail off her face. The amusement died, other emotions taking over her features. Surprise and temptation—he could work with both of those.

He trailed his fingers across the top of her cheek. "I'm glad we got paired together. I'd much rather stare at you bending across the float than Patsy Higgins."

She leaned in a fraction, her breath hitting his lips. "Wow, with a bar that low, I don't even know if that could be called flattery."

Exhilaration surged through him, and he curled his hand around the back of her neck. "Like you don't know that I haven't been able to stop staring at you all night. Honestly, since that day you swore in church, I've had a hard time getting you out of my head."

"You made a rather unforgettable impression, too." She pressed a hand to his chest, and her eyes locked onto his.

Their lips had drifted closer and closer, and now he was a mere inch from closing the gap between him and the feisty, smart woman who was slowly driving him crazy in the best possible way.

Quinn wrapped her hand around his wrist. "Heath—"

"You're going to say this is a bad idea. That we've got to work together or whatever, but think about it. This way we can get it out of the way and focus on the task at hand. And don't pretend you haven't been thinking about it. Your 'bloody hell' gave it away."

"I don't know what's more romantic. You saying you want to get it out of the way or that you're using my swearing against me." She said it in a light, teasing tone, but then her fingers gripped tighter and a hint of nervousness showed through as she licked the lips currently mesmerizing him. "But actually, I was going to say that kissing is as far as this can go. Obviously there's attraction and now that we're working together, it's impossible to ignore or think it'll magically go away—I mean, not even constantly disagreeing is enough to faze it. But I just got out of a relationship, and I'm not looking for anything serious."

"Then we're in the same place. I don't have time for a relationship right now."

"Good," Quinn said, and then her eyebrows scrunched together. "Except that makes it sound like I'm looking for sex without strings attached, and that's not what I mean, either." She glanced to the ceiling like she was looking for an answer and sighed.

He sat back, ready to retreat. He wasn't going to push if she didn't want him to kiss her. Maybe he'd read the entire situation wrong.

"Ugh, now I'm screwing it up before it even starts." Her eyes caught his and held. "I'm saying...I really want to kiss you, but I'm not sleeping with you. I like having a little fun as much as anyone else, and I'm sure you're probably used to girls racing to your bed, but I'm not like that. I'd rather just put that out there now so there's no confusion. If that changes your mind about kissing me—"

He covered her mouth with his and returned his hand to her neck so he could draw her closer. Her lips opened under his, soft, pliant, sweet. He took advantage, sweeping his tongue in to meet hers. It ignited something in her that changed the tempo, no more soft and sweet. Her fingernails dug into the skin on his arms, and trails of heat scored through his body. Her tongue swirled around his, and he groaned—the woman had perfected the kiss.

She straddled him, sinking onto his lap. Her hips bumped into his, and desire fired hotter through his veins. If kissing was all they were going to do tonight, he might as well make it last as long as possible. He savored every inch of her mouth as he slipped his arm between his jacket and her tank top, wrapping it around her and bringing her tighter against him.

Her moan vibrated against his lips, turning him on even more, and then her tongue stroked his. Everything in him wanted to lay her down and start tearing off clothes. The no-sleeping-with-him edict was issued like a challenge he wanted to break, but at the same time, he could tell it'd come out reluctantly and that she'd meant it. So he gave her one more solid kiss, exhaled, and then rested his forehead against hers.

Her chest rose and fell against his, and right now he cursed his leather jacket for being in the way, despite how hot she looked in it.

"Well, then," she said on a shaky breath. "Now that that's out of the way..." She leaned in, gave him a quick peck, and pushed to her feet. She touched her red, slightly swollen lips with the tips of her fingers. "I, uh, just realized I can't make a dramatic exit because you drove me here. So I'll settle for swaying my hips as I walk to the door, giving you a sultry look over my shoulder, and then you following me so you can drive me home."

He simply nodded—that sounded like a solid plan to him. Quinn put an extra sway in her step as promised and cast a come-hither look over her shoulder that only lasted two seconds before she broke into laughter. "Well? What are you waiting for?"

Obediently, he jumped to his feet, surprised his limbs even knew how to work after that. Kissing had always been a nice thing to get to other things, but that had been something else altogether.

He'd never had any woman give it to him straight like that, either. Just lay it out, no games. Every minute he spent around Quinn made him realize he'd never met anyone quite like her.

Now all he wanted to do was get to know *everything* about her, but without either one of them getting too attached.

Sure. That seemed like a probable outcome. And yet he knew he was going to try it out anyway.

Chapter Eight

The second day of float building went much smoother than the first. Quinn had stayed up until two a.m. studying every tutorial she could find. It probably would've gone faster if she hadn't kept reliving the kiss between her and Heath. The way it'd set her body on fire and sent her inhibitions to the back of her mind made it impossible not to think about, though, and having him nearby all morning kept her lips tingling with the memory.

Trying not to lose control with him would be a constant struggle, and yet the thought of never kissing him again made an ache settle over her heart. She didn't want to analyze that too closely, because then she'd have to admit she was already pushing her boundaries farther than she should.

She glanced up at him, watching as he secured the wire frame for the bigger butterfly. Apparently he'd built it last night when she'd been Googling. He let it go, grinning when it stayed in place. He winked at her, and an electric zip shot through her core.

Gah, could the guy be any hotter?

The answer was no, no, he couldn't. Except maybe if he put on his black square frames so the image of hot and nerdy could clash and short-circuit her brain again. He jumped down, landing right in front of her, and then reached out and squeezed her shoulder. "Need help with the purple stuff?"

"The purple floral sheeting, you mean?" Her internet research had her feeling smarter and totally in control of the newbie-float-builders situation.

Heath arched his eyebrows. "The who does what now?"

"I understand if you're not secure enough in your manhood to say it," Quinn teased.

He leaned in until his lips brushed her ear, and goose bumps swept across her skin. "Be careful, or I'll have to take you to my truck and make sure you never question my manhood again."

His hand slid down, pausing right at the curve of her butt. Then he reached behind her and grabbed the stapler. Quinn glanced around. She wondered if anyone had noticed their blatant flirting. The last thing she needed was for it to turn into town gossip that'd get back to her family.

Once our float looks a little less homely, we need to find somewhere we can be alone again. I think I can hold back until then.

He shot her a mischievous grin and dragged his hand across her waist before climbing back on the float. *I...wait. What was I thinking?*

Quinn rolled out the purple floral sheeting. Now that the wire butterfly frames were secured, she could decorate the top of the float and cover the bases Heath had built to hold them in place. Then they'd use the pink and yellow plastic vinyl rolls and festoon to fix up the butterflies so they no longer looked like they'd been set on fire and their skeletons were all that remained. She doubted the people of Hope Springs would go for that kind of float. It definitely didn't say, "Spread Your Wings and Fly."

"Hey, man." A guy Quinn vaguely recognized strode up to Heath. "I can't wait until you get your hunting lodge up and running. My college buddies and I have talked about doing a trip for years, so you let me know when you start booking them, and I'll get 'em down here. It'd be nice to get away from the ol' ball and chain for a few days, you know what I mean?"

Quinn stapled the purple sheeting with more gusto as she thought about this guy and his buddies using her B and B to sit around and complain about their wives. Even though she couldn't remember the guy's name, she'd seen him with his wife, and let's just say she'd definitely gotten the short end of the stick in that pairing.

Jerk.

"Well, it's not a done deal yet," Heath said, casting a quick glance her way. "The committee still hasn't made their decision."

"My uncle's on the committee." He clapped Heath on the back. "I'll put in a good word for you."

Quinn gritted her teeth and fought the urge to turn her stapler on the guy. Heath must've sensed her intent, because he guided him toward the other side of the float, thanked him for his support, and said he needed to get back to work. She tried not to let it bother her, but she couldn't stop worrying the guy might actually have pull, and a mix of resentment and worry rose up, causing her to staple faster and harder.

In her head, she mimicked Heath's *Thanks for your support*, then immediately felt bad. If she knew a way to improve her chances besides simply float building, she'd take it, so she could hardly fault him for the same thing.

Now I need a non-backstabbing way to improve my chances. Let's see, who do I know who's related to a town committee member?

A few names came to mind, but she wasn't sure how influential they'd be. Sadie would be more up-to-date on that kind of info, but with her vow to remain neutral, it might not be easy to convince her to help. *Ooh, I bet her grandparents would know, and luckily, they love me.*

With that thought in mind, she continued stretching paper and securing it in place. She and Heath worked for another hour or so, until the sides and floor were colorful and no hint of cardboard remained, but things were less playful than they'd been before the reminder of their opposing sides.

They'd just decided to take a break when a blond boy who she guessed to be in the six- to eight-year-old range wandered in and waved so big that Quinn worried she'd hurt his feelings if she didn't wave back, even though she didn't know him.

The cutest dog she'd ever seen trailed behind him on a leash, and then they both bounded toward her. It wasn't till they'd raced past that she realized they didn't care about her, but the guy behind her.

The little boy started talking excitedly about how he had a music program this week, and Heath was coming, right?

Quinn glanced from Heath to the kid, noticing similar

features, coloring, and the exact same blue-green eyes, and her stomach fell right down to her toes. *Oh my gosh, he's got a kid. Why didn't he mention that when he was talking about the lodge?*

Usually she'd think that meant he was a deadbeat dad, but as he rubbed a hand over the kid's head and then squatted to be on his level to talk to him, the affection was clear to see.

The adorable puppy jumped, pawing at Heath's knees as if to say he didn't want to be left out, and Heath gathered him in his arms. "Thanks for taking Trigger for a walk. Don't want him staying at home all day and getting fat and lazy."

The dog licked his face and he flinched, but he didn't move him away. Heath glanced up at Quinn. "Quinn, meet Oliver and"—he lifted the dog—"Trigger."

Oliver stuck out his hand, and Quinn shook it. A mitt was on his left hand and his shoelaces were untied, the used-to-be white coated in dirt. "Nice to meet you. And you," she said to the dog, patting his head.

"Guys, this is Quinn."

Oliver spared her another quick glance and then started talking about grounders. Heath nodded and straightened. "Tell you what. Sometime this week we'll go out to the field and practice, okay? Once you get the position down, you'll be stopping them left and right."

"Okay," Oliver said.

"And let's tie those shoes before you trip. Is your mom home today?"

"Nah. She's at work. I got bored so I got Trigger and walked to the store for some candy, and then I saw your truck."

"That's pretty far. I'm guessing you need a ride home?"

Oliver blew out a big exhale. "Yep. Farther than I thought. Took forever, too, because Trigger had to mark his territory everywhere. We both got in trouble when he peed on Mrs. Branson's flowers."

Heath chuckled, and Quinn covered her laugh with her hand. While Heath's having a kid threw her for a loop, as long as he wasn't married, she could deal.

Crap. Here I am thinking like we're in a relationship, when we're clearly not, and we both agreed on keeping things light and easy. Of course, the last hour had felt more tense than easy. Frustration bubbled up as she contemplated her current situation. She couldn't stop thinking about kissing him again, but thoughts about how to get more people on her side for the B and B were rattling around in her brain, too. Now that there was a kid in the mix, her emotions got so tangled up she could hardly pick one from the other.

Heath glanced at her and then attraction rose to the top, shoving her other feelings down for later exploration. "I'm starving. How about I take you two out for lunch, and then I'll bring Ollie home before we get back to float building?"

"Sure," she said, unable to resist the chance to spend more time with him. Not to mention the way her stomach rumbled at the mention of food.

"With milkshakes?" Oliver asked. Heath nodded, and he pumped his fist. "Sweet. I'll go get in the truck." He sprinted away, forgetting to take the dog, his untied shoelaces trailing behind him.

"He's cute."

"Yeah. I just wish his mom didn't think he was old enough to be left alone all the time. I know Hope Springs is a relatively safe place, but it only takes one bad person coming through, or him not paying attention when he's crossing the street... Especially since his shoelaces are never tied."

"So...she's your ex?"

"Hell, no!" His indignant expression softened as realization dawned. "Ollie's not my kid. He's my little brother."

"Oh." Quinn didn't know what else to say, and with the amount of relief flooding her system, she was afraid anything more would give away her realization that her interest in Heath already felt more serious than it should.

Was it bad that the other reason she felt so relieved had to do with the fact that she'd feel worse about taking Mountain Ridge away from a single dad? She would already have enough to feel guilty about if she got the property, after all.

"No kids yet. Just to be clear." Heath glanced toward the open garage door where Oliver had disappeared. "We'd better get out there. Ready?"

Quinn abandoned the float materials, and Heath picked up the puppy, who went to licking the side of his face again. Tucking him under one arm, he put the other hand on Quinn's back, and the butterflies from yesterday returned, no longer drunk but hyper.

The simplest touches drove her crazy, the guy's kiss made the world spin off its axis, and he took care of his little brother and had the cutest dog in the history of dogs. Apparently, it was, in fact, possible for him to get even hotter.

Puff, puff, puff. Two days in, and I'm already in so, so much trouble.

• • •

Heath pushed into the Triple S and searched the crowd for Quinn. Earlier they'd had lunch with Ollie. When he'd invited her to his school music program on Thursday night, Heath had given her an out, telling Ollie she probably didn't have time. But she'd smiled and told him she'd try to make it.

The kid had enough people in his life who fell through, and he hoped Quinn wouldn't be one of them, but the only thing he could guarantee was that he'd be there. While he'd moved back to Hope Springs to get Mountain Ridge, Ollie was one more reason he needed to get the property and make an actual home there, so his brother would always have a place to go. He felt a little guilty for leaving him on his own for so long, actually. Without Cam, Heath never would've gotten through having Dad as a parent, so he'd decided to watch over the kid and do what he could.

If Dad wouldn't take Ollie fishing and hunting, he and Cam would. He hoped Dad would, though, because those camping trips and wilderness survival lessons were his few bright spots in a sea of bad memories.

I'll have to have a talk with Dad about it. See if I can't convince him that Ollie needs those kinds of memories with him, too.

Heath shelved that to-do item for later and focused on why he'd come to Seth's Steak and Saloon. After his and Quinn's second round of float decorating this afternoon, she'd said, "Hey, if you're out of your bathtub moonshine or you want to change it up, you should meet me and everyone else at the Triple S tonight."

So here he was. Usually he played it cooler, but the festival was in three weeks, and then the decision about Mountain Ridge would be announced, and things between them would be irrevocably screwed up. There was something about knowing their hangouts had a time limit that made him not want to waste any of it.

He heard Quinn's unmistakable laugh and spotted her with Cory Brooks on the dance floor. They were caught mid-spin, their arms tangled, and Cory laughed along with her as he tried to untangle them. Within a couple of seconds he gave up and they broke apart and started over.

Without Cory in the way, he got a look at Quinn. Her hair was twisted up, that bright red strand threaded through the black, and she wore a silver sequined top that caught the light and a tight black leather miniskirt that drew attention to her legs. The tall black heels made the muscles in her calves stand out. *Holy shit, woman.*

He didn't exactly love watching her dance with Cory. In fact, a slight twinge went through him when his eyes narrowed in on the hand at her waist, right where his had been earlier today, when he'd guided her out of the garage and in and out of the diner.

It's not like I have any claim on her. The more he watched, though, the clearer it became they were more friendly than trying to feel each other up on the floor, which helped. Sadie and Royce danced next to them, spinning and not missing a step, but they stopped and said something to Quinn and Cory and then they all laughed, Quinn's rising above the rest.

Taking his eyes off her wasn't easy, but he didn't want to come across as too desperate, even as a desperate edge to be near her flooded his chest. He headed to the bar, sat on one of the stools lining it, and signaled Seth over. By the time he had a cold beer in his hand, the song had ended and Quinn and the rest of the group neared. She perched herself on the stool next to him and leaned in to kiss his cheek with her cherry-red lips.

His heart stuttered, the sweet gesture giving him thoughts that went far beyond sweet.

"Hey," she whispered in his ear. "I'm glad you came."

He was going to joke that it was for the booze, but then he decided to be as straight with her as she was with him. "I'm sort of addicted to seeing you now, so I didn't have much of a choice."

He got the uninhibited smile. Judging by her flushed cheeks, she was already a few drinks in—or maybe the color was from the dancing. Reluctantly he moved his gaze from her and greeted everyone else.

Royce sat on the stool next to Quinn and pulled Sadie onto his lap. Before Sadie had shown up, the guy had been all business. She forced him to take time off, and on the road—since it wasn't like privacy in a van was a possibility—he'd often overheard her half of their phone conversations. Heard the reassurances she gave Royce and knew he gave them right back. Heath saw the way they worked together and balanced each other out, too. Admittedly, a couple of times he'd caught himself thinking it'd be nice to have some-one like that waiting at home.

Eventually. First he needed to get things squared away with the lodge and then find the best way to promote it and their tours and other services, and then maybe he'd think about attempting a real relationship.

He couldn't even believe he was contemplating it, con-sidering signing the contract for the band had almost been enough to give him hives. Long-term commitment had never been his thing, and he'd worried turning the music he'd used to escape into work might make him end up resenting it. So far that hadn't happened, though, and a big part of it was how well he, Sadie, and Will got along. They made music they liked, and Sadie was big on being allowed to do things their way—she'd been beaten up pretty badly in Nashville and didn't want to compromise who she was again.

It meant they might never have millions of record sales, and honestly, that'd helped make signing the contract less overwhelming. The only thing he'd never experienced that type of panic over committing to was the lodge. Because he knew he'd be running it with Cam, they'd balance each other out, and work would be half play. For that, he'd gladly hand over his life savings, sign the dotted line, and spend day and night ensuring its success.

That had to be his focus now. No thinking that a relationship—say, with the woman currently flashing him a smile—might be a welcome change from the norm.

She's the only thing standing between you and that lodge. Don't let yourself forget that, Brantley. Or that this thing between us is running on borrowed time.

Quinn helped herself to a drink of the beer he'd barely touched. Then she jumped to her feet and grabbed his hand. "Okay, now you get to dance with me."

He tugged against her, making her stumble into him, and caught her around the waist. "And if I refuse?"

"You won't," she said, leaning close enough that her lips were within reach and then pulling away before he could capture them.

Once they got on the dance floor, he said, "Fair warning. I can't do any of those fancy moves."

"As I'm sure you saw, neither can I. Not even with Cory leading me, and he's good at it. That's why I picked a slow song for us." She hooked her hands around his neck, and her body bumped against his.

He wrapped his arms around her, bringing them tighter together. Maybe dancing wasn't so bad. "You all have known each other for a long time, huh?"

"Yeah, Sadie moved in sophomore year and we were instant best friends. Even before she and Royce were officially together, I knew it'd happen. Whenever I wasn't grounded—which was, like, maybe once a month—the four of us were running around town or headed to another rodeo. Sadie would usually sing the national anthem, and then we'd sit in the stands and cheer on Royce and Cory. Sadie nearly had panic attacks during the bronc riding, which always made me feel even worse about the times I couldn't go with her. I'd sit at home feeling left out and abandoned and wishing that I could go a few measly weeks without being grounded."

"You were grounded that much?" he asked, wondering what she'd done to get into trouble that often.

"My parents thought I was a wild, rebellious child who needed to be contained—even now they think that. I tried to walk the line, I did, but it was just so boring. So I'd sneak out and inevitably get caught. It's not like the people in this town are known for keeping secrets, and as you probably also noticed, I'm not exactly quiet. Even now I'm wondering how much gossip from this weekend is going to get back to them—how much I drank, who I was with, if I was out super late. It'll be like high school all over again."

Heath dodged a faster-moving couple and pulled Quinn out of their path. "I suppose it'll be bad if they find out you spent most of your time with me."

"Definitely. There'd be an intervention with the preacher who's already scared of me."

He tensed, not sure why, since it wasn't exactly a news flash.

"Don't take that the wrong way," Quinn said. "They barely like anyone. But they don't live here anymore, and the Triple S is like the Vegas of Wyoming, so…" She flashed him a smile and then shrugged. "Even if they do hear about it, they won't be too surprised, and I'll play it off as not a big deal. Just a night out with Sadie where I danced with lots of people—you and Cory now count as lots. Then I'll get guilted into taking on some project I don't want to at the office."

She glanced down and then back up, and the lights caught her brown eyes for a moment before they turned and his head blocked the glow. "It's another reason why I want Mountain Ridge so badly. I hate working for my father. It's like living in a fishbowl but not having the gills to breathe underwater as it slowly suffocates me. He's always telling me what I'm doing wrong, no matter how many deals I close or how much I prove myself. I'm damn good at my job, but I don't even like what I do."

The reminder of the property made it feel like she was slipping away, even with her pressed against him, and he splayed his fingers on the small of her back, wanting to touch every inch of her he could. "Why don't you just tell him how you feel? Get a new job?"

A mirthless laugh escaped her. "You don't understand. It's not that simple." She shook her head and sighed. "It's hard to explain."

"You think I can't keep up? I might surprise you."

She nearly stopped moving. "That's not it at all. Most people just don't get it, even when I explain, and that makes it more frustrating."

He locked eyes with her. "Try me." Usually he'd let it go, but there'd been something about Quinn, day one, that made him want to make it better. After seeing her cry at the wedding reception then school her features as if she had to fake being okay a lot, he didn't want her to have to do that with him.

"No matter how Americanized my family is, our Japanese roots are more important. So grown woman or not, when it comes down to it, respecting your elders and the approval of your family is put above everything else. It's not something I can just turn off because it'd be convenient. If I do get Mountain Ridge, I'm not even sure how I'm going to tell my father—it'll be an intense conversation. But at least I can call it leaving for another business opportunity, and he'll still be able to manage a bit of pride that I'm starting my own business and honoring the family name, even if he's not the happiest about me leaving Sakata Real Estate."

Sorrow flickered across her face, and a pang went through his chest. "If I don't get it, I'll have to stay where I am. I can't disappoint him for anything less than my dream job, and I can at least justify the bed and breakfast by pointing out that I'm still working in the same career field he helped train me for."

The song ended, but Heath didn't bother leaving the floor, simply kept holding on and swaying to a beat that was no longer there. "I guess I get that. Regardless of how screwed up my dad is, there's still part of me that wants his approval. Even an acknowledgment that I turned out okay would be nice."

"Most people tell me I should get over it. Like I can simply accept going against my beliefs and my family and see their disappointment and not care. You'd think I'd be immune since they've disapproved of most every choice I've ever made for myself, but like you said, a part of me thinks I can still manage to make them proud." She moved her fingers to the back of his neck, playing with the hair there, and his tensed muscles relaxed. "You don't say much about your dad."

Another song came on, this one faster, and still they continued the slow tempo. He had to raise his voice a bit to be heard over the guitar. "There's a reason for that. It's sort of a buzzkill subject."

She looked like she wanted to push, and he supposed that was only fair, considering what she'd confessed about hers. But he wasn't ready, and he wasn't doing it here.

He tightened his arms around her waist, moved his lips next to her ear, and whispered, "Let's just enjoy the rest of this dance."

• • •

Heath's whiskers brushed her cheek, and darts of heat zipped through her as she clung to his shoulders. Then she was turning her face and pressing her lips to his. All day she'd wanted to kiss him again, and between the dim lights and the crowd of people on the floor, they were sorta blocked from view.

This was how she always got into trouble in high school. She'd tell herself she'd practice better self-control, and then she'd get caught up in the moment and her self-control would stick its tongue out at her.

Speaking of tongues…Heath ran his across her bottom lip and then she couldn't remember what she'd been thinking or why she'd even considered pulling back. With the heavy dose of lust pumping through her system, her thoughts turned pleasantly hazy and every inch of her body tingled with anticipation of more.

More exquisite brushes of whiskers against her skin, another tempting taste of Heath's tongue. More inches of their bodies finding each other on the dance floor.

Suddenly people were shuffling around them, some leaving and some going, and she realized the second song had ended.

Oops. Meant for that to be more of a quick, stealthy kiss.

"You wanna get out of here?" Heath asked.

Yes! But wasn't that code for "and go back to my place and have sex"? She'd tried to be clear last night, but she'd also been afraid that if she'd said she was *never* going to sleep with him the kissing definitely wouldn't have happened, and she'd wanted to see what it was like. Now she was thinking she was better off not knowing. "I…"

"You want to hang out with your friends," he said. "That's totally okay."

"It's not that. I just…" She glanced around. "Can we go somewhere else that's not your bedroom? Remember what I said last night?"

"How about we hop on my motorcycle and see where the night takes us?"

"Can I drive?" That would help her keep control of the situation before it got away from her.

"Hell, no," he said and then slid his hand down and laced

his fingers with hers.

She should be insulted. Or pull away. Anything but blindly follow him. Quinn caught Sadie's eye right before they reached the door. Her best friend's eyebrows arched, and Quinn shrugged.

"Be careful," Sadie mouthed. Then she mimicked a phone with her pinkie and her thumb and added, "Call me later."

Quinn nodded. If this went badly, she was all too aware that she might be calling in tears.

Chapter Nine

Without saying a word, Heath took off the same leather jacket she'd worn yesterday and wrapped it around her. There really wasn't any way to be proper as she got on the motorcycle in her skirt, so she just did the best she could, knowing she was exposing a whole lot of thigh—at least she'd managed to keep her underwear from being on display.

Heath's gaze ran over her exposed legs, the heat in it enough to send jolts of electricity across her bare skin, and then he swallowed, hard. He leaned over the bike and kissed her, sliding one of his hands from her knee to her thigh but stopping a few inches below her skirt, leaving a clashing mix of relief and disappointment.

He twisted his hat around so that the bill was behind him and climbed onto the seat in front of her. The entire frame of the motorcycle bounced as he kick-started the engine. It caught and roared as he twisted the throttle, a loud rumble that vibrated through her entire body. She wrapped her arms around him, and then they were off.

As they buzzed out of town, she didn't even care where they were going. For the past few years—ever since she'd started working at Sakata Real Estate—she'd forced herself to be more responsible. She'd held back going out too much, and while she'd still slipped here and there with a guy who screamed *bad boy*, she'd mostly stayed in line. Done what was expected of her. Even dated a guy because he was family approved and supposedly safe.

Until now, she hadn't realized just how much she missed not knowing where the night would lead. Missed simply jumping in without a second thought to everything she should be doing. It made her want to freeze the rest of the world so she could live in this moment for a while. The part before she'd have to tell Heath once again that she wasn't going to sleep with him, no matter where he took her.

Don't think about that right now. She hugged him tighter and slid her fingers underneath his shirt, gliding them across the firm muscles in his abdomen. The bike wavered, and she grinned against his back. That probably wasn't going to help her cause, but the temptation to throw him off proved too strong. Next she kissed the back of his neck.

A few minutes later he pulled the bike off to the side of the dirt road surrounded by miles and miles of prairie land. "You really wanna drive?" he asked, and she nodded. "Do you know how?"

"I'm a fast learner."

She could practically see the wheels turning in his head. Weighing letting-her-take-charge-of-his-bike versus wrecking-his-precious-motorcycle scenarios. "So now you trust the machine that I built with my own two hands?"

She took one of his hands and kissed the back of it. "Now that I know they can build butterflies, I feel completely confident in your skills."

He attempted to remain straight-faced, but a smile broke through. Then he ran his free hand over the handlebar. "I don't usually let anyone else drive her."

"I'll go slow. And be so, so careful." She held her breath, awaiting his verdict.

He swept his gaze across the prairie. "Guess there's not too much out here you can wreck into," he said. Then he shook his head, as if he were having trouble believing what he was about to agree to—clearly she'd convinced him to let her give it a shot, and a thrill went through her stomach. "Just promise me you'll listen regardless of your constant aim to do the opposite of what I say."

"Okay," she said with a squeal.

As they stood to switch seats, Heath said, "And don't think I won't give you the same treatment you've been giving me."

Putting on her most innocent expression, she batted her eyes. "I have no idea what you mean."

Once they'd resettled onto the bike, Heath leaned over her to explain how to work the gears and gas and brakes. Her first couple attempts resulted in a lurch and the engine dying, but then she gradually got the hang of it. She figured out how to shift gears with her foot, even though motorcycle clutches were clearly not built with high heels in mind. The entire time, Heath's body remained coiled behind her, ready to spring into action if she lost control.

By the time she'd cruised in third gear for a mile or so, she felt like she knew what she was doing, and Heath had even relaxed a fraction. The urge to punch it and fly across the flat prairie land was strong, but she'd promised to go slow, and they weren't wearing gear for that kind of riding anyway.

Soft lips touched the back of her neck, and Heath's hand dropped to her thigh and squeezed. Her breath lodged in her throat, and she slowed the motorcycle, downshifting when the engine almost died.

"Distracting, isn't it?" he asked against her skin, and a shiver ran down her spine. "I think I'd better take over now, before you dump us both on our asses." Not bothering to trade places, he reached around her and took control of the motorcycle. He spun them back toward Hope Springs and drove until they ended up in front of her place.

With her family now living in Cheyenne most of the year, the enormous three-story building loomed, no light, all clean lines and emptiness.

"I just want you to know that I heard you last night," Heath said, his voice low and right next to her ear. "I don't mind keeping things less complicated. But much longer looking at you in that skirt, and I'm afraid I might lose the shaky grip I have on my control."

Instead of running from the flame, she crept closer, turning around on the bike so that they faced each other. She ran her hand over his jaw, the whiskers tickling her palm.

His backward hat gave her a better view of his eyes. Blue right now. Or...well, bluish-green. Pupils dilated. "Thanks for understanding," she whispered.

"Mmm-hmm," he said, carefully keeping his eyes off her legs.

"You know how you said you were addicted to seeing

me? Well, I'm having the same problem. I need to drive back to Cheyenne tomorrow so that I can be in the office first thing on Monday, but I'll be back for a long weekend to help out with the float. I think I can even manage to get back Thursday night to go with you to Oliver's music program, if you want."

"I want." He dragged a knuckle down her arm, and the pulse underneath her skin chased after his touch. "What about all the gossip? The more time we spend together in public, the more people are going to talk. On the dance floor, I could tell what you said about your family and trying not to disappoint them was important to you. That you meant it."

Quinn closed her eyes and exhaled, trying to let rational thoughts float to the surface despite how outnumbered they were by the oh-my-gosh-Heath's-so-sexy-and-I-like-him-so-much ones. "It is. And I did. But we can play it like friends at the music show, and then later…" She tiptoed her fingers up his chest, gently tugged on the cross necklace he had on, and pulled him closer for a kiss.

Within seconds, his lips were moving against hers, stirring every hungry cell in her body into a frenzy again.

When they broke apart, she reached up and swiped a finger across his mouth, not that it did anything to remove the red. "Just so you know, you've now got more lipstick on than I do."

"Good. I'll go back to the bar and show it off, so all the other guys will be jealous."

She laughed. "Or maybe they'll start rumors about how you wear lipstick, and then everyone will ask what else you're doing in your spare time—I bet they'll even throw a few cross-dressing mentions into the mix. You know, that might help my chances with the town committee, so I'm all for it."

"And I thought we were going to play fair," he said, his mouth nearing hers again. One last kiss that made her head spin—and wasn't even close to playing fair—and then she reluctantly broke away.

Her second attempt at a smooth exit was stopped by realizing that she couldn't get off the bike without swinging her leg over his head—which was highly unlikely considering her lack of flexibility. Plus she'd probably end up kicking him in the side of the head, but only after he got a view of her underwear.

He must've read her *oh crap* expression, because he slipped off the back of the motorcycle and helped her down, his hands lingering on the sides of her waist for long enough that her rapid heartbeat thundered through her and drowned out all other sounds.

"Until then," he said, and then he kissed her one more time. Her jelly legs barely made it to the door. He waited until she'd stepped inside to take off, and she stayed in the entryway, watching the fading taillights.

Quinn sagged against the wall and replayed the night, including how he'd let her drive his precious motorcycle and had been surprisingly patient as he taught her how, and then all of their kisses. Whenever she had chemistry with a guy, her attempts to go slow and play it safe got left by the way-side, and she and Heath had enough that spontaneous com-bustion seemed highly likely.

Already she felt more for Heath than she ever had after six months with Grayson. Despite reminding herself this was just a fun way to pass the time—because no matter what happened, one of them would lose their dream because of the other—she was already falling for him. And the crash at the end was going to majorly suck.

Quinn froze at the sound of footsteps, sure she must've imagined them. Then the light snapped on, making her jump and shield her eyes as she simultaneously tried to remember all of her aikido training.

"Well, well. What do we have here?"

Chapter Ten

Quinn whipped around, biting back the expletive on the tip of her tongue, since she knew it'd only make things worse.

When she spotted Maya at the top of the stairs, her tensed muscles relaxed, but her heart continued to hammer against her chest. "You scared the crap out of me, Maya! You sound just like Haha."

Maya's wicked laugh made it clear she'd done it on purpose.

"Everything okay?" The deep male voice came from the direction of Maya's bedroom—Steven.

"Yeah, babe. You go ahead and sleep, I'm going to chat with my sister." Maya bound down the stairs and threw her arms around Quinn.

Quinn squeezed her back. "I didn't realize you'd be here."

"Yeah, the house doesn't close for a few weeks, so Steven and I decided to stay here for a while before getting back to the real world."

"How was the honeymoon?"

A smile spread across her sister's face, stars practically gleaming in her eyes. "Amazing. St. Barts was beautiful, and we just lay out on the beach all day and then stayed in all night." She sighed. Then her eyes refocused. "And how was your night? Your makeup's a little smeared. I suppose you owe that to whoever was on the motorcycle?"

Heat flooded Quinn's cheeks, more from the memory than her sister's correct assumption. Quinn tugged Maya to the couch, dying to dish about her perfect night. "Remember Heath Brantley?"

"The guy who caused you to swear in the church, who just so happens to also be the guy you were obsessed with for a while in high school?"

"The very same one." The smile started to hurt her cheeks, but she didn't bother fighting it back. "He's so freaking hot, and while most guys are in a hurry to get the kiss over with and way more focused on feeling me up, he knows just how to use his lips and tongue. Not that he's bad with his hands, either."

Maya's grin barely caught before her look morphed into one of concern. "You already sound so…" She grabbed Quinn's hand. "I just worry about you. You've got that same twitterpated look and voice as when you fell for that Slade guy."

Slade. The tattooed drummer whom Quinn had dated for a couple of months. Not long as far as relationships went, but it'd been one of those whirlwind types where they met, ended up talking all night long, and spent every spare minute they could together after that. She'd gone to every one of his shows, got completely wrapped up in him—the way she tended to do—and then, when she told him she wasn't having sex until she got married, he'd dumped her so fast she'd nearly gotten whiplash. Since she'd thought they were kindred souls, it'd left her a wreck for about a month afterward. So half the time they'd been together. Whereas he'd probably had a new girl by the end of the night they'd broken up.

"I'm…being more careful now. I know better than to fall so hard so fast. Heath and I even agreed to keeping things light and fun. We know it's temporary, and we're just going to enjoy it while it lasts."

"Mmm-hmm. Like with Adam? That kind of carefree fun?"

"Hey, no fair pulling out my hall of shame exes. He… well, he was perfectly free to see other women, because we'd agreed to no labels, and obviously he took advantage of that. A *lot*. But I'd like to point out that the supposedly safe guy ended up dumping me in the end, too. For the exact same thing."

Maya flinched. "Grayson's the baby of the family, and I knew he was spoiled, but I never thought he'd treat you that way. I'm sorry I pushed so hard for you to stay when you clearly were having doubts."

Quinn tiptoed into the territory she hadn't dared to over the phone. "He told me you guys didn't wait, so I guess that translated to him not having to wait any longer, either."

Guilt panged through Quinn when Maya hung her head—she hadn't meant to make her feel bad.

"Why didn't you tell me? I don't care, you know. It stung a little for him to know more than I did, though."

Maya shrugged. "I waited until we were engaged. Honestly, I meant to wait for the wedding, but I love him so much and..." She shrugged again.

"Tell me all about it—I mean, the important happy details, not so much the blow by blow."

Maya filled her in on her nerves before and how great Steven had been, and told her more about their honeymoon. Talking and giggling over boys, the way they used to in high school, made everything lighter, and Quinn needed lighter after the harsh reminder that every guy she'd dated didn't care enough about her to wait. Especially not guys who looked like Heath. Not when they could so easily find another girl willing to do what she wouldn't.

Maybe I am stupid to think I won't get hurt because we agreed to nothing serious. The time away will be good. It'll put enough space between us to help me keep perspective.

Because that certainly wasn't an option when she was kissing Heath.

Chapter Eleven

Quinn strode through the office, her thoughts on yoga pants and takeout in front of the TV. It'd been a long week already and it was only Wednesday. Lucky for her, she only had one more day to go.

Chichi stepped out of his office. "Is the paperwork done for the Seventh Street property yet?"

"Just got it all turned in."

"And you're headed back to Casper tomorrow and then Salt Lake after that?"

Through a bit of smooth talking, she'd convinced her father-slash-boss that she should close on the Casper property in person. Then, since she was already headed in that general area, head down to Salt Lake City to get updates on their properties there and check out another building for sale, which cleared the last half of this week and the first part of next.

"*Hai.* From the pictures, I think we could get that Utah

property for a steal, flip it with our contacts for not much, and then turn it into a moneymaker. But I don't want to commit unless I see it in person—you know how unreliable photos can be."

Chichi placed his hand on her shoulder. "I'm proud of you for showing such initiative, Quinn-chan. I knew you'd get there eventually, even if you did have to drag your feet the entire way."

Guilt washed over her. The semi-jab at the end didn't even make a dent in it, because in *his* eyes, he'd given her the highest praise. No doubt it'd eat at her the entire week, regardless of the fact that she *would* check out the property as promised. But her priority right now was float building and Frontier Days prep in Hope Springs for Mountain Ridge.

She and Chichi rode the elevator down and exited the building. At least she got a glimpse of the last rays of sunshine. In a few months it'd be dark when she came in and dark when she left—that was when the winter blues hit.

When I get Mountain Ridge up and running, I'm going to set aside time to watch the sunset on that swing, just like Sobo and I used to do.

"Why do you keep parking way back there?" Chichi asked. "Planning a quick escape?"

Always. "Trying to get in a few extra steps each day. Read about it in a magazine." Another half truth and another jab of guilt. Technically she *had* read a tip about parking farther away to fit in a little exercise when you had no time, but the real reason she'd parked there all week was because she didn't want her father to see the dent in the driver's side door. It'd lead to questions, and despite her lies of omission, she didn't want to add an outright lie to the pile.

She supposed she could tell the snake story without mentioning the reason she'd been at Mountain Ridge. But then she'd have to work around Heath's involvement as well, and that'd add another heavy brick of guilt to manage.

Man, my life's getting more complicated by the minute.

Chichi squinted at her car, and her heart took off on a high-speed race. Surely he couldn't see anything from here, but he had this freaky sixth sense. "It looks dirty," he said. "Make sure you wash it before you take any clients out. I bought it to impress people, not so that you could joyride in it and neglect to properly care for it."

There was the reminder of why working with him was like walking along the edge of a sword. If you were careful enough, you could keep your balance and only get a few minor nicks, but the tiniest slip and you'd fall on the sharp blade. Right now it felt like she was one wrong step from a slip, which meant it was time to cut and run. "Yes, Chichi. I'll take better care of it, I promise. Good night." She leaned in and kissed his cheek. Before she could make her getaway, he stopped her with a hand on her arm.

"You remember the company mixer next weekend? I ran into Grayson and he didn't have any idea it was going on. I invited him, Steven, and their father."

"Oh, Chichi, you didn't."

The line of his jaw hardened and his eyes narrowed to steely slits. "Excuse me?"

She shifted from foot to foot, not finding one any better than the other for this conversation. "It's just that Grayson and I broke up. Didn't he mention that?"

"Quinn-chan." Chichi sighed, not bothering to hide his disappointment with his posture or the tone of his voice. "For the first time in your life you managed to be in a respectable relationship. Our families are connected through business, and he told me he couldn't wait to see you, so you fix it. It reflects badly if you show up alone. It's not proper."

"Then I'll get another date. I'm not going with Grayson."

Chichi pinched the bridge of his nose. She wanted to blurt out why they'd broken up, but there was the reminder that they were in business together. Now Maya was married to Steven, too, so any fallout affected more than just her. Still, she'd be damned if she'd hang onto Grayson's arm and act like they were cool. "Just once," Chichi continued, "it'd be nice if you thought about other people besides yourself."

He unlocked his car and lowered himself into it before she could respond. Not that she could with the giant lump in her throat. She'd stumbled on the edge of that sword and now she'd hacked off a leg—it certainly felt like it, anyway. Especially since she *was* trying to think about everyone but herself. It wouldn't be easy to focus on schmoozing clients as Grayson circled his way around the place and charmed everyone. No one would possibly believe he wasn't the person he claimed, not when she'd already proven herself as the wild one.

Fighting back tears, she made her way across the parking lot as quickly as she could without running—because proper women didn't run across parking lots in heels and skirts.

As soon as the door locked behind her, she slumped in her seat. She waited until Chichi pulled out of the parking lot and then threw her car into reverse. The ringing of her phone stopped her from moving, though.

When Heath's name flashed on the screen, happiness pushed against the sorrow, fighting through the gloom.

They'd exchanged a few texts, mostly about ideas for their float, with some flirting in between.

She answered, and Heath's sexy voice came over the line. "I thought you'd get a kick out of the fact that I now have on more makeup than the night you left lipstick all over my face."

Her spine stiffened. Was he calling to brag about another woman covering him in lipstick? No. That didn't make sense.

"Honestly, I can't believe I'm even confessing this," he continued. "I told Sadie that she better take it to the grave. But I suppose she'd tell you anyway. You two don't strike me as being able to keep secrets from each other."

"Oh! The photo shoot!" Without another woman involved, her excitement pitched her voice several octaves higher. She cleared her throat, trying to play it cool way too late. "I forgot that was today. How's it going?"

"I'm wearing makeup, that's how it's going."

She could hear the sneer in his voice, and she laughed. "I want a picture."

"You'll have to wait for the album cover like everyone else. But I'll sign it for you, since you're special."

"Gee, thanks." Quinn glanced in her rearview mirror, contemplating backing up and making her way home. But she tended to get distracted thinking about Heath, and a wreck in the car that Chichi cared so much about wasn't worth it. "Don't tell me they made you shave."

"Hell, no, and that's definitely where I'd draw the line. Although…"

She gripped her phone tighter. "Spill it."

"They combed some sticky crap into it so that it's all in place. Seriously, I didn't sign up for this."

Quinn laughed again, picturing people around him dabbing on foundation and powder while another person combed gel into his beard. She was surprised it was long enough for that—much longer and it'd be untamed, but he kept it trimmed at the permanent scruff level. Her skin tingled at the memory of it brushing her as they kissed.

"How's Sadie holding up?" she asked. "I know the last label she almost signed with wanted her boobs hanging out as she straddled a guitar or something racy like that."

"I feel like Royce is going to show up and glare at me if I even comment on that, and since he's my best reference for—"

The awkward silence hung in the air between them for a moment, and she knew he'd stopped himself short because he meant *for Mountain Ridge*. Sadie claimed to be neutral, but her fiancé obviously wasn't, which would be the same as her speaking in Heath's favor, too, as far as the town committee was concerned. Tiny pricks of worry and resentment poked at her chest and she tried to ignore them.

That's it. Tonight I'm calling Sadie's grandparents. If I don't get a few extra references on my side, I'm going to lose this race at the halfway mark, and I can't have that.

"Anyway," Heath said. "I just…well, I was thinking about you. Between this and the garage, I haven't had much time to work on the float."

"No worries. I'd only feel guilty if you'd been working on it all week." *And I have enough guilt to deal with right now as it is. Not to mention the town committee's probably been watching.*

Did it make her a bad person to not want Heath to have time so that she actually still had a chance? *Great. More guilt to deal with.* But if Royce was vouching for Heath, she needed all the help she could get.

Ugh, this was getting as complicated as work. She shoved those thoughts away, silently chiding herself to be a bigger person. "I'm planning on being there tomorrow evening for Oliver's music show, if you still want me to come."

"Of course. I can't wait. I'll save you a spot."

"Then I'll practically live in the float garage until Sunday evening, at which point I'll have to head to Utah for work."

"I'll be there to make sure we take food and kissing breaks."

Now the memory of his lips on hers was back, sending warmth through her entire body. "You're such a giver."

"Right?" Muffled voices came over the line. "Hey, I've got to go. Apparently they want to get a few more shots. Wish me luck."

"Good luck," she said. And at least as far as the photo shoot went, she genuinely meant it.

• • •

Damn traffic. Between construction and a wreck, Quinn's three-hour drive had turned into four. She pulled up to Hope Springs Elementary, parked in a spot that didn't technically have white lines marking it, and then rushed into the building.

She'd texted Heath right before she'd left Casper, telling him to make sure to save her a seat. With every minute closer it'd gotten to the starting time of Oliver's music program, the stronger her irritation at other cars had become. Ten minutes late, she pushed into the gym, where she could hear applause. She scanned the seats, worried Heath had given up on her and afraid she wouldn't see him with the lights dimmed. But then she caught sight of the familiar black hat and the empty chair next to him.

Now it seemed silly to think she wouldn't be able to spot him in the crowd. In a sea of parents and grandparents, the guy stood out. He had his arms crossed, and the rings on his fingers caught the tiny bit of light in the gym. Lust and a heavy dose of longing that had to do with more than just his looks twisted through her.

Light and fun, light and fun. No getting caught up. She'd had plenty of time to give herself the pep talk over the last few days. Admittedly, watching his little brother's school program together felt a tad relationshipy, but this was Hope Springs. Usual dating rules didn't apply.

Anyway, that's what she told herself as she sucked in and tried to make herself as small as she could as she squeezed through the small gap between foldout chairs. Seriously, couldn't they at least make it possible to walk through without brushing your butt in someone's face?

Her next step landed her on someone's foot, and she offered an apology as the music teacher announced the name of the song the children were about to perform. Finally she made it to Heath and flopped onto the open chair. "Sorry. Traffic and road construction was a bitch."

The people in the near vicinity turned and gaped at her, their expressions heavy on the scolding side.

"I mean, it was...crappy," she quickly amended, then looked to Heath. "What did I miss?"

The eyes that met hers were definitely blue tonight. With a hint of green. For a moment she forgot how to breathe. Then her gaze moved to his lips and she wanted to ignore the fact that they were in public and kiss him with reckless abandon. She'd daydreamed about those lips ever since the last time they'd left hers. She'd worried time apart might change the vibe between them and then they'd have an awkward, unsure period, but it took all of two seconds before he wrapped his hand around her knee and shot her a drool-inducing smile.

"Just the first song."

Before they could say anything else, the music started up. The shrill noise of dozens of recorders cut through the air. "Ah, the lost art form of the recorder," Quinn said. "Good to know someone's keeping it alive."

Heath chuckled, and her stomach did a somersault. They endured three more songs that relied heavily on the recorders. Between every one, a woman excitedly announced the titles.

Quinn leaned in. "I don't trust anyone who purposely puts herself in a position to listen to that every day. Can you imagine?"

Heath snort-laughed, turning it into a fake cough when the people around them shot them glares. He nudged her thigh. "You're going to get me in trouble."

"All I'm saying is it's suspect. I mean, Ollie sounds like an angel, obviously—if angels decided to forgo trumpets— but think of how they sounded when they first started. She's way too excited about every song, too."

"Is now a bad time to let you know I used to date her?" Heath whispered.

Quinn glanced at the woman again, taking in her bobbed brown hair and prairie skirt. So not the type she suspected

Heath would go for, especially since she had to be in her late thirties. Now she trusted the woman even less, but for petty, jealous reasons that she shouldn't feel considering the light-and-fun rule.

Heath put his fist to his mouth and smothered another laugh. "That was too easy."

She shoved him, and he laughed harder. "I'm going to get you back for that."

They got shushed and that only made them laugh more. Finally they managed to quell the laughter. Luckily, the next two songs involved good old-fashioned piano music and singing, a welcome relief to her ears.

They applauded with the rest of the audience when the kids bowed after their final number, and then the performers were dismissed to find their parents.

Ollie darted through the crowd and stopped in front of Heath. "Hey, now that we're done with that, can we go practice grounders?"

Heath gestured to Quinn. "Did you see that Quinn came?"

He spared her the shortest glance ever. "Yeah. So grounders?"

Heath's look took much longer. She could tell he was conflicted, not wanting to say no, but also taking her into account—hopefully he wanted to spend time with her as much as she wanted to with him.

"You know," Quinn said, diving into the deeper end of the relationship pool instead of shying away, like she probably should, "I never learned how to stop grounders. And the weather's so nice tonight, I'm thinking it'd be the perfect time to figure it out."

Heath reached over and took her hand, giving it a quick squeeze. "Let's go teach you two how to field, then."

On the way out of the school, Mrs. Branson stopped Quinn. "Doris told us at quilting group about how you're trying to restore the Mountain Ridge B and B, and we all agreed it'd be lovely to see that place up and running again. If you need any help with sewing, or quilts for the beds, we'd be happy to offer our services."

"Thank you so much," Quinn said, flashing the woman a huge smile. Obviously Sadie's grandma Doris had come through in a big way—the quilting group carried a lot of pull. When she turned away from Mrs. Branson only to see Heath scowling, she tried to wipe the smug smile from her lips.

As they pushed out the door, Heath mumbled, "I should've told her you laughed about my dog destroying her flowers."

He'd said it more like a joke, and she knew he wouldn't rat her out, but real tension underlay the words.

On the steps of the school, Mr. Case, who owned the local sawmill, stopped Heath and told him he could offer him a good price on lumber for the lodge, and then Quinn had a hard time not scowling. She also wanted to step forward, let Mr. Case know she'd need a considerable amount of lumber if she got the B and B, and pledge her business if he'd offer her the same discount. Seemed too much like crossing the line on their truce, though.

Sheila, who owned the diner, interrupted the conversation and said that the B and B would bring in more business for the whole town, and then she and Mr. Case glared at each other. Several others chimed in, casting their verbal votes and arguing among themselves.

Finally she, Heath, and Ollie made it to the parking lot. For a moment the edge of contention hanging in the air made her hesitate. She almost called it a night, but she'd looked forward to seeing Heath for days, and she was determined not to let their property skirmish get in the way, even if it was proving harder than she'd expected.

"Need me to drive?" Quinn asked when she noticed Heath's motorcycle—three of them definitely wouldn't fit on there.

"Miss Sakata, I don't think that's a parking space." Hank, the local sheriff, stood with his hand on the door handle of his truck, which was parked in the spot—clearly marked with two white lines—next to Quinn's car.

"Really?" She made a big show of looking around. "I swore there was another white line on the other side."

He raised a bushy eyebrow, the way he used to when he caught her and Sadie out late at night—she suspected Chi-chi had asked him to keep an eye out for her. The guy also had sway with the town committee, and the last thing she needed was a mark against her.

"I'll move it and be more careful." She shot him an extra-wide smile. Hank's gaze moved to Heath, who gave a short nod and tugged his cap lower. Maybe she wasn't the only one on the cop's radar. Great, add the riot they'd nearly started as everyone exited the school and they were the town problem couple—er, problem couple of friends who occasionally kissed.

"Hurry. Get in, get in," Quinn whispered, unlocking the doors and sliding into the driver's seat of her Mercedes.

"Wow, this is a super-fancy car," Ollie said, bouncing on

the leather bench seat in the back. "I bet you haven't had any kids in here ever."

"No, actually, I haven't. It's my company car that I use to take clients around, so technically it's not mine." She glanced at Heath. "Which reminds me…" Maybe now wasn't a good time to bring this up—it was usually best to ask for favors when the mood was happier—but she'd already started, so she charged on through with it. "You don't happen to have an opening at the shop tomorrow? It's only a matter time before the dent gets noticed, and I'm hoping to avoid that, if possible."

In an attempt to lighten the mood, she added, "If not, maybe I can just find a really classy bumper sticker that'd help with business. Like, maybe one that says, 'Caution: This car makes frequent stops at your mom's house.'"

Ollie snorted in the backseat. Oops. That was probably an inappropriate joke to make with him in the car.

Heath cracked a smile, and then his hand moved to her knee, enveloping it in warmth that spread up her leg and settled in her core. "I'm sure your clients would find that very amusing, but if you want to go the boring route, you can bring the car into the shop first thing tomorrow, and we'll get it fixed up."

Hope mixed in and deepened the warmth—they could power through. They were awesome like that. "Fine, fine. I'll go with boring and not likely to get me fired. Being a grown-up's no fun."

She reversed her illegally parked car and got in line with the rest of the vehicles trying to leave the school. She was about to automatically turn right toward her house and then hit the brakes. "Where exactly are we going?"

"To my place," Heath said. "The balls and the mitts are there. Then we'll head to the old ballpark—it's only a few blocks away."

Quinn made the left. She wondered if this time she'd be permitted to go inside the house. But then she reminded herself that was probably not a fun and light thing to do, either. She'd never done very well following guidelines, even if she'd been the one to set them.

"I'll be right back," Heath said when they got to his place, which answered her question about being allowed inside. Dang Maya. Now Quinn was thinking about how Adam had never taken her to his place. Other women had apparently come and gone in droves.

The car went dead silent when the door shut, and Quinn reached for the radio. With Heath there, talking to Oliver seemed easy enough, but she never knew what to say to kids.

"Are you Heath's girlfriend?" Oliver asked.

The barrier of the rearview mirror made answering slightly easier, although the boy certainly started with the hard questions. "No. We're just friends."

"That's what my mom says about the guys she brings home, but I'm not stupid."

What do you say to something like that? Luckily the front door swung open and Heath came out balancing a couple of mitts, baseballs, and a bat. He got in the car and pointed out the way to a run-down baseball field. Only the metal posts remained behind home base, which was marked by a large rock—talk about an accident waiting to happen.

"Nobody slide into home, okay?" Quinn said, stepping over the rock as she pulled on the mitt Heath had given her.

"There's no sliding in grounding balls," Oliver said with

a sigh.

Heath reached over and gave her shoulder a light pinch. Then he wrapped his arm around her waist. "Obviously you need to learn a lot about baseball. I think we better have some private lessons later tonight. I'll teach you about rounding the bases." His hand slid low on her back and hooked onto her hip. Guess she'd better learn about grounding and getting people out before home plate, because already her defenses were cracking.

Of course, third base…

Heath nudged her toward the outfield. "Okay, go and stand next to Ollie." He explained where to place the mitt and demonstrated how to put their free hand on the top to keep the ball from coming up and popping them in the face.

There's a high chance of balls hitting me in the face? No wonder I always preferred sitting on the sidelines.

Heath tossed a baseball in the air and swung the bat. A metal clank sounded and the ball bounced across the infield, headed toward Oliver.

He stopped it as Heath had instructed and then threw the ball back to his brother, who caught it in his bare hand instead of bothering with a mitt. He tossed the ball in the air a couple of times and turned his attention to Quinn. "Ready?"

The fact that she managed to nod and was willing to even go through with this said just how much she'd do for a chance to spend more time with Heath, current foe status notwithstanding.

• • •

The breeze stirred Quinn's hair around her face. She quickly swept it back and tucked it behind her ears. Then she bent down low, the way he'd shown her and Ollie. He hadn't even tossed the ball yet and she kept flinching.

He hoped she didn't regret agreeing to come with him, because it was one of the coolest things a girl had ever done for him. He'd been putting off Ollie all week and feeling guilty about it. He'd also spent way too much time calculating the hours until he could see Quinn again. The fact that she'd volunteered to join instead of forcing him to choose had made him want to wrap his arms around her and kiss her like they hadn't been in the middle of a crowd of townspeople.

Of course that same crowd had turned the outing into a local debate, and despite his attempt to keep it away, bitterness had crept in more and more with every person who took Quinn's side. He could see her fighting it, too—her jaw tightened whenever anyone said the word "lodge."

By the time they'd made it to the parking lot, he wasn't sure getting into a small, enclosed space together was a good idea. But instead of snide comments or the cold shoulder, she'd made a joke to smooth over the friction. Yes, he definitely owed her, and after they dropped off Ollie, he planned on making it up to her in the most creative ways he could think of. And most of them involved his mouth.

"Just relax a little," he said, rolling the ball in his hand until his fingers found the seams. "I'll give you an easy one."

Instead of relaxing, she shot up. "Don't you dare go easy. I came to ground balls and I'm not going to half as—halfway do it."

He laughed over her slip of the tongue. "All right. You

asked for it."

She squinted one eye closed. Regardless of what she claimed, she wasn't ready for his full swing. He hit the ball toward her, nice and low. It rolled across the ground, hit a stray rock, and he held his breath, afraid it'd pop up and hit her and then he'd spend the night icing her mouth instead of kissing it.

The hand at the top of her mitt knocked the ball back down, though, and she scooped it up and stood. "Get him out before he reaches first, Oliver," she yelled, tossing the ball to him.

There'd been no running bases so far, but Heath dropped the bat and sprinted toward first. If he pushed too hard, he'd get there before his little brother, so he held back and then acted disappointed at getting tagged out. "Dang it, I should've slid!"

"Oliver would've still gotten you," Quinn said, and Ollie grinned. He held up his hand to give his brother a high five and then turned to Quinn to do the same.

Ollie seemed to go back and forth about whether he liked Quinn tagging along, but Heath could tell that he was leaning toward liking it again. Even though she was obviously a bit out of her element with Oliver, Heath loved that she tried. The kid definitely needed more positive role models in his life. He only hoped he didn't get too attached—of course, right now, he didn't see how anyone could spend time with Quinn without getting attached.

"So, ice cream at the Dairy Freeze?" Quinn asked. And just like that, she won them both over for good.

Chapter Twelve

After ice cream at the Dairy Freeze, Heath dropped Ollie off at his mom's place, making sure she was actually home before telling his little brother good-bye and hustling back to Quinn's car.

The instant the door closed behind him, he leaned over the console and planted a kiss on her lips, the contact a relief after hours of holding back. "I wanted to attack you the second you showed up tonight, but we were surrounded by parents and kids, and I knew it'd push the friends cover."

Quinn trailed her fingertips down the side of his face. "I thought you were worried about smearing your makeup. I hear guys turn into total divas after they've had their beards gelled."

His jaw dropped, and she erupted in giggles. "Little girl, I'm going to get you for that." He tugged her to him and rubbed his whiskers against her cheek. She squealed and made a halfhearted attempt to shove him away, but then he kissed her neck, and her squeal turned into a moan.

Desire flooded his senses. He undid her seat belt and pulled her onto his lap. Good thing these windows were tinted, although for what he had in mind, he needed more room to work with.

Her hair fell over them like a dark curtain as she sank onto him, the soft touch of her lips igniting every nerve ending in his body. His elbow banged the door as he wrapped his arms around her waist.

"I feel like I'm in high school again," she said before slipping her tongue in to meet his.

He ran his hands up her thighs, groaning when she rolled her hips. "Is there anyone at your place?"

She froze and then sat back. "My sister and her husband are staying there for another week."

"Damn. My dad will be awake, and he's been in a mood lately…" He was almost willing to risk it. But he couldn't stop thinking about the house she'd grown up in and her fancy car and how his current living situation looked even worse in comparison. He already felt like a loser living at home again. She was probably used to guys who owned fancy condos with lots of square footage and high-thread-count sheets and all the stuff he didn't have.

"We can watch a movie with my sister and her husband. It'll be fun."

Not compared to what I want to do.

She started back over the console, and he held her in place with his hands on her hips. "We can go to my house. Just…ignore whatever my dad says, and close your eyes till we get in my room. Maybe even after that, too. How do you feel about blindfolds?"

The fake smile came out.

"I was kidding," he said.

"You know what? I'm starving."

"After all that ice cream?"

She smacked his chest. "Hey, Jenny Craig. I skipped dinner, so now that I've had dessert, I need real food. Or more dessert. I'm not picky." She climbed back into the driver's seat, and his lap immediately felt empty.

"This is Hope Springs, remember? Everything's closed after nine."

"Well, I guess I'm going to break my rule and make you food, then." She ran her thumbnail along the steering wheel. "Unless you want me to drop you off?"

He wanted to go back to where she gave it to him straight, because there was something different going on now that he didn't quite understand. She sounded disappointed at even the idea of dropping him off, yet clearly he'd pushed too far.

He reached over and took her hand, lacing his fingers with hers. "You're in the driver's seat. For everything. Know what I mean?"

Some of the anxiety melted from her expression. "Okay. Then I choose food and a movie at my place."

"Then I'm along for the ride."

As soon as they got back to the giant house on the ritzy end of town, Quinn called out for her sister. When it was clear she wasn't home, a hint of nervousness crept back into her features.

Before he could ask what was up, she charged into the kitchen. The clang of pans and slam of cupboards being opened and closed filled the air. She frowned at what she found inside the pantry and then pulled out a bag of rice.

She peeked in the fridge and brought out a package of fish. "Here's hoping Maya loves me enough to not care if I use her groceries."

After getting a pot of water boiling, she poured soy sauce, sake, and grated ginger over the salmon and then placed it in a skillet. He'd eaten dinner, but the smell of the food made him hungry all over again.

Watching her move around was entertaining in and of itself. She'd crinkle her brow, tap her lip, and mumble to herself, and then dive back into the fridge or pantry for another ingredient. When she'd settled in front of the stove, he moved behind her, swept her hair to the side, and kissed the back of her neck.

Her tiny gasp made him smile against her skin and do it again. "Just so you know, I'm firmly against cooking for a guy so he thinks of me as domestic," she said.

"Well, don't I feel special? But don't worry, the last thing I'd call you is domestic."

"Yeah, much to my family's dismay. Maya's way better at it."

"So she doesn't have to work at the company with you?"

"She already had"—Quinn made air quotes—"discipline and direction in her life, whereas I apparently needed it. Sometimes it feels like my father thinks if he works me hard enough, I'll decide the life of a trophy wife would be easier." She grabbed a knife, sliced a lemon, and squeezed it over the fish. "Stir the rice, will you?"

Heath grabbed a spoon and stirred as instructed. "You've got the looks for the trophy wife, but I barely know you and I can tell you'd never be happy with that life. Maybe put on your fake happy front and pretend, but it wouldn't be the real kind of happy."

She stared at him, the surprise clear on her features. "How…"

"I pay attention." He gave the rice another stir, sending a few grains over the pan. They sizzled against the burner, the ends curling up and turning black. "So, we'll fry this up and make egg rolls, right?"

Her jaw ticked, although she tried to hide it.

The laugh he'd worked to hold back broke free. "That's for the diva comment earlier. I know egg rolls are Chinese, not Japanese. I actually read up on your culture online." The other night he'd gotten curious. He couldn't believe he'd done it, much less confessed to doing it.

Their gazes met and held. Then she leaned in and kissed his cheek. The simple gesture sent a surprising amount of warmth through him, a much deeper affection than lust that should scare him. Instead he wanted to wrap his arms around her and hold onto it as long as he could.

"So if you"—his tongue stumbled, like it didn't want to admit the possibility, but he forced the words out—"get the B and B, will you be doing the cooking?"

She reached over the stove and lowered the temperature on the burner. "To start with, anyway. I've got recipes set aside that I've perfected with a gourmet breakfast experience in mind, and I actually enjoy cooking once in a while, but it depends on how busy the place gets. As soon as I'm fully up and running—and with any luck, mostly booked—I'll be out delivering the food and talking to the people instead of being locked away in the kitchen, although I'll do that, too, if I have to."

He nodded, noting she already talked about it like it was

hers. He did the same thing. In fact, he'd emailed Cam today with information on tents, hunting packs, and snowmobiles he'd priced so they could figure out start-up costs. Dad had made a comment about both of his boys working at the shop soon, and when he explained they wouldn't be because they'd be running the hunting lodge, and Dad scoffed at their chances, it'd lit a fire under him to come up with an exit plan he could execute as soon as possible.

Conflicting emotions rose and got tangled up in his gut. He *needed* that property—large plots of land rarely went on the market around here, since families had owned most of it for generations and they liked to keep it that way—and it was the only place that backed up to the mountain range.

But he could tell how much working for her dad ate at Quinn. Just talking about it dimmed her usual spark of frantic energy. Discussing the B and B, on the other hand, had the opposite effect.

If she were simply a spoiled girl with no substance to her, it'd be easy to brush her off and think she had no chance. To dislike her for trying to take away his dream. But she was smart and funny and overloaded every one of his circuits with the lightest touch. He liked her—more than he should for someone he barely knew.

His thoughts turned to what would happen if Cam finally came home only to find nothing here for him, though. Most likely he'd reenlist and leave again. He'd been on several dangerous missions he wasn't at liberty to discuss, and Heath wanted to ensure his brother didn't have to keep putting himself in harm's way day after day anymore.

This deal's bigger than just me. While he'd feel horrible about Quinn not getting what she wanted, failure wasn't an option. *Sorry, Quinn*, he thought as she turned off the burner.

Once they'd piled the steaming food onto their plates, they moved to the couch. He expected her to put on a chick flick, so he was pleasantly surprised when instead he got the newest superhero movie.

After they'd finished eating, he wrapped an arm around her shoulder, drew her closer, and pressed a kiss to her forehead. "Thanks for dinner. For the record, I think it's cool that you care about your heritage, but yet you don't conform. Promise me that no matter what happens, you'll never lose that feisty, impulsive side of you."

"You're just saying that because that's the side of me that means I forget about our differences and kiss you."

He curled her tighter to him. "That might have something to do with it."

She smiled, and then he slanted his mouth over hers. He pushed a hand through her hair, and the kiss took on an urgent edge that fanned the need he'd felt earlier. He let her control the tempo, though, not wanting her to pull away like she'd done in the car.

A loud throat clearing interrupted the moment. Apparently Quinn's sister and her husband had come home at some point. Quinn made introductions and invited them to watch the rest of the movie with them. Her earlier comment about feeling like she was in high school again suddenly applied, because that was what the group date made him feel like. Only he'd never done the group dating or hanging out with a girlfriend's sibling thing, even in high school.

As soon as the movie was over, Steven said he was tired and going to bed. When he tried to pull Maya to her feet, she waved him off and told him she'd be up in a minute. She watched her husband go up the stairs and then turned to Heath, and he got the feeling he was about to be interrogated. "So, Heath, you're in Sadie's band, right? And then you work at Rod's Auto Repair?"

"For now." He glanced at Quinn, wondering if her sister knew about Mountain Ridge. She gave a slight shake of her head, apparently reading his mind. "I'm hoping to run my own business someday—technically, I already do. I build custom motorcycles, and once I have a larger garage, I'll be taking on more projects as time allows."

"What're your thoughts on steady, committed relationships?"

"Maya," Quinn said, glaring at her sister. "That's kind of a deep question for a simple movie night."

"I'm just asking. I want to get to know the guy my sister keeps coming back to Hope Springs for."

"That's not the only reason I'm in town," Quinn said. Then she rubbed a couple fingers across her forehead. "It's on my way to Salt Lake."

"Mmm-hmm." Maya turned to him. "You never answered the question."

Clearly she'd heard things about him, and between that and the way he looked, that was enough for her to judge him. He never bothered trying to convince people of who he was and wasn't, and he wasn't about to start now. Except he didn't want to leave things badly with Quinn. Despite the couple of bumps along the way, as well as the giant elephant in the room that always stood between them, they'd managed to have a great night. And it wasn't like he had anything to hide. "I'm sure they're great for some people. Honestly, I've seen and been in my fair share of bad ones, though, and I'm in no hurry to jump in. But that's nothing Quinn doesn't already know."

"Sometimes Quinn needs lots of reminders."

"Okay, that's enough talking about me like I'm not here. Heath has to be up early for work, so I'm going to tell him good-bye." Quinn stood and offered her hand. He took it and let her pull him up. "Sorry," she said once they reached the door. "She's a little overprotective, despite being the younger one. Must be that driven, disciplined thing I mentioned earlier."

"It's okay. I get it, I don't exactly scream boyfriend material."

"In my experience, boyfriend material is overrated. And I know we're keeping things light, even if she obviously didn't listen when I told her that's what you and I were doing."

That statement should be more comforting, since it was what he wanted. Great. Now he was the one wanting to hold on, and the fear was over her not feeling as much for him as he did for her. He'd never been on this side of things, and he didn't like it one bit.

"See you tomorrow at the shop?" Quinn asked, arching both of her eyebrows, and he nodded. She gave him a quick kiss and started to pull back, and then dawning crossed her features. "Oh, wait. I drove, and your motorcycle's still at the school. Let me grab my keys and take you."

Between the sudden neediness and the fact that he'd be tempted to go for round two of making out in the car, where he'd probably get caught up and push too far again, he decided he'd best cut and run before his head got even more messed up over this girl. Cool air and expending energy with a walk would do him some good. "It's not that far. I'll just hoof it."

"But it's late at night. I know it's a safe town, but still."

He laughed under his breath. "Don't worry, I'll be the scariest thing out there. Who'd mess with this?"

Quinn raised a finger as if to say she would, and his best intentions to pull away cracked—another point for getting out of here as quickly as possible.

"Till tomorrow," he said, reaching for the door handle.

"Okay. Text to let me know you got home safely."

He glanced over his shoulder at her. "Are you serious?"

"Yes. The future of my lips touching yours again depends on it, too. I won't be able to sleep knowing I let you walk alone late at night without me as a bodyguard."

No one had ever wanted him to check in. Not Dad, and not Mom before she'd left. None of the women he'd dated. Most of the time he liked not being accountable to anyone, but something about picturing Quinn pacing the halls, worried about him, hit him in the chest, an unfamiliar sensation tugging at his heart. "I'll text you."

An appeased smile lifted her lips, and he couldn't help turning around for another kiss. Who knew it'd feel so damn good to have someone look after him?

Immediately he quashed the yearning that rose up, whispering that he wanted this to be more. That was a dangerous road, especially with Quinn, and he'd learned a long time ago that it did no good to wish for things you could never have.

Chapter Thirteen

"Not cool, dude," Quinn said to Maya as she reentered the living room.

"Just trying to look out for you. You know that Chichi and Haha would flip if they knew you were dating him."

"As you pointed out, we're not in a serious, super-committed relationship anyway."

Maya shrugged, unapologetic.

This was why she hadn't told Maya about Mountain Ridge. Growing up, she'd talked about the B and B, but she doubted Maya had given it a second thought now that Quinn was working with Chichi. As much as she loved her sister, she'd never been good at keeping secrets. Even if she managed to not say anything to their parents, she'd tell Steven, and then Grayson and the rest of the Rutherfords would find out, and as Chichi had pointed out, their business connections were important.

It'd be a miracle if they didn't find out about Heath and

freak out about it, actually. From now on, she'd keep their dates in town to a minimum, the way she'd meant to back before she lost her mind over the guy. The rumor mill would still churn with speculation, but as long as it didn't get to be too newsworthy, maybe it'd stay in the confines of Hope Springs.

If only that didn't mean facing the other problem: whenever she was alone with him, they tiptoed closer and closer to the line she'd have to draw in the sand, and then she worried it'd be over, and she so wasn't ready to stop kissing Heath Brantley.

Maybe they weren't in a serious relationship, but no other guy had bothered to look into her culture. Her heart skipped a few beats just thinking about how sweet it was that he'd cared enough to do so.

"I thought you were over this stage," Maya said. "Don't you remember how awful it was in high school when you and the parents were constantly at war? Because I do. It made everything so tense, and I had to play peacemaker and deal with the fallout when it didn't work."

Maya had covered for her several times in the name of keeping the peace, and she'd ended up grounded along with Quinn more than once. *But Heath likes the impulsive side of me. I like that side of me.*

"I'm just not cut out for the trophy wife life, Maya."

Instead of Maya softening, offense pinched her features. "You think that's what I am? Because I'm *choosing* to support my husband and have different goals that don't revolve around a career?"

"No, that's not what I mean."

Maya stood. "You know what? Go ahead and chase

after the bad boy and then somehow be shocked when he's only interested in sex. But this time when you're crying and brokenhearted, it's going to be really hard to not tell you I told you so."

"Maya, wait."

Her sister didn't slow her stride or even glance back. She charged up the stairs, and if Steven was already asleep, he certainly wouldn't be anymore, thanks to the slamming door.

Quinn Sakata, putting her foot in her mouth since she could talk. Expressing her opinion often meant tension at home, between her and Maya or her and her parents. Sometimes she hit the trifecta and got all three. Then she'd hear the lecture about where rebellion led—ruined reputation, no trust, no husband, going nowhere fast, general ruining of everything.

She'd always hated that being herself was called rebellion. Why couldn't they just call it individual thinking? Several countries had gained freedom because of so-called rebellion. She thought about Sobo Machi, a twinge going through her at missing someone who got it. Someone who would be on her side and tell her to use her strong spirit to fight for what she wanted.

Once I get the B and B up and running, it'll be better. Little by little they'd see she was perfectly capable of making her own decisions. Or maybe they wouldn't, but she wouldn't be living so close to them, so it wouldn't matter.

Her phone chimed and she opened up the text message.

I'm home. About to crawl into my bed and think about what we didn't get a chance to finish.

Under other circumstances, it'd be sweet, but now she was thinking about Maya's accusation. Earlier Heath had said she was in the driver's seat, but how long would it be before he got sick of waiting and decided to take someone else for a ride?

Like with Adam "No Labels" Asshole, her non-relationship with Heath meant she didn't have claim on him, either, so he was free to do so, no need to even tell her about it. Toxic jealousy churned in her gut, the idea of him with another woman eating away at her.

Maybe I should just give up on this…whatever it is… now, like Maya clearly wants me to, and my parents no doubt would insist on.

Her phone chirped again.

There are some sketchy-looking dudes in my neighborhood. Want to come guard my body?

Quinn grinned, a flutter chasing away the icky sensation. Then she thumbed a reply.

Guard. Kiss. I could do a little of both.

Now you're talking my language.

Thanks for checking in. Sweet dreams and I'll see you tomorrow. xoxo

Dirty dreams & I can't wait.

Like the sap she was whenever Heath was involved, she pressed her phone over her heart, as if she could absorb the words and hold them forever that way. A tingle traveled from there all the way down to her toes.

So what if she got hurt in the end? She always did, so that was nothing new. Until then, she was going to enjoy this rush of flirting with a hot guy and anticipating the next time she got to press her lips to his.

Chapter Fourteen

Quinn pulled up to Rod's Auto Repair and got out of her car. The air held a touch of crisp coolness that would burn off in an hour or so, but meant that fall was creeping in. Another week or two and the leaves would change colors and the town would transform into an idyllic little slice of heaven, where everyone would be decked out in scarves and hats, the diner would have a new pie of the day, and the town would prepare for harvest time. Hopefully she'd be here for it, too.

Rubbing her arms and wishing for pants instead of the shorts she'd put on, she rushed across the parking lot and ducked into the repair shop.

A man she vaguely recognized sat behind the desk. He glanced up at her and for a moment she just stared, thinking about how his greenish-bluish-whatever-colorish eyes matched Heath's and Oliver's.

He didn't look quite old enough to be Heath's dad,

although she was relatively sure that's who he was. For a man on the older side, he had a rugged handsomeness that transcended age. At the same time, there was something about the way he eyed her that made her nerves stand on edge and had her wishing for pants again.

Suddenly, it hit her—where she'd seen him before. Back in high school she'd watched a fight break out at the Triple S and they'd dragged him out of the place as he'd spouted enough swearwords to make her look like an amateur. Back then stepping inside Seth's Steak and Saloon, even if only for the best steak in town, ran a very high risk of someone mentioning it to her parents, which usually resulted in a couple weeks' grounding.

The man in front of her had quite the rep for being the town drunkard, and for buying beer for underage teens if you gave him enough to cover a six-pack for himself as well.

"What can I do for you?" he asked, pulling her out of her mixed-feelings stroll down memory lane. "Or are you looking for the nail salon? Because it's a few shops down." He tilted his head as his gaze traveled down her. "You look like you'd belong there more than here."

She didn't know if he meant because she was Asian and should be doing the nail care or because she looked like a ditzy girl who only cared about mani-pedis. Either way, she decided to ignore the jab and go for one of her own. "Wow, the sign was so unclear about you being an auto shop. You should *totes* do something about that."

He huffed a laugh. "All right, darlin', fair point. What can I do for you?"

"Actually, I'm looking for—"

Heath burst in from the door leading to the garage.

"Hey." He turned to his dad. "I got it, Pop. Quinn's here for some bodywork."

His dad's eyes homed in on her bare legs again, and Heath cleared his throat as he stepped between him and her. She wasn't sure what passed between them, but he must've mouthed something. Then he said, "Quinn, this is my dad, Rod Brantley. Dad, Quinn. We're going to be in the garage."

Without leaving time for any further exchange, Heath took Quinn's hand and led her into the garage.

"Sorry about that," he said. "He has this thing for younger women and unfortunately enough of them have fallen for it that he decides to hit on every pretty girl who comes into the shop. It's embarrassing. If we weren't one of the few shops in town, it'd probably be bad for business, too."

While the exchange had been a bit odd, her main worry right now was the tense line of Heath's jaw. She tipped onto her toes and kissed it. "Was there someone else in there? Once you stepped in, all I saw was you."

He wrapped an arm around her and kissed her until her knees threatened to give way. When his appraising gaze ran down her body, heating every place it touched, she didn't mind in the least—funny how that worked. "Dang, you're always short, but when you don't have on the heels, you're almost pocket-size."

She scowled, and he pressed a kiss to the wrinkle between her brows. "No getting pissed off already. I like it—I'd gladly keep you in my pocket." He flashed her his cocky smile, grabbed her hand, and led her over to the far corner of the shop.

Heath shed his leather jacket, revealing a snug black T-shirt that showed off his colorful tattooed arms and the studded black cuff around his wrist, and then stepped into faded blue coveralls with a ROD'S AUTO REPAIR patch over the pocket. Shame covering up all that sexy ink, although the hot mechanic look totally worked for him as well.

He eyed her pale pink top, most likely thinking, like she was, that maybe it hadn't been the best choice for today. "I'd better get you a pair, too. Gotta teach you how to take care of dents, since I'm sure it's not the only one you'll get in your fancy car, especially if you're going to be taking on any more Hope Springs wildlife."

After a moment riffling through a cupboard, he brought out another pair of faded blue coveralls. Regardless of the fact that anyone could tell from a mile away that they were too big, he held them up to her.

"I'd look like a hobo in these," she said, kicking out at the spare fabric piled on the floor near her feet.

"A very cute hobo."

"So a very cute hobo snob? Seems like an impossible combination."

"Yet you manage to pull it off." Heath tossed aside the giant coveralls. "So, you just wanna watch, then?"

"Oh, I'll be watching, but I can help, too. I don't mind getting a little dirty."

His eyes sparked at that, a dozen ideas she assumed were dirty flickering through them. How did they manage to turn everything into an innuendo when they were together? And what would he do when he found out she couldn't follow through? Call her a tease? A prude? A bitch? She'd been called all three and every other variation in between.

Just focus on the here and now. "Do you want me to pull in the car?"

"I'll do it. We're full-service here."

She dropped the keys into his hand and then watched him get into her car. Within a few minutes he had it up on lifts, his tools out, and her car door open. "The paint's not scratched, which is good because we'd need to order it in," he said. "But I think we'll be able to just open up the door and pop it out."

"Yeah, that's totally what I was thinking. Guess we actually agree on something."

The smile he shot her ignited an intense spark of want that she'd never felt so strongly with any other guy. If she'd been sitting, she would've crossed her legs and gulped about a gallon of water, but all she could do in the garage was stand there and let it overwhelm her.

The temperature and staggering attraction only increased as he pulled out his tools and got to work on her car door, making it that much harder to pay attention as he explained every step. Disconnecting wires—like she'd ever try that herself. Then the screws and tabs—maybe she could do that step, but he seemed to magically know where everything was, and she hadn't even known her car door *had* screws or tabs until now. Her gaze drifted to his whiskered jaw, his perfect lips. To those hands and how good he was with them.

He set the inside of her car door aside and then only the metal shell remained. He picked up a mallet-like hammer. "See the dent? Now we're just going to work it out."

We. Right. He tapped it out and then studied the other side. She stepped around after him and ran her hand over the smooth surface. "Wow, like magic."

"That's me. A regular magician," he said. "By the way,

how long has it been since you had an oil change?"

She grimaced—she'd meant to take it in last month, but she'd been busy, and with all the miles she'd put on going to Casper and then here a few times...

"Guess we'll take care of that for you, too," he said, swiping his hand across the small of her back as he moved to return the tools to his kit.

A few minutes later, they were both under the car. "Okay, twist that off," Heath instructed.

As soon as she got the bolt loose, dirty oil ran down, coating her fingertips before running into the pan. She turned to him, holding her blackened fingers in front of his face.

"Hey, I told you that you should wear the coveralls."

"Well, you're wearing them. Let's see how much they help." She swiped the black across his cheek. He grabbed her wrist and twisted her hand toward her face. "Heath, no!"

With a quick push, her dirty fingers were against her cheek. He dragged them down her neck, her attempts to break free met with iron resistance. "What? You can dish it out, but you can't take it?"

She reached into the dirty pan with her free hand, getting more disgusting oil on her fingers, and then flung it at him. Playing with toxic materials was probably a don't, but she still laughed at his shocked expression. Then he grabbed her and rubbed his dirty face on hers, his whiskers tickling her neck and making her squeal.

She shoved his chest, leaving more smudges. In one lightning-quick movement, he clasped her hands, forced them behind her back, and encircled both of her wrists with one of his large hands.

He lowered his mouth to hers and kissed her, an intoxicating attack of lips and tongue that had her moving closer instead of attempting to break free. Her chest rose and fell against his, and she wasn't sure if it was just her heart beating that fast or if she was feeling his, too.

Then the door to the garage swung open, and his dad stepped inside. "If you're done farting around, two customers just came in and I could use some help."

"I'll wrap up this oil change and be right there," Heath said, without so much as glancing at his dad.

Rod shook his head and went back into the office.

"Sorry," Quinn whispered. "I'll pay for the oil change. I don't want you to get in trouble."

"Oh, I can get into trouble just fine by myself. Don't worry about it." He quickly finished up, still explaining the steps, although they were more hurried now. About ten minutes later, she knew how to change oil—in theory. Really, she knew more about how Heath stuck out his tongue and furrowed his brow when he concentrated and how he pushed back his sleeves when he worked, which was nice, because then she could watch the line of his forearms flex and twitch with his movements.

He was deliciously dirty, too, black smudged and sexy. She lifted her own blackened fingers, thinking she might have to hit that nail salon for a manicure when she got the chance. While Heath pulled her car out of the garage, she cleaned up in the bathroom and then headed outside to meet him.

"Thank you," she said as he handed over her keys. The car now looked as flawless as the day Chichi gave it to her. "I'll be working on the float for the rest of the day, so come by whenever. If you even can. I seriously don't mind taking care of it."

Heath glanced at the station. "I'll be there, but not until around two or three. My dad gets all testy when I don't put in full days, and I already missed a few for the photo shoot this week." He sighed. "I really can't wait until I'm done with it."

His eyebrows drew together, and then she realized what he meant, which brought the reality of their situation crashing into her again. She tried to mentally shake it off before it could fully catch hold, not letting herself analyze it too deeply. Luckily he leaned in for a good-bye kiss instead of using their unspoken conflict to walk away and leave her even more unsettled.

Lips moving against hers, he pulled her closer, his hands drifting down to her butt. He gave it a gentle squeeze, and then a giant grin stretched his lips. "I'll be there to help with the float as soon as I can."

She nodded and then reluctantly climbed into her car. Once she was behind the wheel, she realized she'd totally failed at keeping her and Heath's interactions discreet.

Not that many people are out right now anyway, and that kiss...well, who cares if people saw. A traitorous thread of apprehension rose up, and she hated that she couldn't truly not care if her parents heard about it.

With a sigh, she started her car and headed to the float garage. When she got there, she could hardly believe the change that'd happened over the last week. The rest of the floats were impressive and huge and complete, but her and Heath's float wasn't looking half bad. He'd added a few more skeleton butterflies that needed decorating, but she could take care of those while he was working, and then they should be done with the hardest part.

Quinn grabbed the box of decorations and got to work wrapping butterfly wings. Patsy Higgins came over and studied her, a deep crease forming between her eyebrows, and Quinn's pulse climbed into the danger zone. The woman held her future in her hands and she couldn't tell if she was happy or upset or…

"What?" she finally asked, the suspense killing her. "Is there something wrong with the butterflies? Am I doing it wrong?"

"I was more wondering about the two giant handprints on your backside."

Quinn spun, trying to look at her butt. After sticking it out and twisting until her back screamed at her, she finally caught sight of a giant black handprint. She turned the other way and, sure enough, there was a matching one on her other cheek. That explained the canary-eating grin as she'd told Heath good-bye—here she'd thought he was just that ecstatic to be kissing her.

Oh, I'm so going to get him back for this. Her mind spun for a good payback, and as if fate had decided to step in and help, an image popped into her head. "I'm going to go grab a coffee at the diner," she said to Patsy Higgins. "You want anything?"

"A coffee with cream and sugar would be divine right about now."

"Coming right up." Not bothering to try to hide her marked backside, Quinn marched into the diner and ordered two to-go coffees with cream and sugar. Then she walked over to the announcement wall. The flyer for the

Hope Springs Beard-Shaving Rendezvous sat between the hot rod show and the mud run sign-ups.

As usual, the event was Saturday after the parade, and it was a fund-raising event for Hope Springs search and rescue. Basically, people sponsored guys to shave their beards. The guy who earned the most money was going to win a coyote hat, too.

Well, she'd pay good money to watch Heath have to shave, and she'd bet a lot of women would, too. Other men had written down their names and phone numbers. Good thing she happened to have Heath's number.

She borrowed a pen from the cup by the cash register and wrote Heath's name and number, nice and large, then smiled to herself.

Ah, revenge. All the sweetness of an ice cream sundae with none of those pesky calories.

Chapter Fifteen

By the time Heath arrived at the garage to help Quinn, the float had completely transformed. It might not be the ugliest thing in the parade, after all. She'd wrapped the remaining butterflies in colorful paper and festoon and lined the sides with it as well—the fact he even knew the pink fluffy stuff was called festoon made him feel like he should turn in his man card.

When Quinn bent over to staple the metallic pink, purple, and yellow fringe to the bottom, he noticed his handiwork on her back pockets—he wondered if anyone had mentioned it. She straightened as he approached, her hands going to her hips, and that answered that. He grinned at her mock anger.

"You think you're pretty funny, don't you?" she asked.

Happiness swirled through his chest, and he nodded.

"Well, I'm not telling you how I got you back, but one day you'll see, and I'll be there to give you a smug grin like you're giving me now." The overtly innocent way she batted her eyes combined with the evil smile sent a ping of worry through him—but the mischievous glint in her eyes gave him other ideas that outshone it. Mostly ideas about putting his hands right on his handprints and picking up where they'd left off earlier that day.

"I figured you'd change if you knew," he said, leaning in for a quick hello kiss.

"Why bother? Everyone already saw them. So much for keeping things under the radar."

That stopped him cold. "Shit, I'm sorry. I didn't think about that."

She shook her head. "Honestly, how I ever thought we could hide it, I don't know. Nothing stays hidden here."

The disappointment in the way she said that hit him in the gut like a sucker punch. When had he ever cared if he was someone's dirty little secret? He started to pull away, and she wrapped her hands around his biceps and held him in place.

"It's just my family," she said. "You know how you didn't want me to meet your dad?"

He exhaled. "Yeah, and I'm sorry I didn't warn you—I had no idea he'd be up so early. Usually I'm the first one to the shop."

"No worries. But he probably doesn't care who you date, whereas my parents are control freaks about it."

Truthfully, Dad didn't care, although he had to make a snide comment about Heath "really stepping in it" when he put two and two together and realized exactly who Quinn was, and that she was the other bid for the property.

"But you know what? I'm over it," Quinn continued.

"Let them find out through the grapevine—I've been settling for boring for far too long." She leaned in and brushed her lips across his. "Oh, but remember this moment and how super cool I was when my revenge comes to light, 'kay?" She tapped him on the chest and then turned and resumed her work with the float.

Heath picked up a staple gun and started in on the glitter-coated letters that went along the side.

"You're putting those too far apart," Quinn said. "It looks like an acronym, not a word."

He stepped back. "Looks fine to me."

"The *E* and the *A* in 'spread' have uneven spaces, especially compared to the *S* and the *R*. You've got to measure them."

"We're back to this? I should've hurried up and done it all while you were gone."

"I would've just redone them when I got in."

He sighed. Then he got out a stupid ruler and measured, moving them closer together. A self-satisfied smile curved her lips before she went back to stapling the fringe, and he rolled his eyes. She drove him crazy in every possible way. How could they disagree on everything and still have so much chemistry?

Then again, there were things—like parent issues and always feeling like you constantly fell short, and pouring your heart and soul into achieving a dream—where she understood him better than anyone. Plus she made him laugh, he could talk to her about the things he usually kept to himself, and she made him text so she'd know he'd made it home safely. And while she was a perfectionist about the float, she was easygoing when it came to their hangouts, something he never would've guessed after their first town committee meeting.

"Oh, Heath, I'm so proud!" Patsy came over and patted him on the back, and every hair on his neck and arms pricked up. This much excitement was usually reserved for people who volunteered for something, and he hadn't volunteered for...

He glanced at Quinn, who gave him an exaggerated grin.

"Ye-ah," he said, "the butterflies turned out really well."

She swiped a hand through the air. "Not the butterflies. The beard-shaving rendezvous. I was hoping for an even ten, and I'm so glad you stepped up. I was surprised, but you've really dedicated yourself to this celebration, and I promise that it won't go unnoticed."

He automatically lifted a hand to the beard he trimmed now and then but hadn't been without since he was eighteen.

"I'm going to sponsor him," Quinn announced proudly. "I want to help him win that hat. Plus, anything for the town, you know."

When Patsy turned to her, he widened his eyes and dragged a finger across his neck. Quinn's grin only grew.

Patsy put one hand on each of their shoulders. "I'm so proud of both of you. I had a feeling you'd hit it off, too, and I was sure working on the float together would give you that push you both clearly needed. Although, young man"—she turned to Heath—"maybe we should keep our hands where they belong."

"Yes, ma'am," he spit out through his plastered-on smile.

After Patsy walked off, Quinn erupted into laughter. "Oh my gosh, your face was so priceless. I'm kicking myself for not getting a picture."

"Laugh it up, squirt. Because you basically declared war."

She leaned in so close he could feel the warmth coming off her. "Bring it on."

. . .

Heath had hoped they'd get a chance to be alone after hours of working on the float, but Quinn said that Royce and Sadie had invited them over for dinner, so they parted for showers and a quick change, and then he picked her up at her place.

When she got into the truck, the scent of her exotic perfume hit him, just as intoxicating as she was. Tonight she had on skintight jeans and a black top that slipped off one shoulder, displaying a red bra strap. Her spike heels matched, and he barely suppressed a groan. The woman was starting to give him one-track thoughts.

"What are you doing way over there?" he asked.

She scooted across the bench seat until she was right next to him—much better, although it didn't help the one-track thoughts. Later tonight, he was definitely going to have to drive her back to his place so they could be alone.

After reaching a steady enough speed that he didn't have to constantly shift gears, he wrapped his hand around her thigh. He wanted to mark it, too. Just put handprints all over her body so everyone knew she was with him.

As they drove past Mountain Ridge, she glanced out the window at the crumbling bed and breakfast. Only for a few seconds, but the longing in her eyes and the way she lifted her fingertips to the glass made a twinge go through his chest. During their flirty texts, riding his bike, playing baseball, working on the float—he always managed to forget the thing that constantly stood between them. Sure, it buzzed in the background now and then, but right now, with the actual land in view, the details of the mountain range he loved taking shape, it wasn't in the background anymore.

A ticking clock, a high-stakes, all-in poker game, it now took every inch of space.

If it weren't for the looming barrier, he probably would've hesitated to jump in as much as he had, because it already felt like a more serious relationship than he'd ever experienced. Like they'd been dating for months instead of only knowing each other for a couple weeks.

Their gazes met, and he could see as plain as day that she'd been thinking about the impossible situation they were in, too.

He wrapped his hand tighter around her thigh, trying to tell her it'd be okay, even though he knew that for one of them, it wouldn't. Which meant they wouldn't be okay, either.

When he pulled up to Royce's and turned off the engine, the silence between them stuck out even more. If he knew what words to say, he'd use them. Since he didn't, he simply got out and extended a hand to help her out of the truck.

As soon as they stepped inside the house, Sadie pulled Quinn into a hug. "I love that you're coming to Hope Springs so much lately. I think I'll tie you up like a calf, the way Royce taught me, and just keep you here."

"She'd kick out of your weak knots in a couple of seconds," Royce teased, and Sadie smacked his arm.

"I'm voting for not being tied up at all," Quinn said, stepping back to stand next to Heath.

He leaned in and whispered, "I don't know. I think it sounds like a good idea."

She turned to him, cheeks flushed and eyes wide. But then nervousness broke through, and she looked away, suddenly fascinated by the bracelet on her wrist. He'd thought a flirty line would ease the weirdness that'd crowded the space between them since passing Mountain Ridge, but it only seemed to make it worse.

"The burgers and hot dogs are already done," Sadie said. "It's such a nice night, we thought we'd eat out on the back deck."

The four of them headed outside and sat around the patio table. The mouthwatering scent of food made it hard for Heath not to devour his burger in two bites. The potato salad was the best he'd ever had, too—he even teased Sadie that she'd been hiding her culinary skills so he and Will didn't make them invest in one of those big tour buses with a kitchen.

"I keep meaning to tell you that I got a couple of new mares at the sale last week," Royce said, glancing at Heath. "They should be good packhorses for the hunting tours."

Quinn dropped her fork, and it clattered against her plate. "You make it sound like the lodge is a done deal. If I'm not mistaken, *I'm* still in the running. Or do you know something I don't?"

Royce opened his mouth and closed it. Then he looked to Sadie.

"Oh, no," she said. "I already told Quinn that I'm Switzerland about this. Although you'll recall I did say something about it at the sale."

Heath had been around Royce and Sadie enough to

know there was some tension between them over his and Quinn's dispute as well. Great. This situation was tearing up everyone. Like he needed to feel worse about it.

"I just don't see how the town committee could possibly think that a"—Quinn's lip curled—"*hunting lodge* could bring in more business than a cute, cozy place where families will come for an extended stay. A place that facilitates visits to town to spend money in local shops, at that."

Irritation rose up, leaving a stinging trail through every internal organ it passed. "That's because you've always been in your nice big house, not paying attention, or perhaps just sitting back and judging the people who come from all over during hunting season. The sporting goods store would benefit from the lodge, people could experience more of the beautiful mountain range with our tours, and there are already two nice hotels for families to stay in if they want to visit Hope Springs."

"The Mountain Ridge Bed and Breakfast is not a hotel, though! It's a family vacation experience that'll give people happy memories for *years*."

"So will bringing home a prize buck," Heath said.

Sadie reached over and slid both of their knives and forks away. "I'm thinking a subject change is in order."

Quinn continued to glare at him, the muscles in her jaw twitching.

"How's the float coming?" Sadie asked, her voice crammed full of over-the-top cheer.

Heath almost said that Quinn was as close minded there as about Mountain Ridge, but that wouldn't help turn the conversation around, and as crazy as she made him, he hated the valley that'd opened between them. He forced himself to look at Sadie and put on an air of affability. "It's coming along nicely. This afternoon Quinn turned my metal monstrosities into butterflies."

The hard lines of her features softened. She ran a hand through her hair and blinked, her glistening eyes opening a hollow hole in the center of his chest. "I'm sorry, guys. I'm so stressed out trying to balance everything and…" She swallowed and her hand fisted on her thigh.

And she wanted Mountain Ridge more than she'd ever wanted anything. He knew. Man, how he knew.

Cautiously he reached under the table, covered her fist, and slowly worked it free so that he could turn her hand palm up and slide his fingers between hers.

When she lifted her thumb and stroked it over the top of his hand, he knew they'd be okay. For tonight, at least.

"Can I have my utensils back?" she asked, turning her attention to Sadie. "I'm over feeling stabby, I swear."

Sadie pushed them back toward her and then did the same with Heath's. A slightly awkward tension remained in the air, but Sadie steered the conversation toward music and the next batch of kids coming to Second Chance Ranch, and before long, things were easy again.

But the ghost of the argument remained, promising to haunt them for as long as they continued trying to make whatever this was work.

Chapter Sixteen

"What are you doing?" Sadie asked when she and Quinn were alone in the kitchen.

"Getting the corkscrew," she replied, earning her a raised eyebrow. She sighed. "I don't know. I thought we could pretend we weren't opponents and just enjoy our sorta relationship while it lasts, you know? But I'm trying to balance work and building the float, and suddenly on top of everything else, I'm worrying what will happen to Heath and me after the festival's over—or if we'll even make it that far—which is only making my stress and mood swings that much bigger."

Sadie came over and squeezed her shoulder. "You must really like him."

"I do. Only you saw how it is between us. Earlier today we were in the garage and he was showing me how to fix cars and everything was so perfect. But then we drove past Mountain Ridge, and it stirred up all these emotions.

I started thinking what if I don't get it? What if I can never leave my job? Then Royce is so clearly on his side, and that means you—"

"I'm on your side, Quinn. I'm *always* on your side. It's hard because it'd be good for the ranch to work with Heath, and being in Dixie Rush with him is the most fun I've ever had with my music. I know better than anyone how hard it is to hold onto band members, so I need him to be happy and stay in Hope Springs, but you're my best friend, and I want you happy, too."

Stupid tears sprang to her eyes, and Quinn hugged Sadie—she'd needed to hear that someone was on her side, because she knew her family wouldn't be.

"I know your relationship with your dad is complicated," Sadie said, "and I know how much you want *that* B and B. But if it doesn't work out, we'll brainstorm and find something that does. Even if it takes us a while." She pulled back and looked her in the eye. "Okay?"

Quinn nodded. "Okay. And thank you." She leaned back enough to sneak a peek through the archway, catching a glimpse of Heath and Royce on the couch. She and Sadie had always dreamed of being with guys who were friends so they could hang out all the time and do fun group couple things. They'd even lamented the fact that she and Cory didn't have any romantic chemistry.

"I like him more than I should," Quinn said, and her heart tugged to drive the point home. Sadie came to stand next to her and watched the guys for a moment, smiling when they did. "Maya so nicely reminded me that I fall fast and always end up hurt, but I think I outdid myself this time. I can't even let myself be alone with him for too long for fear the make-out sessions will get out of control. Maybe I should hold on to the frustration from our earlier argument, so he won't be surprised that all he gets when he drops me off is a brief kiss good-bye."

Sadie draped her arm over Quinn's shoulders. "Babe, you need to stop being such a wimp and just tell him about your stance on sex."

"But then it'll be over, and I'm not ready. It's like a roller coaster—there's ups and downs, but I'm experiencing the biggest thrill of my life, and I know it's going to end eventually, but while I'm on it, I just wanna hold on tight and enjoy the ride. Even if there will be no riding." With panic digging sharp claws into her chest, the joke didn't quite land the way she wanted it to. Probably because she knew she'd want to stand in line to experience it all again, only that wouldn't be an option after the point of no return.

"If he's dumb enough to end it over that, I'll be, like, triple on your side. But pushing him away while trying to keep him close isn't going to work, either."

Her shoulders slumped, and her head fell back against Sadie's arm. "Why do you have to know me so well? It makes it impossible to deny everything you say."

"Hey, you were there pushing me when I wanted Royce back. I'm just returning the favor."

Quinn took the bottle of wine from Sadie and plunged the corkscrew into the top. "Then I'm warning you right now to keep your cell phone on tonight, because if telling him goes badly, you're going to need to come and pick up the pieces."

• • •

As soon as he and Quinn were in the truck again, quiet descended. Quinn had never been quiet before, and he wasn't sure how to take it, but he knew it couldn't be good. He wondered what she and Sadie had talked about—he knew his bandmate liked him, but he also had no doubt she'd choose Quinn over him if it came down to it.

Judging by the silence, it was a choice she'd have to make soon.

"Still mad?" he asked.

"I was never mad."

He shot her a look.

"Frustrated, yes. Mad at the situation, even. But not mad at you," Quinn said. "I overreacted when Royce mentioned the horses because my dream bubble was popping before my eyes and I totally panicked. I'm sorry that it turned into a big fight. I never meant for that to happen."

"I'm sorry, too." He let out a long exhale, trying to dispel the frustration he'd also felt. "I suppose it was only a matter of time before we couldn't hold it in anymore. Most of the time I manage to forget that you're my competition." He took her hand and lifted it to his lips. "You make me forget."

"Right back at you. I tried to pretend it didn't matter that much, but I suppose that's ridiculously hopeful."

"Maybe. It's been a long time since I wanted to be hopeful, though."

She glanced at him, a hint of sorrow in her eyes, and the smile she gave him was the one she worked to put on. A stab of despair lodged in his chest. Hope was foolish—how many times had he learned that?

Still, as he made the last turn to her house, he wanted to hold on to it. Which was why the second he threw the truck in park, he gathered her to him and captured her lips with his. She looped her arms behind his neck, kissing him back like she thought it might be their last. Apparently they were thinking the same thing. So he took his time running his tongue over hers, memorizing the taste, the feel, the way she sighed and sank deeper into his embrace.

The windows fogged around them, providing another layer to cut them off from the outside world and the reality it held, and then Quinn broke the kiss. "Heath…" The fortifying breath she took made an icy lump form in his gut. She was about to tell him she couldn't do this anymore. He didn't want to examine too closely the urge to beg her not to do it. "I'd like to run into my house and have that kiss be the last thing between us this weekend, so I can pretend that everything's all good, but I'm afraid that'd only set us up for a worse crash in the end."

She swallowed. "I've had so much fun with you, and we still need to work together, so I'm hoping that this won't screw everything up too badly."

His nerves stretched thin, ready to snap.

"Sadie told me I should stop being such a wimp and just talk to you before it got out of control. Which I knew she was going to do, which was why I asked her to let us come over. I didn't expect the fight over Mountain Ridge, but that's neither here nor there, so…"

Heath gripped the back of the bench seat, digging his fingers into the fabric. "Quinn, are you trying to drive me crazy? Just spit it out."

She glanced down, her dark hair falling and obscuring half her face. "Do you remember the night at the reception? The fight I had with my ex?"

His teeth ground at the mention of the guy. Maybe she was going back to him. Convincing himself he didn't care would've been easier if the pit in his gut hadn't opened up. "I remember."

"The reason he dumped me was because after six months, I still hadn't had sex with him. The truth is…" She finally looked up and swiped her hair behind her ear with a shaky hand. "I'm not planning on having sex until I'm married." It burst out of her the way one would admit to being a murderer. "I'm sure you were thinking light and fun meant lots of no-strings-attached sex, but all I can offer is hanging out and kissing and that's it."

He blinked, unsure how to take that. Waiting. No sex. Yes, it changed his plans some—he'd be lying if he said he hadn't thought about sex with Quinn.

"So there you have it. When I said I wasn't having sex with you, I meant long-term. I usually wait until I'm in a more committed relationship with a guy to tell him, but so far that hasn't gone so great, and I figured I might as well be up front instead of being terrified of being alone with you."

"Terrified?" He tried not to be offended at that.

"Not like scared of you. But I sometimes jump right in without thinking things through, and with you…well, it's easy to get caught up in kissing, and…" Her gaze moved to his lips, and she released a shallow breath. The temperature in the truck climbed, and now all he could think of was getting caught up in kissing. "Some guys get crazy angry when I tell them to stop. I like you, so instead of springing it on you mid-make-out session, when we're both struggling to maintain control, I decided it was better to tell you now. Hopefully that way there won't be angry words exchanged that'll make it impossible to work together. And this way you can tell me it's over, kick me out of your truck, and then make your escape if you want."

Escape? She actually thought he'd bolt?

Then again, was he truly up for this? Another complication?

"I'll leave you to let that sink in, and then you can call me this week and let me know if you still want to keep dating or whatever, or if you think we should try to just be friends. Because I'm sure that's totally possible after kissing. People do it, right?" She slid across the seat and pulled on the door handle. He lunged over her and held the door in place.

She slowly turned her head toward him, vulnerability filling every inch of her face. Such a contrast to her usual feisty, carefree nature.

"I'll admit I don't have much experience with waiting in that area," he said. "But I'm willing to try. For you."

"You are?" she asked, and her voice cracked.

He placed a hand on the side of her face and brushed his thumb across her cheekbone, his affection for her firing through every cell in his body. "I've never met anyone quite like you, Quinn. Honestly, I completely lose my mind around you—which is probably dangerous, but I'm not sure our relationship is something I can walk away from, even with as much as we have stacked against us."

"Right? I keep thinking, why'd it have to be you bidding against me, but then we probably wouldn't have gotten to know each other this well, and that thought makes me sad." She fisted her hands in his shirt, one on either side of his waist. "You're really willing to try a relationship that doesn't involve sex? Even after I signed you up for a beard-shaving contest?"

"Most likely *because* you signed me up, which means I've got serious mental problems."

She laughed and then smashed her lips to his. Then she climbed onto his lap and deepened the kiss. This whole thing was so impossible, yet the thought of giving it up made it hard to breathe. How'd he let her in so quickly when his first instinct was to keep people out?

And how was he going to not explode from sexual frustration when the woman could do such wicked things with her tongue?

Chapter Seventeen

Quinn frowned at the run-down building. It needed more repairs than Mountain Ridge B and B, which was saying something. The last owners of the commercial two-story structure in front of her had completely let the offices inside go.

"It's in worse shape than you led me to believe," Quinn said, and the real estate agent showing it gulped—rookie mistake. It shouldn't make her proud to unnerve the guy, but it did, and *that* was something she wasn't proud of. Although it did make it easier to bargain, and a good price led to praise from Chichi, which didn't come easily.

"The inspection passed," the agent said as he led her inside.

"That doesn't mean people are going to rent spaces. It just means the homeless have a less scary place to squat right now." Quinn ran her fingers over a dusty surface and frowned at the exposed wiring hanging from the warped ceiling panels—another tactic to show she wasn't messing around.

"They might be willing to take a little off for remodeling."

"Try *a lot*. In fact, I'm going to give you a figure, and if the owners are smart, they're going to dive on it, because they won't get more, and I can only imagine what they're sinking into the place every month between taxes and the mortgage."

Already Quinn was calculating how little she could persuade their regular contractor to do the job for, and how long it'd take until the offices would be in nice enough shape to lease. At the end of the tour, she made an offer that gave her plenty of wiggle room for the back-and-forth negotiations that'd inevitably take place.

By the next afternoon, though, the owners had agreed to sell it to Sakata Real Estate for a lowball price she could hardly believe, and her contractor was already scheduling the renovations.

A deal like that used to give her a rush, but now all she could think about was how much more satisfying it'd be when she could fix up her own property, and how it'd be homey instead of cold convenience. Of course that led to thinking about Heath, as most things did these days. She could still hardly believe he was willing to try a relationship without sex.

Her heart skipped a couple beats when she remembered his words. *I'm not sure it's something I can walk away from, even with as much as we have stacked against us.*

While she wanted to believe they'd figure everything out, plenty of guys claimed they could wait, only to change their minds a few months in. Anyone even willing to try was hard to find, though, and Heath had surprised her at every turn. She couldn't help hoping that maybe that meant this time it would actually be different.

Her phone chimed—Heath's ears must've been burning.

I get to see you tonight, right?

Giddiness bounced through her as she read the message again. She typed that she'd be there as soon as possible and then got into her car. She called the office to update them as she maneuvered onto I-80, wishing she could fast-forward to the moment she pulled up to Heath's house.

• • •

The worry over having Quinn at Dad's place was still there, but Heath's need to see her overshadowed it. He let her in and stepped aside so she could take in the tiny, messy living room, where Dad sat in his usual spot drinking a beer.

"Hello, Mr. Brantley," Quinn said, shooting him a smile.

"Why if it isn't the feisty girl who flung oil all over my shop. You want a beer, sweetheart?"

"Sure. Unless you've got moonshine in the tub," she said, winking at Heath. He gave her hand a quick squeeze before letting it go.

"I'll grab one for you." Heath hesitated at the edge of the room—he'd be back in all of thirty seconds. How much could Dad say in that amount of time?

Probably too much. Keeping his ears perked up, he grabbed two beers, took care of the lids, and then strode back into the living room. Quinn was on the couch, and Dad had a hunting magazine open and in front of her as he told her she'd never felt power until she'd shot a rifle. Then he added that he'd take her shooting one day so she could experience it for herself.

Over my dead body.

Quinn simply smiled. "I think I'm going to have to give Heath that privilege. But we'd be happy to have you tag along when we go." She looked up at him. "Right, babe?"

He loved how easily she handled Dad. Even more that it meant her adding a "babe" on the end of that question. "If that's what you want, darlin'."

Dad tilted the neck of his beer bottle toward her. "She's a real spitfire — better hold on tight."

"I plan to," Heath said, handing her one of the beers. Then he gestured for her to follow him. She told Dad that she'd see him later and then followed Heath back to his room. With every step, he worried this was yet another bad idea, but she'd said her sister was still staying at her place, and he didn't want to deal with other people. If Mountain Ridge fell through, he was going to buy himself a house as soon as possible.

It really can't fall through, though. Cam needs it. The last email made it clear how excited he was to not have to deal with such a structured life anymore. The multiple tours overseas had burned him out, especially with the close calls he and his guys had had over the past few years. He'd said he couldn't wait for the day orders weren't barked at him — which definitely wouldn't be an option if he had to work at Dad's shop. They'd always clashed, and Heath was actually scared what would happen if they tried to work in the same place now. It'd be an explosive fight waiting to happen.

Cam had also written that it'd be the first time he'd be completely in charge of his own life, and that'd hit Heath hard. While he had often felt unsettled over the years, he'd always chosen where to go next and what to focus on. He wanted his brother to have that—if anyone deserved it, it was Cam.

Heath glanced at Quinn, wishing for the hundredth time that getting the lodge didn't mean she wouldn't get her B and B.

Not wanting to have a repeat performance of the night with Royce and Sadie, he shoved away thoughts of their rivalry so he could focus on the here and now.

Right as he was about to ease the door to his room closed, Trigger came scampering down the hall. He knew he'd be a bouncy yippy ball of energy, but he didn't have the heart to slam the door in his face.

Quinn bent down and picked up the fur ball, making an *aww* noise as she straightened. "You're seriously the cutest little thing ever." Trigger licked her face and she laughed.

"Oh, sure, you give him the first kiss." Heath wrapped an arm around Quinn's waist, careful not to smash Trigger between them, and pressed his lips to hers. For the first time since she'd left a couple of days ago, his frayed nerves calmed. "I missed you," he said, then mentally smacked his forehead. He really needed to stop saying crap like that.

"I missed you, too," she said, making it all okay.

"Sorry about my dad. Again."

"He's not so bad. In fact, I think he's the first parent of a boyfriend who's ever liked me, so there's that." Her eyes widened with a hint of panic. "Not that you and I are…you know what I mean."

"I do. And we are—I thought that was pretty clear after our last discussion. I'm not dating anyone else, and I sure as hell don't want you to."

Trigger wiggled, and Quinn set him down on the bed, where he bounced up to the top and bit at the edge of the pillowcase, attacking it like it was going to be his next meal. Heath knew the little bugger would be a distraction.

Quinn watched him for a couple seconds and then returned her gaze to him. "Good. I'm glad that's settled, then." She sat on the foot of the bed, and he dropped next to her. She rolled the bottleneck between her fingers. "Tell me more about your family. Now that I've met your dad, I can jump to a few conclusions, but I'd rather you tell me."

He sighed. "The only steady thing in my life was that it's never been steady. Even when my dad and mom were married, one of them was always storming out. They got married young—because she'd gotten pregnant with Cam, and then they had me about a year and a half after he was born, because apparently they didn't learn from the first accident."

Quinn flinched, probably because he'd referred to himself as an accident. He'd been reminded about it a lot every time he did something wrong, but he was over it.

He took her hand. "It's okay. I got a thick skin a long time ago. But there were good times when Mom would come home and make cake for dinner. When Dad took us fishing and hunting. But then he got hurt, started drinking to deal, he and my mom fought even more, and then she left."

"That sucks. My parents sometimes smother me, but I never really thought about what I'd do if they hadn't been there."

"Again, it was a long time ago."

"You don't have to play Mr. Tough Guy."

"Who's playing?" he said with a grin.

She leaned in and kissed his cheek. "Okay, so your home life sucked a bit and you left as soon as you could—makes sense. Where'd you go?"

Rehashing the many bumps along the way to find a different life didn't appeal to him, but he supposed he might as well get it out of the way. "Everywhere. Tried college, but it wasn't for me. After that I moved from job to job as the mood struck me. Mechanic work, construction. Whatever I could find. Then I'd start to feel tied down, so I'd move again."

He reached over and tugged Trigger away from his pillow so it wouldn't end up in shreds. "Actually, I was worried about committing to Dixie Rush at first. Even this little guy seemed like a big commitment." He patted Trigger's head. "But I've found when I find something that truly fits—like the custom bikes and the band—it doesn't feel so claustrophobic. The lodge would be the same way, especially since I'd get to run it with Cam. He's the closest thing to a constant I have. He made sure I ate and went to school, and he keeps in touch through emails and the occasional call. I'd do anything for him."

Quinn nodded, and he wanted to peer inside her brain and see what she was thinking. "Including living with your dad to save money so that you could get the Mountain Ridge property for you and your brother—brothers, really, because I know you also worry about Ollie."

Now it was Heath's turn to nod. "He needs me here to do what Cam always did for me. I want my dad to step up, but it's unlikely, so I don't mind taking some time to help with baseball and make sure he gets enough food and attention—I enjoy looking after him more than I expected, actually."

Quinn's phone chimed, and she glanced at it. Then she swore.

"Everything okay?"

She flopped back on his bed with a groan. "I have this stupid work party on Friday night and my father's trying to make it so that I have to go with Grayson, even though I told him we broke up."

Heath's jaw clenched at the mention of her ex. "Why would he want that?"

"Because our families work together, which is why I haven't told him the reason we broke up. And for reasons I can't even begin to understand, my father thinks it's improper for me to show up to a work function without a date. Like being single means I'm irresponsible, when really it means that I control my own life."

Heath tried to keep his voice even. "So are you going to take a date?" He thought they'd just agreed they *weren't* dating other people.

"I could use someone in my corner," she said.

He cautiously nodded. The thought of that jerk being even a fake date made him want to rip off the guy's arms—he certainly didn't deserve to touch her. And the thought of another guy that might not be a jerk sent the same throbbing heat through his gut.

Quinn pushed onto her palms, and her brown eyes bored into him. "Would you come with me? I know you've got a Dixie Rush show on Saturday, but you can come up Friday, stay the night at my place in Cheyenne—in my guest room, of course—and then we'll drive down and do one last decorating sprint of madness before the concert so that we'll be ready for the following weekend."

The hope shining in her features sent a sharp twinge through his chest. "I thought you wanted to keep us a secret from your family. Pretty sure that'd blow our cover."

"So? Let's blow it. I'm done with having to constantly hide who I am from them. I'm a grown woman, and I can decide who I date. And I want to date you."

"While I'm happy about that fact and all, I'm not so sure springing our relationship on your dad at a company party is the way to go. He made it pretty clear when he came into the station that he thinks I'm a worthless grease monkey. I'd be totally out of my league at a fancy party—I'd probably just make it worse." He had no doubt it'd be a fancy party, too.

Quinn's brow crinkled, and he could practically see the wheels in her head turning, running through the most likely disastrous scenarios. Then she covered his hand with hers. "But you'd make it better for me. I've got to make small stands so that no matter what happens with Mountain Ridge, I'm in control of my life—it's time for me to prove that. And dealing with Grayson would be much easier with you by my side. My father can't constantly try to get us together if I show up with my own date, and that way I don't have to fake amicability with a guy who not only dumped me because I wouldn't have sex with him, but told me I wasn't worth the wait."

She bit her lip. "I want you there. I *need* you there. So… what do you say?"

He knew what he should say. That's why he was surprised by the words that came out of his mouth. "If you need me, I'll be there."

Chapter Eighteen

Forrest Scott lifted each of the parts Heath had asked for, turning over the boxes several times to inspect them before eventually scanning them and pressing a couple of buttons on the plastic-coated keyboard on the counter in front of him. The guy seemed to know whenever Heath was in a hurry and go twice as slow, but since it was the only parts store in town, finding a faster place wasn't an option.

The antsy feeling he'd been struggling with all week only intensified his absolute lack of patience. Usually it preceded a change of address or new job or both. Between the motorcycle job he was in the middle of, Dixie Rush, the Mountain Ridge decision still up in the air, and Cam's return creeping closer—not to mention sticking around for Ollie's sake—leaving wasn't an option, though, so the restless sensation needed to go away.

It'll be better once I've got the lodge and don't have to live with Dad anymore while trying to focus on so many jobs at once. I'm sure that's why I'm feeling so on edge. It didn't help that this morning Dad had told him he'd overheard several people in town talking about Mountain Ridge, and that he'd put his money on Quinn getting her B and B. He claimed the town was biased against them as it was, and they'd go for money, well-educated, and highly reputable over handing the place to a guitar-playing mechanic who'd dropped out of college. Then he'd added that Heath might as well start thinking about eventually taking over the auto shop—that it was a more realistic goal.

Finally Forrest gave him the grand total. "I hear you're dating Quinn Sakata," he said as he swiped Heath's debit card.

Heath gave a noncommittal head wobble, his defenses kicking up. In order to be on time for her party all the way in Cheyenne, he needed to get these parts installed in the old Toyota he was working on and hit the road. Well, before he did that, he'd also need to shower and put on a *suit.* He hadn't worn a suit since his grandma's funeral, and even then it'd been a too-big jacket and one of Dad's ties.

The looming party where he'd be completely out of his element wasn't helping with the itch to flee, to say the least.

"That girl is *wild,*" Forrest said. "Used to be with a different guy every week back in high school."

The spot between Heath's shoulder blades tightened. He wanted to tell him to stop talking about her like that, but curiosity crept in, too. Just how wild? Not that he cared—while he didn't want to think about her with different guys, her past was the past, and his was far from unblemished. He understood if she'd settled down and wanted to go slower now, because he'd been choosier about whom he'd slept with over the years, too. But she'd said she was waiting until marriage and made it sound like she'd never had sex. Or had he just assumed?

Maybe she used to have sex in high school, but had a change of heart somewhere along the way and decided to wait until she was married to sleep with anyone else.

Or maybe he was being played. When it came down to it, how well did he know Quinn? He'd seen the way she could throw up a mask. What if this was part of her master plan? Trick him into falling for her so he'd pull his bid on Mountain Ridge and she could have her bed and breakfast.

Even as he thought it, his brain screamed no. That he could tell the difference between her mask and when she was genuine. That he knew her better than that.

But the doubt in the back of his mind blazed a path for every doubt he'd ever had, about her and about himself, and now Dad's words about Quinn being the sure bet pushed forward. After all he'd done to try to show the town he'd changed—after jumping through every single hoop—he couldn't help but feel bitter.

"Yeah, have some fun with that one," Forrest said with a stupid grin on his face as he extended the plastic bag with the auto parts.

Heath snatched it from his hand and pushed out of the parts store, his mind spinning. Was playing the damsel in distress another way to sink her hooks into him?

Maybe he should just fail to show up to her party and piss her off enough to end things before even more of his heart was on the line. After all, why wear a suit and face down a room of people who'd hate him on sight for a girl when the relationship was going to end in a week or two anyway?

· · ·

Quinn paced the lobby of the building where the company party was being held. She'd told Chichi she had a date, but she hadn't bothered telling him who. In fact, she'd avoided talking about anything but the Utah property all week, claiming to be buried in paperwork.

Which was at least true.

As she made another pass, her five-inch stilettos echoing against the marbled tile floor, she wondered if Heath had changed his mind. The hour-long silence after she'd texted to tell him that he'd have to wear a suit and tie seemed like a bad omen.

Looks like I might have to go in there and face the music by myself. The Rutherfords were already here—she'd seen them entering the building as she'd pulled into the parking lot. Grayson had texted a few hours earlier, saying he hoped to see her and that he'd like to apologize in person.

Fat chance. Of course, it'd be much easier to hear his weak apology with Heath by her side to help run interference.

She glanced at the time. Much longer and her father would hunt her down. She considered calling Heath, but she figured he'd get there when he'd get there, so she should just bite the bullet and force herself to go mingle until then. Putting on her fake, I'm-so-happy-to-be-here front, she took two long strides toward the large room where the party was being held.

The unmistakable growl of an engine filtered through the glass doors, and she stopped in her tracks. Not many people invited to this shindig drove vehicles that made that kind of noise.

Sure enough, Heath's truck came into view, and the fake smile she'd had to work to hold up turned genuine and effortless. Suddenly standing in the lobby waiting for him felt too needy, though. Then again, she didn't want him to have to wander into the room alone—she could only imagine how unfriendly everyone would be.

How unfriendly Chichi would be.

Oh, hell, this is the worst idea I've ever had. She'd wanted to feel stronger—independent—but now she felt like the impulsive teenager she'd been in high school, constantly disappointing her parents and forever on the verge of trouble.

But then Heath stepped into the foyer and her breath left her in a rush. The suit and tie covered his tattoos, but his piercings and scruff were still in place, and the enticing combination sent desire tumbling through her.

"Sorry I'm late," he said. "I got caught up at work and—"

She threw her arms around him and crashed her lips over his. His large hands encircled her waist and then drifted down as he deepened the kiss. "If you just marked my butt again," she mumbled against his lips, giving her head a tiny shake. "You know what? I don't even care."

The grin he gave her made her stomach take a trip to her throat. "That dress is...*damn*."

She smoothed a hand down the purple fabric, making sure everything was still in place. It was on the snug side, but she loved the way it accentuated what little curves she had instead of overwhelming them like most dresses she tried on tended to do. "Thanks," she said, then reached up and grabbed Heath's black tie. She tugged him down to lip level so she could kiss that addictive sexy mouth again. "You look pretty *damn* yourself."

Before she got carried away and dragged him into the nearest office so they could make up for all the kisses they'd missed in the days they'd been apart, she forced herself to step out of his embrace. She took his hand and let out a long exhale. "Sorry in advance for what I'm about to drag you into, but I'm so glad you came."

"No matter what happens, I got you," he said, tightening his grip on her hand. His strength transferred to her, calming her nerves and giving her the feeling she'd wanted when she'd originally come up with this idea.

The buzz of conversations and the faint classical music playing in the background increased as they approached the large room filled with people she worked with in varying capacities. She took a deep breath and stepped inside.

They kept to the outskirts, managing to avoid Chichi and Grayson. She introduced Heath to a few of her clients, and he easily charmed them. When she introduced him to Mr. Churchill, who leased half of their ritziest building for his company, they started talking motorcycles. Apparently he owned several, and when he heard Heath built them, his entire face lit up. Pretty soon, he'd pulled several of his colleagues into the conversation.

Quinn was laughing at one of his cross-country motorcycle trip stories when she caught sight of Chichi, his disapproving glare in full force. He nodded at Mr. Churchill as he broke into the circle, then put his hand on Quinn's back and guided her away from the crowd. Heath stood back a few feet, clearly not sure whether or not to follow.

"You're making a spectacle of yourself, laughing like

that," Chichi said.

"People love to laugh," she said, keeping her voice much quieter than he'd kept his. "They'll remember me now when I call their office."

"Yes, but they'll think of you as the silly, inconsequential girl. Not someone they should listen to."

Her smile turned to glass and shattered but she kept the mirage of it there on her lips. Her mind spun for effective words to defend herself without sounding disrespectful, but then a stern-looking man with gray hair approached and Chichi turned his attention on him, giving Quinn the chance to escape.

Heath's gaze met hers, and she kept the corners of her mouth propped up, refusing to let her mortification show. "My father," she said. "Breaking out the Victorian insults since 1992."

Heath put his hands on her shoulders. "Quinn—"

"I'm a real estate shark. I close deals. I…I don't need pity." To her dismay, her voice cracked. So not sharklike.

Heath stepped closer and gently tipped up her chin. "Good. Because I'm not pitying someone who drives a Mercedes, wears designer shoes, and wants to turn my hunting lodge into a frilly B and B." There was a teasing yet challenging edge to his words.

"Good," she said, her voice now convincingly firm again.

"Great," he mimicked in the same tone.

A laugh broke through, and then she quickly clamped her lips. He leaned down, and his warm breath hit her ear, sending a chain reaction of delicious shivers and stuttered heartbeats. "By the way, I love your laugh."

She closed her eyes and let the compliment sink down

deep where her father couldn't touch it—she'd no doubt need to hold on to it and remind herself of it in the future.

"Shall we go drink some froufrou champagne?" he asked.

At her nod, Heath took her hand and placed it at his hooked elbow, even offering a tiny head bow that made her giggle. And even though it meant he'd witnessed the kind of humiliating exchange she and her father often had, she wouldn't trade his being there for the world.

Chapter Nineteen

Heath handed a fluted glass to Quinn. He'd worried he'd gone too far with adding the mock B and B insult, but it'd had the desired effect. For all her talk about being a shark, her dad's words had clearly cut her.

It'd taken all his willpower not to interrupt the two of them. He knew her dad was big on respect, and he didn't want to get off on the wrong foot with him—well, that ship had probably sailed long ago—but he didn't want to make it worse or to draw more attention to the chiding. Plus there were Quinn's conflicted feelings on disappointing and honoring her family to consider.

But how didn't Mr. Sakata see the way Quinn lit up the room, or that people were drawn to that? They'd do business with her because she was fun to be around, on top of being smart. Not to mention sexy as hell.

Now he hated himself for doubting her earlier, all because someone had called her wild. No one could fake the hurt on her face after her dad had scolded her. Not to mention he loved her so-called wild side—she was adventurous and free, something she clearly wasn't allowed to be at her job.

No wonder she feels suffocated working for her father. It's like he's trying to slowly stamp out who she is.

At this point, even if she were conning him, he'd happily be her mark. He tightened his grip on her hand, wondering how he could fix everything. How he could hold onto her, no matter what the town committee decided.

"Incoming," she muttered, and Heath braced himself.

Ah, it's just the ex. No problem. Grayson stopped in front of them, and Heath wrapped his arm around Quinn's waist.

"Hello, Quinn," Grayson said. "It's nice to see you."

"Have you met Heath?"

"Her boyfriend," he said, extending a hand and fighting the urge to crush the guy's bones in his grip. He loved that she hadn't offered a fake, "Nice to see you, too," and got straight to introducing him.

"Yeah, sorry I haven't called you back, but I've been so busy." She nestled closer and put her hand on his chest, fitting against him perfectly. When he glanced down at her, she wasn't looking at her ex to see his reaction—no, she was looking at him like he was the only person who existed at all. It was the first time he'd felt like a total rock star without his guitar in his hands.

His heart expanded and filled up with her, and for such a tiny thing, she somehow filled every inch of space. Somewhere along the way, he'd completely fallen for the girl.

The yuppie left in a huff, and a mix of satisfaction and happiness danced through him, leaving him pleasantly light-headed. Before he could fully enjoy the buzz, her father approached. This time Mr. Sakata clearly noticed she was with him, and the man couldn't look less thrilled about it.

Heath swore he heard Quinn mutter, "No more strings," under her breath before raising her voice and squaring off in front of her dad. "Chichi, this is Heath. Heath, this is my father, Kenji Sakata."

"Nice to meet you," Heath said, extending his hand.

A muscle ticked in Mr. Sakata's jaw as he reluctantly shook it. "The mechanic, right?"

"He's a very talented mechanic who also builds these amazing custom motorcycles," Quinn said.

Did the girl seriously not know that mentioning motorcycles was the least endearing thing ever when it came to fathers?

Mr. Sakata turned to Quinn, his mouth pressed into a tight line. "Maya mentioned you'd been in Hope Springs a lot, but I didn't realize why. Now I see."

"I've been helping the town prepare for the Frontier Days parade, too. Heath and I built and decorated a float and have been working closely with the town committee."

"We'll talk about this tomorrow. Come by the house at ten."

"It'll have to wait. I'll be in Hope Springs until Monday."

Frustration rose to the surface on father and daughter alike, barely contained, and Heath tightened his arm around Quinn, a dozen swearwords running through his head. Somehow he'd involved himself in a power struggle that spelled imminent disaster on all sides.

They stood there, gazes tangling for a moment, and then the flurry of the party broke through as a couple who practically dripped money approached. Clearly they weren't very good at sensing tense situations, because Heath was sure this one could be spotted from miles away. Mr. Sakata's entire face changed in a flash, much like Quinn's did when she had to power through something she didn't want to, and he greeted them warmly and thanked them for coming.

As soon as the other man pulled Mr. Sakata into a conversation, Quinn steered Heath away. She greeted people, introduced him, and made small talk, more subdued than she'd been at the beginning of the party, but still easily winning them over. Every time she bit back a laugh or cut one off before it fully caught hold, though, it ate at him.

Mr. Churchill came over to talk to them again and asked Heath for his card so he could have Heath build him a motorcycle. While most of Heath's clients came from word of mouth or the website he needed to do a better job of maintaining, he'd made up a few cards. After being in his wallet so long, they looked a bit crumpled, but they had the necessary info. Mr. Churchill promised to pass on Heath's name to the guys he rode across the country with as well, and then his wife came over and tugged him away.

The crowd thinned, and Quinn glanced at her phone. "I think it's time to make a break for it before we have another awkward interaction with my father." She cast him a worried sideways glance. "Sorry about that, by the way, but you have no idea how much your being here helped me."

"Even though you're going to regret it later, when you have to actually deal with it?" he asked.

She winced and then quickly tried to recover. "Yes. Now, what do I have to do to get you to take me home?"

"Little girl, be careful what you ask for, because you just might get it." He guided her toward the exit, out the door, and over to his truck. "We'll get your car tomorrow."

"No need. I took a taxi here so we could ride back to my place together."

He gripped her hips and boosted her into the truck, his heart pumping double time as he climbed in after her and fired up the engine. It'd been a long week, and he was glad to finally be alone with Quinn again. With her by his side, the restlessness that'd plagued him all week disappeared.

She gave him directions to her place, which was only a few miles away.

Once in a while her lifestyle versus his hit him hard, showing him just how different they were. Like right now, as he took in the recently built townhouse she called home. But then she leaned in and dragged her nose across his cheek before placing a soft kiss on his jaw, and differences didn't matter anymore. "Do you have a suitcase?" she asked.

"Duffel bag." He reached behind the seat to get it. "Gonna carry it for me?"

"If you need me to," she replied with a grin. He slid out, shouldered the bag, and took her hand. This was new territory for him—staying the night without having sex. He felt like he was walking a fine line, unsure what would be considered stepping outside of it. Wanting to push the boundaries but not enough to push her away.

She flipped on the lights and then pointed out the guest room. "I figured we could change into less binding clothes and hang out."

Hang out. Sure. Not think about the way that purple dress emphasized the nice curve of her butt or how her sexy legs would feel wrapped around him. Definitely not think about getting her out of the dress. He tugged at his tie, in desperate need of more air, although he didn't think it actually had anything to do with the fabric noose around his neck. "I could use a wardrobe change."

"See you in a few minutes, then." She lingered in the doorway to her bedroom, one hip against the frame, and sank her teeth into her lower lip. He watched, mesmerized, his fingers twitching to grab her and make quick work of that dress.

Then she swung the door shut, and he closed his eyes, trying to cool the molten need searing burning trails through his body.

• • •

Quinn leaned against her door, taking deep breaths in an attempt to cool the desire that'd turned to need somewhere along the way. She'd been tempted to forget her rules before, but right now, she was playing with fire. Sexy, tattooed, ripped-abs fire.

She reached back and tugged at the zipper on her dress, hoping focusing on the task would help, even though she knew it was highly unlikely *anything* would help at this point. A few inches down, the zipper caught. She craned her neck, trying to get a look, but she couldn't see it, even after making herself cross-eyed. She pinched the tab between her fingers and pulled down again, and then up when it refused to cooperate, but the zipper wouldn't budge either way. She attempted to wiggle out of the dress with the little gap she'd made, but the dress was far too snug and also refused to move up or down more than a couple inches—apparently it and the zipper were in cahoots.

Real funny, guys, she thought, and then wondered at her

mental state. At least she hadn't said it aloud, though, right? That kept her right above the completely bonkers mark.

She tugged her dress back into place the best she could, walked out of her bedroom, and then knocked on the door to the guest room. "Not trying to torture you or anything, but I'm stuck in my dress. Could you help me with my zipper?"

Rustling noises came from behind the door and then it swung open, revealing a shirtless Heath.

"Holy shitballs," she said, her eyes glued to the muscles covered in ink. As if it had a mind of its own, her hand lifted to the tattoo running across his left pec. She traced the colored lines of the fiery bird and flames, realizing it was a phoenix. His skin twitched under her touch, sending a surge of power through her. After feeling so helpless earlier at the party, it was especially addictive.

The feathered wing merged into swirls on his sleeve, a mix of stars, a cross, and other images that flowed flawlessly to the next, outlining the ridges of his muscles. She followed the trails of ink, entranced by the feel of the slightly raised skin under her fingertips.

"Quinn." His voice was low, husky, and the dark eyes that met hers made heat pool low in her stomach, leaving her aching for something more. Which meant she should step away.

But her feet remained firmly in place. "Just checking out your tattoos."

"That's fine as long as I get to do the same to you," he said.

"I don't have any tattoos."

His eyes locked onto hers, and what little color she could see around his dilated pupils was most definitely blue tonight. With a hint of green. "I'm afraid I'll have to see for myself."

Her heart slammed against her chest, so hard she wouldn't be surprised if it burst right out of her.

He placed his hands on her shoulders and then curled his fingers around them. "Don't worry, I'm aware of your boundaries. If I get too close to crossing the line, all you have to do is say so, okay?"

She meant to say, "Okay," but her tongue seemed to be stuck to the roof of her mouth, so she simply nodded.

"Now, didn't you have a stuck zipper?"

She turned her back to him, sweeping her hair to one side so he could take a look without it in the way. He wiggled the tab of the zipper, but it didn't budge, so he began gently pulling at the fabric. Just when she thought she was going to have to cut herself out of the dress—a shame, since it was one of her favorites—the zipper slid down. Cool air hit her exposed skin, and with the amount of heat currently radiating through her body, it was especially welcome.

Heath slipped his hand inside the dress, his callused fingertips dragging across her skin, and her internal temperature shot up again, the cool air no longer enough to faze it. He moved his hand around to her stomach and then pulled her back flush against his chest. His obvious arousal heightened hers, and rapid breaths sawed in and out of her mouth. He brushed his fingers across the bottom of her bra and her heartbeats fractured and raced to the spot where his hand warmed her skin.

His lips hit her neck, and a moan escaped her. He moved his hand lower and lower, at a tortuously slow pace, but stopped with his fingertips against the top of her panties.

"I…" As much as she didn't want him to stop, she knew

she'd never be able to if they went any farther. Her entire body pulsed with want already, and her thoughts were beyond fuzzy. "We've reached the line."

He withdrew his hand, but instead of getting mad or cutting their make-out session short, he turned her around, pushed her against the opposite wall, and covered her mouth with his. The kiss was like their arguments—he'd make a move and she'd reply, both of them fighting for control.

Weeks of frustration. Lust. Passion.

Something more she was scared to even think…

He boosted her up on the wall, and her legs went around his waist. Then the kiss morphed into more of a team effort. Given and taken breaths and swirling tongues that danced in tandem and made it clear just how well they worked together.

Her dress slipped off a shoulder, and Heath kissed down her neck, across her exposed collarbone, to the swell of her breast. He palmed the other one, his thumb brushing across the thin lace and sending corresponding jolts through her core.

She dug her fingers into his shoulders and rolled her hips, eliciting a groan from him. The threads of her control snapped one by one, until only a tiny frayed string remained. "Heath," she said, the word coming out on a labored breath. "Line."

He rested his forehead on her shoulder for a moment, and then he slowly let her down, shaking his head in a dazed way, his chest rising and falling as rapidly as hers. "Sorry. Got a little carried away."

"Me, too." She bit her lip. "No yelling?"

He cupped her cheek. "Definitely not. Never yelling about this." He gave her a hard kiss on the mouth, shoved his hands in his pockets, and backed away. "But maybe a cold shower. Yeah, I'll be back in a few."

Quinn changed into her least sexy pajamas—flannel pants and a tank top—and scanned her movies. Not sexy. Not horrible.

That narrowed it down quite a bit. Finally she settled on *The Heat*. Good, funny, and better yet, no sex scenes to completely derail her attempts to not think about it.

When Heath came out, his hair was damp and his shirt clung to his skin. She bit back a groan.

"Hey, no making sexy noises," he said, sitting down next to her. Apparently she hadn't done such a good job of biting it back. She wasn't doing a good job of not thinking about sex, either.

She ran a shaky hand through her hair. "This whole relationship is totally impossible," she said. "I'm still not sure why you haven't run."

"Because I'm not stupid." He draped an arm around her shoulders and tucked her next to him. They cuddled and watched the movie, exchanging glances now and then as if they were checking on each other.

As the movie wound down, she studied his sexy profile and thought about how incredible the night had been, from the party to the hottest kissing session ever to snuggling on her couch. For the first time since she'd put in her offer on Mountain Ridge, she wondered what was at stake if she actually got it and if it was worth the risk.

Her heart was on the line, she knew that much. In fact, the tingly euphoric haze currently flooding her senses made it clear that despite telling herself to be careful, she'd accidentally fallen in love faster and deeper than she ever had before.

Chapter Twenty

The doorbell jerked Quinn out of a dead sleep, the amazing dream featuring Heath fading away even as she tried to hold it in her mind. She squinted against the morning light glowing around her blinds, threw back the sheet and covers, and pulled on a robe. She padded out of her room, casting a quick glance at the closed door of the guest room.

As amazing as her dream had been, the fact that Heath had come to her work party and then spent the night without pressuring her for more was a real-life dream coming true. She let the grin on her face stretch into completely enamored territory and then headed toward the door as the bell rang again.

The peephole showed Chichi and Haha on the other side, their austere expressions already in place. Quinn's blood pressure spiked as she cast another glance down the hall. If they found out Heath was here, separate bedroom or not, they'd completely freak. Any chance of them eventually liking him would be gone for good. Even though the odds of that ever happening were slim, she wasn't quite ready to extinguish the glimmer of hope that they'd somehow survive their staggering amount of complications and pull off a full-fledged relationship.

"We're not leaving until you talk to us," Chichi said.

With a futile attempt to telepathically tell Heath to stay put, Quinn cracked open the door. "It's not a good time," she said. "I made commitments in Hope Springs, and I've got to get going. We'll have to talk Monday morning at the office."

"What were you thinking bringing that tattooed mechanic to a work function?" Clearly Chichi didn't take direction very well. "Were you trying to hurt me? Because if you were, you certainly achieved it."

Guilt came, fast and hot, shame heating her face. She'd needed Heath last night, but asserting her independence at the party had been a disrespectful move, one she knew embarrassed her father. She only meant to show him he couldn't choose her dates, not hurt him.

"Does he even have a degree?"

She gritted her teeth. Saying no seemed like a betrayal, even though it was the truth.

"You honestly think you'll be happy with a guy like that?"

Quinn glanced from him to Haha, although she wasn't sure why. She certainly wouldn't get any help. They always presented a united front.

Panic choked her as a noise came from the back of the house. *Please, please don't come out of the room.*

"I've provided for you, and this is how you repay me?" Chichi continued, never one to keep a rant short. "You have your nice office and your new townhome and your car.

Commercial real estate is difficult to get into, I'll have you know, but I paved the way for you."

"I appreciate it, Chichi. But I still need to be free to live my own life. To not be treated like a child." She hadn't planned on saying any of those things, but they slipped out, and as scared as she was to have them out there, she liked that after two years of constantly biting them back, they weren't clogging her throat anymore.

"You're acting like a child. Throwing it all away for a guy. You think it'll last? That he'll take care of you?"

Of course her father didn't think she could take care of herself. She opened her mouth to respond, but a lump lodged in her throat.

Chichi threw up an arm in exasperation. "You're letting your impulses control you instead of thinking about the future. I thought you'd learned, but now I see that I've given you too much freedom. Played into your whims too much."

Too much freedom? Whims? When it came to work, she did her due diligence just like everyone else. And the decisions she'd made this past month were because she *was* thinking about her future. A future that didn't include working for her father until every ounce of happiness had been squeezed out of her one crappy year at a time.

"Until we get this worked out, I'm going to need the keys to the car," he said, extending his hand. "It's for work and clients, not for joyrides to Hope Springs."

Clenching her jaw, she grabbed her key ring, removed the key and fob to the Mercedes, and placed them in his open palm. Instead of twenty-four, she felt sixteen again. He'd never treat her any differently, no matter how many deals she closed or clients she brought in. In his eyes, she'd always be the rebellious daughter who needed to be kept in line "for her own good."

"I'll see you Monday," she said. "I might be late, since I'll have to take the bus." Without waiting for a reply, she swung the door closed. Never before had she ended the conversation before Chichi dismissed her. A mix of guilt and pride that she'd stood up for herself hit her, leaving her somewhere between feeling like she could take on the world and bursting into tears.

Her family would always be important to her, and she hated the thought of what this might do to her relationship with her parents, but it'd been a long time coming. She might not have a car anymore, and she wouldn't be surprised if her father demanded she move out of her townhouse. But if it meant being in control of her life, she'd find a way to stand on her own two feet, no matter what it took.

• • •

The silence that hung in the air after the door slammed made Heath wonder if Quinn was having a breakdown. He'd thought her dad was harsh last night, but to come to her house and scold her like that?

Clearly I still don't understand their family dynamic. Heath knew some of it went back to their culture and how strongly they felt about respecting their elders, but Quinn was a grown woman.

Who hadn't defended him. Not that he needed her to, but he'd held his breath as he'd waited for her answer after Mr. Sakata had asked if she honestly thought she'd be happy with a guy like him. The silence had filled his gut with lead.

Then there'd been the question about him providing for her.

He wasn't a provider type guy. He'd barely started to think maybe he could be a relationship type guy. He'd known from the start he wasn't good enough for Quinn—that they had significant differences that'd make a relationship difficult. Perhaps impossible.

He tugged on his jeans and a T-shirt and then exited the room. Quinn was staring at her coffeemaker, watching the stream of brown pour into the glass pot.

She spun around and pulled out her fake smile. "Morning. Small complication with my car—I might not be able to go to Hope Springs, which I guess means the Dixie Rush concert is out, too, which really sucks, because I've been dying to hear you guys play your songs in a live venue. There's always next time, though, right?"

"Quinn."

Her smile cracked, and her gaze dropped to the floor. "So you heard."

"I heard."

She shrugged. "It was bound to happen someday. Might as well be when everything in my life is on the line. It'll make it that much easier to walk away from my job if I actually get Mountain Ridge, right?"

He flinched, and she put her hand on his arm. "Sorry. I didn't mean to drag the property into it. We've both invested a lot of time and energy into trying to achieve our dreams, and I'm proud we never resorted to playing dirty. I'm still all about the winner getting good luck wishes and a congratulatory kiss. I'll be okay either way."

The squeak at the end of her sentence made it hard to think she believed that. Pressure built, pressing against him.

The urge to bolt was strong, but that'd make him a dick. It'd also make him just like his dad, and he refused to use the cut-and-run method on Quinn. Cracks were forming in their attempt to pretend they'd be okay regardless of what the town committee decided, though, widening more and more the closer they got to it happening.

If she doesn't show this weekend, they'll for sure award it to me. Sometimes he felt guilty that he could work on the float during the week when she was busy with her job, even though he knew he could use all the extra points he could get. "Let's not worry about Monday right now. Let's hop in the truck and stick with the weekend we planned."

"According to my father, I never think about the future anyway. Might as well go with it, since I'm going to be accused of it." She poured two mugs of coffee and added cream and sugar to hers before taking a gulp that had to have burned off her taste buds.

Ten minutes later, they'd both showered and Quinn sat in his truck, her wet hair piled into a high bun that displayed that one stripe of red. Despite how messy and complicated things were becoming, he couldn't get over how beautiful she was. How much he wished he *was* a different kind of guy. One who could make her happy long-term.

Again he heard that heavy silence after her dad had asked her, how quiet she'd been when Mr. Sakata had asked if he even had a degree.

As much as he wanted to not care, it was like ripping off a scab that now needed to heal all over again. It was one thing for his dad or even hers to feel that way, but he thought Quinn saw more.

He needed to prepare himself for the inevitable ending.

With several cracks already in place, all it'd take was one more complication to add enough pressure to burst apart and crumble, and with their opposing position and someone being on the losing end, it was only a matter of time.

This was exactly why he should've stopped himself from falling *before* he'd gotten all wrapped up in her. And definitely before he'd started thinking that he'd give anything to find a way to get over their vast differences and the committee's decision and take a real stab at making things work.

• • •

Quinn's fingers were coated with glitter, and she was pretty sure she'd have a permanent mark in her palm where she'd gripped the unforgiving handle of the industrial-sized stapler. Her forearm ached with the repeated stapling motion, and a sneeze that wouldn't just come out already had been holding her nose hostage for the past minute.

Her phone chimed again, and even though she was sure it was Maya, she glanced at the display to confirm. Her sister was currently the only family member still on speaking terms with her, and with how often she'd texted to tell Quinn that their parents were upset and she needed to call them and make things right, Quinn sort of wished she'd stop talking to her, too.

Of course Maya thought a massive blowout years in the making could be solved in a matter of hours. Because if it were her, she would've already smoothed it out with an apology. Strike that. She never would've dared to yell or slam a door in the first place.

For the first time, a hint of that resentment she'd never

felt at her sister for being the good one rose to the surface. *Great. Now I feel totally cut off from my family.*

At least Maya and Steven had closed on their house a few days ago, so Quinn would have the Hope Springs house to herself.

Or maybe not totally to herself... She smiled over the float at Heath. He gave her a weak smile in return and refocused on testing the butterflies for any spots that might need tightening in case the trailer encountered a bump on its way down Main Street. Their afternoon in the garage wasn't like the other times they'd worked on the float. Their usual banter and flirty glances back and forth weren't there, only the sound of staple guns, crinkling paper, and the occasional "pass the festoon" between them. She'd even take arguing over the awkward silence.

Every time she asked if he was okay, he claimed he was fine, but she wondered if he regretted bringing her to Hope Springs. If he'd decided she was too much drama now that he'd seen how much Chichi liked to play puppet master in her life and how hard it was for her to break free of it.

For about the hundredth time that day, she wished Sobo Machi were there so she could talk to her and get her advice. How did you move mountains but not lose your family? Because as angry and frustrated as she was with them, she couldn't imagine not having them in her life. Going along with whatever had been so easy the past few years, despite how unhappy she'd been. Choosing her own happiness over theirs was selfish, right?

Then again, living in constant resentment and suppressing who she truly believed she was meant to be wasn't going to move any mountains, either. She just hadn't realized she'd feel so lost. There was also an edge of desperation, too, because she'd have to go into the office on Monday and face Chichi, and if she didn't get Mountain Ridge…

Yeah, there was nothing after that. Her future was suddenly a black hole. For someone who didn't consider herself a planner, that terrified her more than she'd expected.

She stapled the last flower in place and then stepped back. "Wow. We actually pulled it off. With a week to spare." Not that she would've had actual time during the week to work on it, but at least it wouldn't require a caffeine-fueled all-nighter the day before the parade now.

Heath jumped down and came to stand next to her. Hesitantly, she reached out and snaked her arm around his waist. *I need us to at least be okay. Please show me we're okay.*

He looked down at her, and her heart caught. Then he drew her closer and lowered his lips to hers. "Never could've done it without you."

"Right back at you," she whispered.

Heath rested his forehead against hers and took in a deep breath, and she wrapped her other arm around him in a tight hug, fighting the urge to cry and not even knowing why.

After a minute like that, he pulled out his phone. "Looks like we've got just enough time to clean up and get to the concert. You still up for it?"

She nodded. "Yeah, I've been looking forward to it all week. I know you guys kept it mellow for the wedding, and I'm eager to hear you play and sing all out."

They put away the tools and piled the few materials they had left over in the massive box that'd been bursting when they'd first gotten it. Their "Spread Your Wings and Fly" float might not be quite as impressive as the others in the garage, but it no longer stuck out as the ugly stepchild.

As skeptical as she'd been about working on the float with Heath in the beginning, they'd made something beautiful, upbeat cheesy message and all. It was hard to celebrate finishing when it signaled how close they were to the end of what had forced them together in the first place, though.

With the town committee's verdict right around the corner, things were shifting. Their best intentions might not be enough to stave off the bitterness that'd follow for one of them, but she couldn't help hoping they'd make it through the storm. Weren't those the kinds of experiences that were supposed to make you stronger?

She didn't see how, but that was the thing about hope. You didn't need to have everything figured out to hold on to it.

Chapter Twenty-One

The music made everything better. Recording the album had been hectic, with long hours of playing the guitar until his fingers ached and protested at the thought of another song—but studio time was expensive. So he'd played on, Will had hammered away on the drums until he'd said his arms felt like noodles, and Sadie had sung until she'd almost completely lost her voice.

But tonight, in this tiny venue with the good down-home country boys and girls, music took away Heath's worries about Quinn and the property and left nothing but the rush of being onstage.

Sadie belted out a song about simple life, and he felt the urge to shout an amen. Maybe he was a simple country boy, but he liked that about himself. He didn't need money and fame and glory, and he sure as hell wasn't going to try to be anyone else. He hit the chords harder and bobbed his head.

The crowd buzzed with energy, clearly taken with Sadie's

magical voice. When he first mentioned needing a singer for the band he and Will piddled around with on the side, he'd thought they'd play and have fun. He'd never expected the recording contract, although he should've known she had the star power to make it happen. Still, he was glad they were relatively unknown as of yet. If their album blew up after it released, he'd have to find a way to deal with the extra time commitment, but he'd cross that bridge when he got there.

Right now he'd enjoy the music while it was about it and nothing else. As the song came to a close, he scanned the crowd for Quinn.

Her shiny dark hair was stick straight, and she'd done up her eyes and put on bright red lipstick, so she looked the way she had the night they'd danced at the Triple S. Even with everything up in the air between them, he wanted to jump down, scoop her in his arms, and kiss her. Their memories together flooded his mind, from having her riding behind him to teaching her to drive his bike to the smug look on her face when Patsy informed him about the beard-shaving contest.

Good memories he'd have long after she'd moved on to someone more appropriate for her.

Don't think about that now. He winked at her, and she beamed up at him, and then they started the next song, which was appropriately about lost love and the resulting broken heart.

· · ·

Obviously she and Cory had decided to go for a drink at the

worst possible time. Not that the bar had been slow at any point since Dixie Rush started playing. The place was wall-to-wall bodies, most everyone decked out in cowboy hats and boots.

In her black leather zippered pants and red stilettos, Quinn definitely stuck out. People probably thought she'd mistaken the show for a rock concert. The rustic decor, complete with a moose head staring over the bar and judging everyone who came for a drink, struck her as slightly ironic, too. Everywhere she looked was another reminder that she and Heath were so crazy different.

Cory waved at two bartenders, but they charged by without a second look.

"Move aside and watch the master work," Quinn said. She hoisted the top half of her body onto the bar, caught the eye of a beefy bartender with a belt buckle the size of a football, and shot him a flirty grin.

He shoved a drink at someone else and then sauntered over. "What can I get you, darlin'?"

Cory rolled his eyes and spun to face the guy. "Three of whatever beer you've got on tap."

The bartender glanced at Cory, looking none too happy to find him there. With a sigh, he turned and grabbed three glasses. The last song came to a close, Sadie and the boys thanked everyone for coming and left the stage, and the crowd chanted for an encore.

Quinn leaned back against the bar and whistled to add to the buzz—they'd put on a hell of a show. Pride over Sadie's success and happiness that her best friend was living out her dreams flooded her. Some of it was for Heath, too, of course.

See, he's got so many jobs already. He doesn't need

another one.

The evil thought had come out of nowhere, and she tried to shake it off. He had as much reason to want Mountain Ridge as she did, plus he had his brothers to consider.

Ugh, whatever happens, I know it's going to be hard for whoever doesn't get it to be happy for the other person. For the past couple of hours, she'd tried to convince herself it wouldn't be a big deal, but her thoughts broke through before she could stop them, showing her how unlikely that was.

The crowd roared as Sadie, Heath, and Will stepped back onto the stage. Sadie wrapped her hand around the microphone and said, "Okay, one more. This one's going out to my fiancé." She winked—no doubt at Royce, although Quinn could no longer see him in the crowd—and the familiar notes of Sadie's favorite Carrie Underwood song filled the air.

Finally Quinn and Cory got their beers, with Cory carrying the extra glass for Royce. As soon as the song ended, people shoved toward the stage, vying for a chance to talk to the band.

Of course Heath's line consisted mainly of women. Almost every one of them stopped to pose for pictures, too, which somehow always meant putting their hands all over him. Seriously, did they have no boundaries? Quinn watched a leggy redhead lean into him and laugh, pressing her silicone-enhanced assets up against him.

Most of those women would have sex with him in a heartbeat, too, she could tell. He talked a lot about getting bored easily. How he hated feeling tied down and often felt the urge to move on. The word "claustrophobic" had even been mentioned when he spoke of commitment. *It's only a matter of time before he decides he's sick of waiting.*

She glanced at Cory. "Why are guys so afraid of settling down with one woman?"

He choked on his beer and sputtered for a moment before getting it under control. "Jeez, Quinn. Warn a guy before you spring that on him."

"I just want to know."

Cory wiped at the front of his shirt. "No, you wanna know about Heath, not me."

"Well, I figure you guys have enough in common that you could provide some insight." Quinn nearly asked him what he'd do if a girl he really liked asked him to wait for sex, but she was afraid she knew the answer, and with her insecurities flaring, she didn't think she could hear it without having a panic attack. Not with all those pretty women surrounding Heath.

"Look, he likes you," Cory said. "It's obvious."

"But enough to make it work, even though we want the same property and I'm not willing to go as far as other women?"

Cory shifted from foot to foot, suddenly very interested in his beer.

"Once the right person came along, it'd be different for you, right?" she asked, a sense of desperation tugging at her and diminishing her oxygen supply. "If you really cared, you'd make sacrifices?"

"That's the theory."

"Theory?" Her voice came out more high-pitched than she meant for it to.

"I'm not playing anymore." Cory nudged Royce over. "You talk to her."

Royce was different—he was a guy who committed to relationships and would work like crazy to maintain them. He'd do anything for Sadie, and they'd fallen in love when they were teenagers. When it looked like he might lose her again, he'd been willing to give up everything to be with her.

Royce glanced at her before his gaze automatically returned to Sadie. She had a mix of men and women approaching her.

"How do you deal with it?" Quinn asked.

"I trust her."

That thorn dug at her. Because she didn't trust guys in general. All they'd ever shown her was that she *couldn't* trust them.

She'd hoped for a better pep talk, but Royce had never been what one would call verbose. He also didn't believe in sugarcoating things. Quinn tipped back her drink, draining it in a few large gulps. Then she decided it was her turn to head over and congratulate the band on their good show. And only a little bit so that she could wrap her arms around Heath and let the groupie wannabes see that he was already taken.

$\bullet\ \bullet\ \bullet$

By the time he and Quinn made it out of the bar, the long day was taking its toll. His limbs dragged, and he wanted to crawl into bed. If he were being honest, he'd love to have Quinn sleeping next to him, but then sleeping would be nearly impossible.

Plus it meant getting in deeper, and he was already in over his head.

He opened the door to his truck for Quinn, put his guitar in the back, and then walked around the hood and slid behind the wheel. "Where to?"

"I guess my parents' house. Fingers crossed they didn't change the locks in order to teach me a lesson." She sat back with a groan. "How am I going to go into the office on Monday morning? It's going to be so horrible."

"So quit."

"I can't just quit—not without a fallback. Of course, I don't even have a way to get back to Cheyenne." She pressed her fingertips to her temples and rubbed circles there. "I really screwed up things good this time."

Ouch. He hated that her words stung. Now he was turning into some sensitive guy he didn't even recognize, taking offense at everything when he wasn't even sure if it was aimed at him.

"You can take my truck to Cheyenne," he said. "You're coming back for the parade next weekend anyway, and I'll just drive my motorcycle till then." He put the truck in reverse and glanced in the rearview mirror.

"That's okay. I don't want to be obligated to you."

He hit the brakes, threw the truck in park, and looked at her. "Obligated? What the hell's that supposed to mean?"

She shrugged. "I just mean I don't want to owe you anything. It always comes along with certain expectations."

"That's what you think of me? That I'll come to collect, bartering sex for a week's use of a truck? I thought maybe…" He shook his head. "You've got about as high an opinion of me as your father."

"That's not true. In my experience, though, that's the way it works. It's a truck or a necklace, and then it's *look at all I did for you. I'm sick of waiting. It's been such and such* *amount of time. Just come on.*" She tucked her knee under her and twisted to face him. "And how am I supposed to even expect you to wait when you've got women throwing themselves at you all the time? I'm not stupid."

"So you think I'm a caveman who can't control my impulses? Explains why you didn't bother defending me to your dad."

Her face dropped. "I told you that my relationship with my family is complicated. Respect your elders—it's the number-one rule I've been taught my entire life. My father's now ashamed of me, and if he knew you'd stayed at my house all night, he'd probably disown me outright."

"Bet it'd be less shameful if I was rich with good connections and a fancy college degree. Then I'd get accepted into the family the way your sister's husband was, right?"

Her silence confirmed what he'd suspected.

"I've tried to understand your culture, and I understand why you want the B and B and how much it means to you— hell, I even respect what you want to do with it. But you still look at me as a hick who wants to ruin your property, admit it." Irritation dug under his skin, pulling it too tight. "You've been spoiled too long, used to jobs and fancy cars handed over to you. I hope you never have to learn what it's like to fight just to have the bare minimum, but damned if it wouldn't give you an ounce of understanding what most people—me included—have had to deal with their whole lives."

Fury sparked and ignited, her eyes glowing with it. "Here we are. Back to you telling me I'm a pretty snob. Real understanding, Heath. Why don't you just get to the real point?

You're not a commitment type guy, you told me that from the beginning, and without sex on the table, you're not getting anything out of this relationship anymore, so you might as well end it before you have to feel too bad about it."

"If that's what you think of me, there's nothing more for me to say."

He narrowed his gaze on the flickering Coors sign in the window of the bar, waiting for her to tell him she didn't think that. But then a cool gust of air wafted inside the cab, followed closely by the slam of the door, so loud it made his ears pop. She flagged down a truck, and Heath was about to jump out and stop her—angry or not, he wasn't going to let her hitchhike with some stranger who might hurt her.

But then he saw it was Cory, and he decided that letting her go was for the best. This way they could both walk away before saying more awful things that'd destroy every good memory they'd ever had together.

Besides, when it came down to it, they just had too much stacked against them. This kind of ending was the one they'd been headed toward anyway.

Chapter Twenty-Two

Heath finished up the last vehicle of the day and scrubbed a hand over his face. The restlessness he'd experienced last week had not only returned but increased, until getting through each torturously slow hour made him want to throw tools and destroy instead of fix.

The past several days he'd been so miserable he could hardly think straight. He wasn't sleeping, either, but instead of using the extra hours to get ahead on all the work that was piling up, he could hardly summon enough motivation to fake his way through each menial task.

Like Quinn has to do every day, he thought and then curled his hand into a fist. He'd tried to avoid thinking about her, but it was proving impossible, and now that thoughts of her seeped in, he couldn't get them to shut off. He didn't know how she kept it up. Faking being okay was exhausting, and it only added to the empty, hollow sensation that'd taken up residence in his chest.

Busy. I just need to keep moving. No more thinking. He closed up the auto shop and headed to the float garage, even though he knew it'd be impossible to not think about Quinn as he stared at their butterfly concoction.

The float looked the same as the day they'd finished it, and while he'd already been pulling away and dealing with the dull ache the thought of breaking up brought, that was nothing compared to the real thing.

He wanted to believe the horrible ending wasn't all his fault—Quinn was the one not willing to ever see his side of things. Not willing to have the tiniest bit of faith in him or take a risk.

But what did blame matter when it didn't change the devastating result?

She'd been right that he wasn't usually a commitment type guy. Wrong that he wasn't willing to wait, though—hadn't he told her that enough? After every guy who'd hurt her in the past, maybe not.

He'd seen how much she cared about her family, too—how much it hurt that she'd disappointed them by simply being herself—and he supposed he could've been more understanding about that. Could've done so many things differently and probably should've. Including attempting to prove to her family that he could make her happy, regardless of not having a degree or a lot of money. At least he could've tried.

I lost her. A sharp pain shot through his chest, and he stared at those damn butterflies and the perfectly spaced lettering and thought about ripping up a section so he could have an excuse to call her and force her to be around him for a little while longer.

And then what? Have another fight so we can finish

destroying each other?

How were they supposed to work things out when one of them was about to lose their dream *because* of the other person?

Misery wrapped its arms around him, dragging him toward the darkness that'd wanted to claim him ever since Quinn had walked away.

"Heath. Just the person I wanted to talk to." Patsy stepped in front of him, cutting off his view of the float he'd been looking more through than at. "I can't seem to get ahold of Quinn. When's the last time you talked to her?"

That awful fight in the truck hit him all over again—like lemon juice on a cut that somehow got deeper by the day instead of gradually healing—and he wanted to go back to that night and fix it. Undo calling her spoiled. He'd seen how everything she had came at a cost, and how hard she was working to pull away and stand on her own two feet, and he'd still thrown it in her face. And instead of getting angry over the implication he couldn't control whom he had sex with, he could've assured her again that for her, he could wait. That he'd do just about anything for her.

"Heath?" Patsy pushed up her glasses and stared at him, obviously waiting for an answer, although it took him a moment to remember the question.

"Last Saturday." The words scraped his throat. "That's the last time I talked to her."

Patsy looked supremely confused, like he'd spoken a different language. "Well, I need to know for sure that she'll be at the parade. She will be, right?"

"I…think so?"

"You think so? I thought you two were tog—"

"We're not."

Patsy pressed her lips together and gave a tiny, knowing nod, the look on her face saying she could tell he'd screwed it up.

Yeah. I'm still the town bad boy, and I suck at life. Thanks for rubbing it in. Since he didn't think snapping at the woman who ran the town committee would do him any favors, he strode out of the garage, got onto his bike, and buzzed home.

Usually working on his custom motorcycle jobs improved his mood, so he attempted to put the finishing touches on his current project. But then he started thinking of his and Quinn's first kiss, only a few feet from where he was working, and another wave of misery slammed into him.

He tossed his tools aside, the clang of the metal echoing off the walls and vibrating in his ears. He brushed the dirt off the seat of his pants and stormed into the house, wanting this week to just be over already. If he could get through the festival and start dealing with whatever came after, maybe he'd have a chance at moving on. At finding joy in something. Anything.

"Why don't you bring your girlfriend around anymore?" Dad asked as Heath flopped down on the couch. "Afraid I'll embarrass you?"

So much for getting away from his thoughts of Quinn and how empty everything in his life now felt. Explaining they were no longer on speaking terms meant dealing—yet again—with how true it was, so he simply shook his head.

Of course Dad wasn't satisfied with that answer. "Tell me you didn't let her go—you won't ever find anyone that good again. Take it from someone who's an expert at letting good ones get away."

Heath tugged the brim of his hat lower and reached for one of the two remaining beers in the six-pack Dad had already made most of the way through. The glass was slick with condensation, so at least the beer should still be cold. "It's complicated. Just leave it alone."

"Here I thought you *didn't* want to end up like me."

Heath started to stand, and Dad put his hand on his shoulder, pushing him back onto the couch. "Look, I know I screw up a lot, and when it comes to you and Cam, I should've done things different, but I'm proud of you both. You turned out real good, despite everything. I only push you so you have a better life than me."

"You should think about all the things you should've done differently and try them out on Ollie. He needs a dad more than I do right now."

Dad's features hardened, and Heath thought he was about to yell or start with the insults, but then his shoulders deflated. "You're right, and I'm going to try, I am. It'd be easier if I knew that I'd at least given you an ounce of good advice at some point, so here it is. You'll regret letting that girl go for *years*. Holding on to anger or the idea that you're right and that's all that matters, it makes you bitter, and it's hard as hell to get over once it's got a grip on you. You make it right before it's too late." Dad got up and headed back to his room, leaving Heath staring at the TV.

Did I just imagine that? Dad admitting he messed up? Trying to give me good advice without a follow-up insult? He looked at the spot Dad had vacated—the spot where he spent the majority of his time.

Heath didn't want to be sitting on a faded old couch years from now, a beer in his hand, thinking about how he should've fought harder to hold on to the best thing that ever happened to him. Even if the best thing that happened to him was an infuriatingly stubborn, beautiful woman who knew how to push every one of his buttons.

He closed his eyes, picturing her when she gave him the real smile and replaying her loud no-holding-back-in-an-attempt-to-be-proper laugh. He thought about that look she'd given him at the party, the one that made him feel like he was the only person in the room.

The only time he didn't feel antsy or the urge to move on to the next thing was when he was with Quinn. She brought a sense of steadiness to his life. His lack of experience with love must've made him blind, because as he ran through their memories together, there was no doubt he loved her.

The kind of love that there was no coming back from.

He didn't just love her, either. He needed her, like he'd never needed anyone before.

He had to get her back. Had to prove he could commit and give her what she needed in return, and that he didn't care how long he had to wait if he got her in the end.

He was far past an apology-filled phone call, he knew that much. Which meant he had to pull out the big guns, and there'd be an even bigger chance of falling on his face.

But even if he crashed and burned, he had to try.

. . .

All week Quinn had struggled at work. She struggled at home, too, for that matter. The hours trickled by, and she'd done so much faking she was okay that she worried her face would freeze like that and she wouldn't be able to smile for real if she ever had occasion to again.

She'd tried to throw herself into her job, and Chichi had rewarded the deal she'd closed with a satisfied nod. Things were still tense, but apparently Maya had told their parents that she and Heath had ended their relationship—her sister had asked if he was worth it during her hundredth "Please make peace" phone call, and Quinn had confessed that it was over, so it didn't matter anymore.

So now her family was practically celebrating the very thing tearing her up inside. As she headed to Chichi's office for the impromptu meeting he'd called, a knot the size of Texas formed in her gut.

Bracing herself for the worst, she knocked on the open door. He gestured her inside and she sat in the chair across from him.

"I know I was harsh on you, Quinn-chan, but it's only because I care. I'm giving you back your car, and as long as you continue to earn it, it's yours."

So he could just rip it out of her hands whenever he liked and use it to control her every decision? Did he really think she'd be swayed by material possessions so easily? Apparently Heath had. Not that she'd done a good job of showing him otherwise.

A stab of despair shot through her chest—she missed his voice. Missed being able to call or text when she needed someone to talk to. She'd cried over the phone to Sadie a couple of times, and she was grateful for their talks, but a large Heath-shaped hole remained. The pain from her shattered heart routinely stole her breath and made her think she'd never fully recover, no matter how much time passed.

The keys jingled in Chichi's hand. "Aren't you going to

take them?"

"I didn't bring Heath with me to the party to dishonor you, and I wasn't dating him because I'm impulsive. I care about him. He was so good to me—he even looked up information on our culture and asked me questions and respected my values more than any other guy's ever done. And he was right. He was understanding and I didn't give him the same in return. I'm the one who screwed it up."

All week, as she'd been crying, she'd told herself he'd been wrong—that he'd harshly judged her—but now... Well, those jingling keys seemed to be telling a different story, because while she didn't want the strings, the urge to accept the car and go on like nothing had happened nearly overwhelmed her.

Yes, she'd worked hard to get to where she was, but she'd had a lot of support, both emotional and financial. She didn't know what it was like to struggle for every material possession. While he'd asked questions about how she'd run her B and B, she'd never asked him the same about the lodge. Never tried to see his side or find out his vision for the place.

The one thing she *did* know was what it was like to constantly fight with a guy because of her stance on sex, and while she and Heath had argued plenty about nearly everything else under the sun, he'd never treated her decision like it was a silly idea he could eventually change her mind about with words or pressure.

She'd accused him of awful things—implied he could never be faithful and turned the kind offer to use his truck into bad intentions—even after he'd proven he was different. How could she have been so blind?

Chichi's eyebrows drew together, the confusion clear. So

she decided to give it to him straight, regardless of it being uncharted waters for them.

"Do you know how many of my other boyfriends have actually respected my values? How many haven't pushed for more or tried to buy me off, like I'm for sale?" As difficult and awkward as it was, she met Chichi's gaze. "Not a single one. Heath's been the only one who followed through when he said he wouldn't push for more than I was willing to give. The only one to attempt to understand our culture and help me with how conflicted I feel about what you want versus what I want.

"I've tried to do my best to honor you, but I never feel good enough. I'm too old to be chided for laughing at a party, and my clients like me. I close deals. I keep longer hours than most of the other employees. I do that all for you, and it's still not enough. I'm not happy here, Chichi. I haven't been for a long time."

She lowered her voice, trying to take away some of the sting but keeping the conviction behind her words. "I'm trying to respect you, but that doesn't mean blindly following whatever you say, or only dating who you want me to. You've taught me to think—taught me the skills I need to take care of myself. I'll forever appreciate that, and I'll always love you, but now it's time for me to use those skills and take care of myself."

Quitting hadn't been her intention, not without securing the B and B first, but she'd crossed a line she couldn't—and didn't want to—come back from. "Consider this my two weeks' notice."

"Quinn. If you quit, I can't simply give you back your position when you change your mind in a few months. No more special treatment."

"Hire someone who'll appreciate the job more than I do—that shouldn't be very difficult. I wish you nothing but the best, and I hope that in time, you'll try to understand that I can't live under your thumb anymore." She leaned over the desk, kissed his cheek, and then walked out of the office.

It'd feel a lot more victorious if she hadn't ruined everything with Heath before standing up for him, but at least it was a step in the right direction.

About a hundred more of those, and maybe she could gather enough courage to face him and say everything she'd held back the first time around.

Chapter Twenty-Three

Buying a used car the day after quitting her job had been a tad impulsive, but with everything on the line, Quinn figured it was a necessary evil. It was old and made a growling noise when she accelerated that didn't sound right, but she knew she'd need to keep most of her savings while she figured out what she was going to do with the rest of her life.

As soon as the car was hers, she'd driven to her place, packed a suitcase, and hit the road. On the way to Hope Springs she'd called Patsy Higgins and asked to meet her at town hall.

Just before stepping inside the brick building that'd started the chain of events that'd occurred over the past month, she took a moment to center herself, hardly able to believe what she was about to do. Especially with no backup plan. Hopefully the gesture would convince Heath to give her another chance, because the only thing she knew about her future right now was that she wanted it to include him.

Patsy Higgins met her in the lobby, led her to a small room, and motioned for her to take a seat. "I'm happy to see you. I was starting to worry you wouldn't make it to tomorrow's festivities."

"I wouldn't miss it for the world," Quinn said. "As for the Mountain Ridge property, though, I'm withdrawing my bid."

Deep lines creased Patsy Higgins's forehead as she pushed her glasses up her nose. "Two offers that had everyone debating for weeks, and now you're giving it up, too?"

"*Too?* What do you mean too?"

"Heath withdrew his offer this morning."

No, no, no. This was going entirely wrong. "He didn't mean it—I know he wants it. Let me find out what's going on and get back to you."

"Maybe I shouldn't tell you this, but you already got it, Quinn. You won by one vote. We were going to announce it tomorrow at the barbecue."

The B and B popped into Quinn's head, the way she'd planned on it looking after she'd restored it. She saw breakfasts and dinners around a large table, guests coming and going, and laughing and joking with new people as they discovered the beauty of Hope Springs, no having to hold back. The montage ended with her sitting on the swing and watching sunsets in honor of Sobo Machi.

Despite her earlier decision, the idyllic images beckoned to her, whispering how amazing it'd be.

But then she thought of Heath's arms around her. How he'd constantly surprised her and showed her not all guys were jerks when it came to sex. She thought about running her palm across his whiskers, the way he kissed her, and how she'd never felt as free to be herself as when she was with him.

She wanted him more than she wanted the B and B—he was her new dream. After so long focused on nothing else, the thought was foreign, and honestly a bit terrifying, but also thrilling and bursting with possibilities.

Quinn scrambled to her feet, knocking her knee into the table on the way up. She rubbed the throbbing spot, even though it did nothing to make it feel better. "Just please do me a favor and don't announce it until I get a chance to talk to Heath."

Patsy Higgins frowned, clearly not a huge fan of the idea, but she finally nodded. "Good luck."

After a quick detour at the sporting goods store, Quinn stopped by Rod's Auto Repair, but Heath wasn't there. Just his dad, who eyed her ridiculous neon-orange hat—only making her feel more self-conscious about it—and said he hadn't seen him since last night.

She tried his house and then the garage. Her heart squeezed as she took in his motorcycles and stray parts and thought about their first amazing kiss surrounded by this place that represented Heath and his passions so well—she now considered grease one of the most amazing scents in the world. A clear sign there was no going back. She called Sadie, but she didn't know where Heath was, either. Finally she decided to forget her attempt to surprise him and called his cell.

It went straight to voicemail.

She nearly gave up her search, thinking she'd just sit on his porch and wait him out, when she got another idea.

Tugging the ugly hat firmly in place, she jumped in her new/old clunker car and headed toward Mountain Ridge.

A tight band formed around her chest as she spotted the familiar black truck. No motorcycle, but a ton of pale wooden boards. Quinn pulled up behind the truck and swung open her car door. After a quick check for snakes, she stepped into the sea of long yellow grass that swayed in the breeze and brushed against her pant legs.

A constant tapping noise echoed through the air, coming from the direction of the B and B, although the fading light made it hard to see anything.

Well, except her hat—the neon bill lit up like a beacon. She was fairly certain it cast a horrific orange glow on her face, too. She probably looked like one of those tanorexic girls. Just how someone should look when declaring her love.

As she stepped into full view of the B and B, her breath escaped her in a whoosh. Pale wood made up the porch and entryway, and the swing had been repaired and hung.

She cleared her throat, and Heath spun toward her, his jaw dropping enough that the nails he'd had between his lips fell to the ground. "Quinn." He moved in front of the entryway, like his body was big enough to cover up the work he'd done. "You're not supposed to see it yet."

She stepped over a large rock and rested her hand on the smooth new porch rail. "It's not supposed to be a B and B. You're just going to have to tear it down so you can build your lodge."

Heath's gaze zeroed in on the attention-grabbing hat she'd bought at the sporting goods store before going on her wild goose chase.

She tapped the bill. "See, I'm all prepared to celebrate

you getting your *hunting* lodge. Add a vest and a shotgun, and I'll be ready to trek into the mountains with you—better teach me to shoot first, though."

He rubbed a hand over his mouth, a grin spreading underneath. "I never expected one of those hats to look so hot. And that image…" He shook his head. "But it's not happening. I want you to have your B and B. I set up the porch first, so you can sit here and swing while I whip the place into shape."

"Well, I went to the town committee and withdrew my bid. I want you to have your lodge." She took another couple of steps, the stairs no longer creaky or dangerous. "You were right about everything—I didn't even try to understand. But I want another chance. And I know I defended you way too late, but just so you know, I told my father that I cared about you, and that I thought you were the best guy I've ever dated." Another step and she was on the same level as him, although since she was in her ballet flats, he still towered over her. "More than anything, I want you."

Heath tossed the hammer aside, closed the space between them, and pulled her into his arms. "I was the idiot. I should've never let you go. I want a real relationship with you, and I want you to have your dream." He swept her hair off her face and cupped her cheek. "I'm in love with you, Quinn. You're what I never even knew I was looking for, and I want you to be the one steady thing in my life. I need you by my side. I'll do whatever it takes to make us work, I promise."

Her throat grew tight, and tears sprang to her eyes. She'd hoped eventually he might fall in love with her, though she'd expected it to take time and patience—which had never been her strong suit—but she could've done it for him.

Because he *was* worth it.

It was a relief she didn't have to worry that saying how she felt would scare him away, though. "I love you, too."

He drew her to him and claimed her mouth, the kiss urgent and fevered before it morphed to a methodical rediscovering of each other's lips and tongues.

She wrapped her arms around him, squeezing him as tightly as she could so he'd never get away again. "You've got to build your lodge, Heath. I'll find another job, and I'll be okay. Think about your brothers."

"I did. I already talked to Cam. I told him the entire situation, we brainstormed, and he's going to help me expand my custom motorcycle business. It'll keep us here so we can help take care of Ollie, and if we have a slow month or two, we can always work at my dad's shop."

"No," she said, shaking her head. "I don't want you to have to do that. Your relationship with your dad is as tricky as mine is, and I know you and Cam have wanted this for a long time."

"So have you. And my dad and I...well, we had a talk, too, and we're working on it. Besides, it's already done. I withdrew my bid and your B and B's getting restored."

"It's not done. I undid it."

"Then I'll undo your undoing it."

Quinn exhaled, trying her best not to get into a fight with him, since they'd finally gotten back together, but why did he have to be so damn difficult? She searched for a way to persuade him as she glanced around at the property they'd somehow reversed arguments on after weeks of being immobile. The fact of the matter was, she didn't have a job and was worried she'd have a hard time finding one in

Hope Springs. But she refused to let him settle for less than his dream because of her.

Suddenly, different images superimposed themselves over the land, new possibilities forming before her eyes, and a swirl of excitement went through her stomach.

"You know, this crazy idea just popped into my head," she said. "There's a whole lot of land, and say you were interested in a business partner—and I happen to know a highly qualified person looking for a job so she can stay in Hope Springs with her boyfriend—she could run the main building where people would come to eat and relax or take part in fun activities. She might even be able to deal with a certain amount of rustic charm, hunting gear, and…stuffed animal heads."

She ran her hand down Heath's chest and rested her palm over his heart. "Then there could be cabins for people who wanted their own space. They could decide if they wanted to join in on meals and activities, or just enjoy the scenery, or head into the mountains with a sexy hunting guide."

He swept his gaze across the land, the way she'd done, and when his eyes met hers again, a grin broke free. "It's so crazy it might just work." He brushed his thumb across her bottom lip, and her heart fluttered wildly in her chest. "Would these cabins have frilly curtains?"

"Of course. Hung up by antlers."

Heath laughed, and then he tilted his head and kissed the corner of her mouth. "I accept. Negotiations will take place later, though." He tilted his head the other way and gave the other corner the same treatment. "I want to kiss you some more before we have our first argument after going into business together."

Chapter Twenty-Four

Heath caught Quinn's eye as the barber shaved another line of hair from his jaw. Ollie stood next to her, shoelaces untied as usual, Trigger at his side. And in a new and unusual development, Dad was there, too, his hand on the top of Ollie's shoulder. When the kid had shown up this morning, bouncing around and talking about the parade, Dad had gotten up from his spot on the couch and said he was coming, too.

It was the second time that week he'd shocked Heath, and he honestly hoped he'd keep it up, although Heath planned on keeping his expectations cautiously low. At least it showed Dad had listened the other day, and he wasn't the only one. Heath liked to think he would've pulled his head out and found a way to get Quinn back eventually, but he'd needed that kick.

When Quinn had come over and hopped up on the tailgate next to him to watch the parade, Dad had given a nod, and there'd even been a glimmer of pride in his eyes. The property came up, and they told Dad about their plan to go into business together. He'd grumbled about finding a replacement for the shop when Heath told him it meant he'd be quitting—as well as moving out—but all in all, it'd gone pretty well, and part of that was because Quinn had been there by his side, holding his hand.

So there she, his dad, and his little brother stood, a makeshift family with plenty of issues, but they were his, and once Cam got here, it'd be complete.

Quinn bit her lip, obviously trying not to laugh. Just wait till she found out what he'd signed her up for. It was the next event, and he'd be the one getting the last laugh.

He held his breath as the barber moved the blade to the spot over his Adam's apple. It was one thing to be a participant in a beard-shaving fund-raiser; it was another to trust someone else to do the shaving, especially when said person used the kind of blade that meant serious damage if he slipped.

I'm sure he's done this a hundred times. They wouldn't get an amateur up here to shave guys in front of all these children if there was a chance of bloodshed.

Then again, they'd had him and Quinn build a float when they'd never done it before. Not exactly the comforting thought he was searching for, but they'd managed to pull it off. As their float glided down Main Street, their butterflies had bounced in a way they hadn't planned but that made them look like they were fluttering. A few people had even commented on how cool it was that they'd added that effect, and he and Quinn had grinned at each other and accepted the praise like they'd done it on purpose.

After the parade they'd had a quick meeting with the

town committee, explaining their revised plan to develop Mountain Ridge. Quinn told him she wanted it to be his vision and she'd help him however she could, even if it meant making the old Victorian more rustic or tearing it down if that was what he needed to do. He'd never demolish the building she loved, though, and he let her know it was together or nothing.

So the lodge would be less log-cabin-esque than most fishers and hunters would expect and have space for people who brought their families with them. But then they'd also build several cabins of varying sizes, from big enough to accommodate families to places more suited for one or two people. They'd still be welcome to go for activities and food at the main building anytime, though. The town committee loved the idea of having the best of both worlds, so now it was only a matter of pulling it off.

No doubt they'd argue about aspects of how and why during the construction, but he knew that they'd work it out, and that in the end, the property would be that much better for it. With both of them going in, neither of them would be as financially strapped, either, and he wasn't as worried about the times he'd be on the road with Dixie Rush. Between Quinn and Cam, they'd be better able to keep things running smoothly.

Cam was going to get such a kick out of Quinn, too. He'd already given him crap about being whipped when he'd told him he had to do whatever it took to get her back, so he could only imagine how often he'd hear it once his brother saw how far gone he really was, but Heath didn't care. He'd never been so happy to be whipped in his life.

Quinn whistled as the barber wiped off the last of the

shaving cream. Some of the other guys onstage had lost more than a foot of hair. His beard would be back to its full glory in about a month or so, but his skin still felt pretty bare when the air hit it.

The coyote hat went to a guy in his sixties who'd shaved off a Santa beard, and then Patsy thanked all of the participants and dismissed them. Heath grabbed his black baseball hat—glad he didn't have to wear the coyote one around the rest of the day for fear of offending someone—and tugged it on.

Quinn met him at the bottom steps of the stage and smoothed her hand down his cheek. "Holy shit, there's skin under there."

He slid his hands into the back pockets of her jeans and shook his head. "You kiss your mother with that mouth?"

"No, I kiss rugged men with it." She leaned in, her breath hitting his lips, and then she pulled back and made a big show of looking around. "Too bad there aren't any around."

He lunged for her, and she let out a squeal. He boosted her in his arms, and she linked her fingers behind his neck. "No amount of shaving could take away your ruggedness, babe," she said, and then she sealed her words with a kiss.

Onstage, Patsy announced how much the contest had raised for the Hope Springs search and rescue and the crowd cheered. Once they settled down, she said, "Now it's time for the annual mud run. And we've got a late entry." She glanced in their direction, and Heath lowered Quinn to her feet. Her eyes widened as people turned to stare, and Patsy's eyebrows scrunched together. "Quinn, I do hope you brought your running shoes, because I don't think it's a good idea to do the mud run in those heels."

Quinn spun to face him, her mouth dropping open, and he kissed her cheek before she could say anything. "Don't worry, I grabbed your sneakers from your car and put them in my truck."

"Oh, what a relief," she said, her words chock-full of sarcasm. She fisted his shirt and planted an attack kiss on his lips. "You're lucky I love you. And you're running with me, by the way."

Heath wrapped his arms around her waist and kissed the sensitive spot just under her ear. "Little girl, you know I'd never give up a chance to get dirty with you."

Epilogue

Quinn placed the pot of sukiyaki in the center of the table and then wrung her hands together. Heath came up behind her, wrapped his arms around her waist, and tucked his chin on her shoulder. "It's going to be fine."

"I need better than fine." For the past two months, she, Heath, and a small construction crew had worked themselves to the bone restoring the Victorian they were currently standing in. The cabins were only framed right now, but within another month or two, they'd be finished as well.

Cam would be getting home in a few days, which had her bouncing between nervous and excited. Right now, though, her anxiety over her family coming to dinner at Mountain Ridge eclipsed it by far. It'd taken a while to open up the lines of communication between her and her parents, but after a few hard phone calls, things were gradually getting better. They'd settled on a hesitant truce.

Truces were easier to keep with lots of space.

Quinn spun in Heath's arms and placed her hands on his biceps. "Kiss me so I don't have to think about it for a minute."

"I'll make you forget it for five," Heath said, and then he took her face in his hands and kissed her like the future of the world depended on it. With every passing day, she became crazier and crazier about him. Which made it that much harder not to give in to her desire to sleep with him. He'd continued to respect her boundaries, although they'd both had to request time-outs to cool down after heated make-out sessions.

About a week ago, she'd almost convinced herself she didn't need to wait until they were married, because she believed they'd tie the knot eventually. But in her heart, she knew waiting still mattered to her. Instead of holding back, or having to fake not being frustrated by it, she'd talked to him about it. He assured her he loved her and understood it was important to her, and even though she would've said it was impossible, she loved him even more.

She trusted him completely. They talked about the future. Things were perfect.

Everything but her strained relationship with her family. The sound of tires brought reality crashing back. Her heels echoed against the floor as she walked to the entryway and peered out the large window set into the bright yellow door she and Heath had debated over. He said it was too bright, she bought it anyway—compromise at its finest.

They'd mowed the grass to help with snakes and cleared a small area for parking. And by "they" she meant Heath, because he was much better at that kind of thing. Although thanks to him, she'd learned a ton of basic home repair skills, and as long as the problem didn't involve scales and a forked tongue, she was equipped to handle most anything.

As her parents, Maya, and Steven started up the porch steps, Quinn opened the door. She invited them inside and greeted Chichi and Haha with a kiss on the cheek and then hugged Maya—she hadn't realized how much she'd missed her sister, and when she pulled back, she noticed she wasn't the only one blinking away tears.

Then she moved to Heath's side and introduced him, even though everyone but Haha had met him before. With that out of the way, she invited them to sit down at the large dining room table she'd already set.

"You look well," Chichi said and the compliment nearly blew her over. "You look happy."

Tears rose, dangerously close to breaking free. "*Domo arigato.*"

"*Do itashimashte.*"

Haha smiled at her, and then they all grinned and the tight knot between her shoulder blades loosened.

Quinn reached under the table and grabbed Heath's hand. He squeezed back, a silent *I told you it'd all be okay.*

They kept to polite small talk over dinner, but every minute things got easier. Her father asked Heath about the renovations and the cabins, and while most people wouldn't have seen any change in his expression, she noticed the slight twitches in his features that made it clear he was impressed. Heath even got a full nod—that was like a high five in Chichi land.

After dinner, Quinn got up to get dessert from the kitchen. She hoped they wouldn't all attack Heath in her absence, but she knew he could take care of himself. She brought out the cake she'd made, dished out pieces, and then settled back in her seat.

The slight knocking against her chair made her look down. Heath's knee was bouncing up and down—he must be more nervous than he claimed to be. She placed her hand on his shaking knee and he shot her a tight smile.

Uh-oh. Something's...well, I'm not sure what's going on.

Heath turned to Chichi, his nerves transferring from his bouncing knee to his expression. Then he cleared his throat. "Excuse me in advance, because I'll probably butcher this, and who knows if it's even the correct way to say it, but it took forever to memorize it, so I'm just going to say it anyway." He cleared his throat again. "*Musume-san to kekkon sasete kudasai.*"

"Holy shit," Maya said through a bite of cake. "Did he just ask for Chichi's permission to marry Quinn?"

Chichi and Haha both glared at Maya—about time someone else got in trouble for cussing. Honestly, though, replace "shit" with "shitballs," and Quinn had been thinking the exact same thing.

She tightened her grip on Heath's knee. "Do you know what you said?" Maybe he'd meant "someday." Or maybe Google Translate was playing a huge prank on them both.

"Yes, and I meant it." Heath looked across the table at Chichi again. "I know your traditions are important, and I'm trying to do it the right way. I promise you, I'll take care of your daughter. I'll do whatever it takes to make her happy. I love her. I want to marry her."

Silence hung in the air for one heartbeat. Two. Three...

Chichi wiped his mouth with a napkin, his expression betraying nothing. He looked at Quinn, and her rapid pulse throbbed through her ears. She couldn't move. Blink. Breathe.

Then her father turned back to Heath. "Quinn-chan *ga iito iunara, idarou*."

The tears were coming now, no chance at stopping them. Heath glanced at her, eyebrows raised, probably wanting to know if her tears were sad or happy ones.

"He said that you have his permission if it's what I want."

Heath withdrew a black box from his pocket, opened it, and dropped to one knee. "Quinn Sakata, I love you and I want to marry you." He shot her a nervous smile. "Remember we now own property together, so it's going to be super awkward if you say no."

She laughed and nodded her head. "I want. I absolutely want."

Heath slid the ring on her finger, and then he stood, scooping her into his arms as he did. He kissed her—a more chaste kiss than usual with her family as witnesses. Then he moved his lips to her ear and whispered, "I can't wait to officially make you mine. And in case I haven't made it clear, you babe, are definitely worth the wait."

Acknowledgments

I'd like to thank my cousin Mary Lo Thomas, for answering a ton of questions about her culture, and for being excited about the concept of the book and Quinn's background. I'd also like to thank Clinton Thomas for his input and for always being supportive about my writing. You two rock!

Thanks to Donald Kim Norman, MaryAnn Price, and her friend Asuka-san, for helping me with the Japanese. (And Erin Poehlman for getting me in touch with MaryAnn). Domo arigato!

Shout-out to my brother, Tod, for answering all of my mechanic questions, and thanks to my dad for explaining hunting zones and licenses, as well as always checking up on me to see how my writing's going. Thanks to my mom, who sometimes gets spoiled on scenes because I ramble on and on about them.

When I asked for names for the band, I got a ton of great options, but Rebekah Millet came up with Dixie Rush, and it fit so perfectly I knew I had to use it—thanks, girl! And thanks to my followers for answering my random questions and helping me through the editing process. During the writing and editing of every book, I end up sending dozens—cough, hundreds—of emails to Rachel Harris and Melissa West, and they never fail to help and make me laugh. Love you girls! Big hugs to the CKM and the Colorado Indie Authors for your support, and same to my TZWNDUBC girls.

Of course I can't go without thanking my fabulous editor, Stacy Abrams, who's edited book after book with me and always makes my stories shine. You are a lovely person and friend and I'm so glad I know you! Thanks to the rest of the Bliss team, including Alycia Tornetta, Tara Quigley, and Debbie Suzuki. Oh, and Jessica Cantor for all the awesome covers that fit my characters so perfectly. Entangled Publishing has been so great to me and I'm so lucky to have a home there.

I also have to give a shout-out to Gina Maxwell for pushing me through writing sprints and for all her texts, emails, and tweets that make me laugh and keep me sane. My wonderful kids and husband also keep me laughing, and they never fail to support and encourage me, and I love them like crazy. I'm so lucky you all are in my life.

Lastly, big thanks to my awesome readers! You guys are the best, and I appreciate every single one of you.

About the Author

Cindi Madsen is a USA Today bestselling author of contemporary romance and young adult novels. She sits at her computer every chance she gets, plotting, revising, and falling in love with her characters. Sometimes it makes her a crazy person. Without it, she'd be even crazier. She has way too many shoes, but can always find a reason to buy a pretty new pair, especially if they're sparkly, colorful, or super tall. She loves music and dancing and wishes summer lasted all year long. She lives in Colorado (where summer is most definitely NOT all year long) with her husband and three children.

You can visit Cindi at: www.cindimadsen.com, where you can sign up for her newsletter to get all the up-to-date information on her books.

Follow her on Twitter @cindimadsen.

Made in United States
North Haven, CT
21 August 2022

23000455R10153